ℓ 𝒟 𝑎𝑙

VA̅   A̅R̅Y̅
 D̅   +5

D1359208

Sun Dance

*Also by Fred Grove
in Large Print:*

Bitter Trumpet
The Buffalo Runners
Buffalo Spring
Comanche Captives
Deception Trail
A Distance of Ground
The Great Horse Race
Into the Far Mountains
Man on a Red Horse
Match Race
Phantom Warrior
Search for the Breed

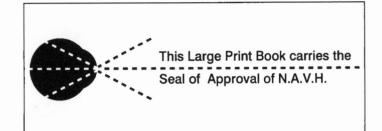

This Large Print Book carries the
Seal of Approval of N.A.V.H.

Sun Dance

Fred Grove

Thorndike Press • Waterville, Maine

LP
Gro

Copyright © 1958 by Fred Grove

All rights reserved.

Published in 2003 by arrangement with
Golden West Literary Agency.

Thorndike Press® Large Print Western.

The tree indicium is a trademark of Thorndike Press.

The text of this Large Print edition is unabridged.
Other aspects of the book may vary from the original edition.

Set in 16 pt. Plantin by Al Chase.

Printed in the United States on permanent paper.

Library of Congress Cataloging-in-Publication Data

Grove, Fred.
    Sun dance / Fred Grove.
      p. cm.
    ISBN 0-7862-5714-8 (lg. print : hc : alk. paper)
    1. Comanche Indians — Wars — Fiction. 2. Texas —
Fiction. 3. Large type books. I. Title.
PS3557.R7S85 2003
  813'.54—dc21   2003053040

1/03
Gale

Sun Dance

National Association for Visually Handicapped
------------------------ *serving the partially seeing*

As the Founder/CEO of NAVH, the only national health agency solely devoted to those who, although not totally blind, have an eye disease which could lead to serious visual impairment, I am pleased to recognize Thorndike Press* as one of the leading publishers in the large print field.

Founded in 1954 in San Francisco to prepare large print textbooks for partially seeing children, NAVH became the pioneer and standard setting agency in the preparation of large type.

Today, those publishers who meet our standards carry the prestigious "Seal of Approval" indicating high quality large print. We are delighted that Thorndike Press is one of the publishers whose titles meet these standards. We are also pleased to recognize the significant contribution Thorndike Press is making in this important and growing field.

Lorraine H. Marchi, L.H.D.
Founder/CEO
NAVH

* Thorndike Press encompasses the following imprints: Thorndike, Wheeler, Walker and Large Print Press.

CHAPTER 1

A wrongness drifted up from below, faint, mysterious. Frank Chesney, squatted down among the scrub oaks, strained harder to see and tried to remember each detail of the box canyon as he'd seen it in daylight. The crumbling shoulder of red sandstone above the tiny seep spring. The footing beyond, so broken and discouraging to travel that he doubted even antelope watered here.

He could see nothing that should not have been, no change through the dimness; but in this late-evening silence every faintness was magnified. Somebody — something was stirring down there. It wasn't the sound of his picketed horse, cropping short grass on the other side of the slope behind him. Nor a change in the drums of the distant Comanche village which he caught now and then as a throbbing, quivering pulsebeat on the warm wilderness wind.

It came to him that he had delayed here too long. And that was a knowledge that went in hand with his trade, a trade where the main trick was to stay alive; knowing when to move and when to wait, which he did by now, almost by instinct.

The "hoom-hoom" of a hoot owl echoed not ten rods down the canyon. He leaned forward and hunted through the tricky haze, bringing up the Spencer carbine, remembering with a thin wryness that, of all voices, the human echoes more than any other in broken country.

A quiet caution grazed him as he stood, a man of medium frame, muscular through the arms and shoulders, and hands as blunt as and lump-knuckled as a hard-rock miner's, a man in long boots who'd learned long ago to force down impatience in Indian country.

"Hoom-hoom . . . hoom-hoom."

There was a boldness in the call; it sounded nearer.

He snapped his glance around and wondered, resentfully, Am I being mocked before they close in? Comanches fought at night, no matter what some officers at the fort believed. Kneeling, he felt along the ground until he found a marble-sized pebble, which he lobbed high, beyond the silver smear of the spring.

A moment and he heard a softly plopping tick. At once, the annoying "hoom-hoom" answered below. He stayed motionless, in the grip of an aroused puzzlement.

8

Then, for the first time, he made out movement. An indistinct shape. Automatically, he eared back the heavy musket hammer.

"Frank . . . Frank . . ."

The voice carried the same tone of the hooting call.

Frank let the carbine sag slowly. His mouth relaxed in an expression of mingled relief and self-disgust. Cradling the Spencer, he started down the slope in long, hasty strides. The man below moved to the spring and waited. Against the dusky light he might have passed for a stocky white man in hand-me-down felt hat, ragged shirt, shapeless trousers.

"Nobody but a damn fool Delaware would come in here," Frank chided him gently, looking at jet-black eyes in a high-boned, smallpox-pitted face the hue of plug tobacco. "I was getting ready to shoot you, Jim Dan."

There was no immediate answer. "You no shoot," Jim Dan muttered at last. He almost never spoke much and when he did communicate, it might be a mixture of horse-barn English and sign language, with a word of Spanish pieced in here and there; often just the fluid, descriptive signs. He turned, jerking the ends of his long, loose black hair, his wanderer's face tilted up, half sad, half secret, and said, amused, "You no shoot," his right hand letting the short barrel of his Burnside carbine point downward.

"Hell I wasn't," Frank told him. "Next time you speak up faster. How'd you find me?"

Jim Dan appeared to grin under his floppy hat brim. All this, it occurred to Frank, was like some untiring primitive game to Jim Dan, instead of more serious business.

"Old Ingen camp," the Delaware explained, pointing off toward the Comanche village on the flats. "Water — here. One time Jim Dan — you — camp here. Remember?" He paused, again secretive, pleased, half grinning. "Jim Dan see you leave canyon."

"Mean you've been hiding out all day?" Frank demanded, thinking of the early hour when, afoot, not daring to ride in daylight, he'd made his way to the brushy lookout on the bluff.

"Damn betcha! Ingen" — Jim Dan made the sign for Comanche, the wriggling motion of a snake — "Ingen, him ride 'round. Close. Plenty Ingen!"

"It's a big village, all right. And they're sun dancing, Jim Dan."

"Medicine dance?" The Indian looked dubious.

"The first Comanche sun dance. I saw their round medicine house. Like the Kiowas make it. The k'ado. You know, with cottonwood poles. Plenty Comanches. Looks like No-ko-nies, Pena-te-kas, Qua-ha-das . . ." He checked himself abruptly. "Who sent you? Major Vier?"

Jim Dan jogged his head.

"What's his hurry this time?" Frank wanted to know.

As if white man's talk merely hindered him, Jim Dan began drawing swift, graceful air pictures. I do not know why pony soldier chief send me to find my friend. But ten sleeps ago strangers from Tehanna country come to soldier house. Big talk. Long talk. That's all I know.

Frank swore under his breath. "Vier sent you out here — risked your neck — just to save a few days? When he knew I'd be in?" Frank made a sudden chopping motion, thinking. Well, that's Vier for you. He never could wait. But this time he's in a real big hurry.

"We'll wait 'til full dark," Frank finished.

In answer, Jim Dan's hand shot out. His grip was light, but firm, urgent, and Frank read a new concern in the earnest face.

"Now!" Jim Dan breathed. "Go now! Ingen dead — back there!" He struck the long-bladed butcher knife hanging at his belt.

Frank stared at him wonderingly. "You kill a Comanche gettin' in here?"

Jim Dan's explosive blast of breath was answer enough. Alarm crowded in, reinforced instantly as Frank discovered the rent down the Delaware's left sleeve.

"Let me look at that."

Frank was already taking hold of the arm, scowling over the ugly, liquid-looking slash that ran from elbow to wrist. He grunted, "Come on," and started up the slope, his mind on the meager contents of his pack.

After a little while, with Frank leading his gelding, they found the brushy pocket where Jim Dan had tied his animal, a flop-eared beast, wiry, tough, big-barreled, Frank remembered, with the endurance of two cavalry mounts.

There was, Frank considered as they walked ahead, this much about a box canyon. People knowing country as the Comanches did theirs had no reason to nose in here, which was why he'd chosen such a nowhere place to hole up; but quitting its cover, the getting out, was something again. Farther on, working up to the broken jaws of the canyon's beginning, he stopped to look.

He stood a minute or more, slowly playing his glance about. He was going to mount when movement on a low brow of hill some scant rods off fixed his eyes.

Flattened against a slab of rock, he watched an Indian and pony shape to bold silhouette. The buck kept turning his head, peering into the thickening gloom. A little time passed and then another mounted Indian materialized; he seemed to float right up against the skyline.

Frank drew a careful bead. Don't do it, he thought. Don't come up this canyon, looking for your dead brother.

The Indians sat their ponies like rock, just peering.

"Kill them both!" Jim Dan hissed.

"And stir up the camp? No."

In the next instant, Frank realized with a surge of relief that the Comanches were making ready to go. And even as he watched, they clapped heels to flanks and unshod ponies' hoofs clacked on loose shale. He watched them as blurs coming down the hill, blending with the darker twilight there. But there was still danger — if they passed the canyon's mouth, if his or Jim Dan's animal shrilled a greeting. . . .

Frank waited. Then he breathed again, deeply. They were going off, turning the base of the hill, the muffled cadence of the riders' chanted grunting reaching him faintly. Hoo-ah-hoo-ah! With straining eyes, he kept them in sight until he could distinguish only formless wedges, until even they winked out and all pony sound dribbled off, lost, and there was only the moan of the wind and the drum throbs.

Jim Dan said, "Frank, you funny man. Talkin' old Broad-hat, huh?"

"Just because I scout for the army is no call to kill every Indian I see."

"Comanches kill you," came the straight reply. "Damn betcha! Quick! You got trouble. You no white man; no Ingen. Heart, mixed up. But Jim Dan take your hand."

Frank couldn't answer that. He mounted at once.

Afterward, heading east as the gold-yellow moon climbed, they rode upon a stretch of prairie strewn with prickly pear. Here, Frank stopped for the first time. Ignoring Jim Dan's muttered protests, he got down and drew his hunting knife and cut off stickers and peeling and made a moist poultice which he spread along the trough of Jim Dan's wound, and rewrapped.

14

Gleaming eyes met his, darkly approving. "You Ingen now."

"That's what Major Vier says. Except he don't mean it the way you do."

Frank straightened up, turning his attention to the rear. The Comanche village was miles behind them, but the strong moon cast a light like half day. He listened a while, then said, "You hear anything?"

Jim Dan walked away from the horses, halted. After a pause, he returned and shook his head.

"Give 'em time." Frank stepped to the saddle, hesitated. "How do you figure this sun dance?"

"Bad. Big bad."

As Frank rode on, the thing built in his mind. Comanches were skeptical for Indians. The People, they called themselves. Individualists, all right. Every man his own prophet. They had no tribal religion. No warrior societies like the Cheyenne Dog Soldiers, the Kiowas' Ko-eet-senko, the Ten Bravest. For them to take up the unfamiliar sun dance meant war was in the making, the bands called together, possibly, for one last desperate cut at the crowding white man. Chances were, the reservation Comanches would stir up, too.

Hell, he thought irritably, you can't

blame 'em. Their way of life was going fast and when it changed, finally, so would his own. Everything would be gone like last winter's snow, after the hide boys finished cleaning out the southern herd. It was that clear cut, he thought, that near.

Along toward midnight they drew up once more, loosened cinches, let their hard-used horses blow. Nobody spoke. Frank, an unlighted pipe clamped between his teeth, saw Jim Dan take a slow circle around the horses. Every few steps he'd lift his nose high to sniff. And always he ended faced into the southwest, whence the wind came, like a suspicious old buffalo bull smelling trouble he could sense but not see.

An impression seemed confirmed within him. He turned, though not speaking.

"What do you hear?" Frank asked.

"Ponies — mebbe."

Frank walked across to him. He bent his head to listen. Wind rustled over the short grass like a multitude of murmuring voices, both near and far, clamoring to be heard. Just this for a spell. Yet, though he couldn't be certain, he thought that once he picked up a kind of hard underroll. He said, "Well —" pushing the question at the Delaware again.

"Ponies," Jim Dan grunted firmly.

"Could be wild ones. Antelope."

He had his answer as Jim Dan went to his horse and cinched up.

From that moment on they seemed to be racing the moon, checking at intervals to rest weary horseflesh, to probe the eternity of space for any change in the tone of the night. Twice, Frank figured he heard an afar drumming, a faint vibration, only to lose it on the persistent wind. The landscape shifted as the light increased imperceptibly. Broken buttes and scattered mesquite gave way to rolling swells of prairie. They passed black pools of cupped buffalo wallows.

First daylight struck as a pencil streak of gray in the eastern murk, and when it broadened he had the naked sensation of a blanket being furled back, leaving them exposed on the prairie sloping in direction of the river. This was the Red, shallow and broad, and sight of the far-side bluffs, broken and humped, warmed like a drink in the belly.

Green cottonwoods beckoned in the bottoms. Once across . . . A bullet whined from behind and Frank, jerking, heard the pop of a rifle. He slowed down, swerving.

Now he spotted them. A clump of dust-raising riders veering out of the southwest, larruping ponies, driving at an angle to wedge between river and horsemen.

He pulled the Spencer free. There was another whining bite and he yelled, "The trees — come on!"

As he kicked his animal into a laboring run, he sensed there wasn't much bottom under him. A lumbering gallop, a sidelong look, and he realized they couldn't reach the timber in time. He yanked up short.

"Get down!" he yelled. "Throw your horse!"

Jim Dan hauled in, his eyes roving wide. He wheeled, pointing, and Frank saw the old wallow. Digging his boot heels, he jumped his gelding over to the wallow's rim and came down with his rawhide rope.

He swiveled the brown head back close to the saddle, lifted the off-side fetlock and drove with the point of his shoulder. The tripped horse landed heavily, grunting. Frank looped one striking hind foot, now the other, drew fast, and snugged across to the front cannons.

Jim Dan was finishing the same tie-down.

About four hundred yards off the Comanches came on, hooting, screeching defiance. Suddenly, as if by command, they stopped in unison, just beyond carbine range.

"Qua-ha-das," Jim Dan called, his voice held low.

Frank counted some seventeen, but it was hard to tell in that mass.

One warrior, wearing a buffalo-horn headdress and riding a yellow mustang with black mane and tail, began a slow, taunting circle. He motioned for the men in the wallow to show themselves and fight. All the while his contemptuous cries carried shrilly on the wind.

"Dirty names," Frank said, across. "What's he callin' us?"

Jim Dan placed hands to his head, raked them downward in a combing motion, and finished by rounding them vastly.

"Squaws," Frank said, watching the leader return to the war party. "Fat squaws. Because we won't come out where they can get to us."

There followed a time-killing period while the Comanches talked and gestured. Some got down and sat cross-legged on the buff prairie, backs turned in scorn at the wallow. They seemed in no hurry, and yet there was purpose here also, for the ponies needed resting before the fight commenced. Standing out in the center, still mounted, sat the war-party leader.

Frank said, "Know that Indian on the yellow horse?"

I think he is Black Star, Jim Dan replied in

19

gestures and sometimes a word. Qua-ha-da chief. I saw him once when the Qua-ha-das camped with Old Owl's Pena-te-kas. A white man was with him. A one-eyed white man.

Frank was watching the Comanches. Now he turned his head and stared hard before he spoke. "White man? One-eyed?"

A nod. Yes. Bad white man.

"Bad? What do you know about him?"

Not much. Pena-te-kas tell me a little. Qua-ha-das don't come in much. They're mad. Wild. Stay way out. Llano Estacado. They laugh when other bands take white man's rations.

"What's this white man's name? I mean, what do the Comanches call him? He's got an Indian name if he lives with 'em."

Jim Dan pondered a moment. "Red —" he said uncertainly in English. "Red — the Red One." Something attracted his attention yonder and he laid his old Burnside carbine across his horse.

Looking, Frank saw the parley breaking up. The sitters sprang up, vaulting to ponies' bare backs. He could feel cold sweat starting in him as the Comanches massed and bunched forward, striking a steady trot. Dust scuffed. A few feathered headdresses weaved in the wind.

He saw the pace quicken. It became a hard lope. Faster. Now a gallop as dust rose higher. Until the tough war ponies were flattening out lower in full run. Wild-eyed pintos, duns, roans, blood-red bays. The Qua-ha-das charged in a bunch. Never in a strung-out line, like the pony soldiers. Yells broke.

Frank fired. Nothing happened. He fired again and again and a pony went down, its rider flipping, ridden under. He heard the blast of Jim Dan's carbine. But the wedge never faltered. For a long count, Frank thought they'd be overrun.

All at once the Qua-ha-das split, each segment of riders sheering off, fanning out. One by one, an instant before sweeping past, each crouched warrior threw himself out of sight on the off side of his pony. Each hung by a naked leg hooked over his pony's backbone and a hair rope plaited into the long mane, so that only a brown face or lean arm was exposed as he loosed arrows or fired his rifle under his pony's neck.

In the wallow the air was filled suddenly with streaky, feathered whisperings and angry buzzings and the constant yammer of insulting yells. Frank fired at a scarlet-striped face, saw a greasy shape tumble and roll in the early sunlight like twisting metal.

21

As swiftly as they'd formed, the Qua-ha-das were gone, cantering out of range, gone to circle back and prepare, Frank knew, for another charge.

He slipped seven fat cartridges into the tubular magazine in the butt stock of the Spencer, inserted another in the chamber, cocked the hammer and looked up. One pony was down and two shapes sprawled on the yellow grass. Beyond, the ponies were coming together again.

Frank's chest was wet with sweat, his hands as slippery. He was pounding inside.

Jim Dan grunted without turning his head, "Qua-ha-das know you." His voice sounded grave.

"You heard it?"

"Bloody Knife," the Indian said, sawing the edge of his hand two-three times in front of his face.

A brief silence. Jim Dan had said all he was going to. He was curious to know, but his Indian manners forbade him to ask.

"Happened after I left the Colorado country for good," Frank said. "Before I came to the pony soldiers' house. I hunted buffalo, sold hides for a living. Far out in Tehanna country. One day a Qua-ha-da party jumped our camp. Killed one of my partners and two skinners before we drove 'em off. A young Qua-ha-da chief sure enough hankered for my hair, and he came close. He took chances; he was very brave. We fought with knives around the wagon." Frank studied the Comanche horsemen a moment. "I got him. It was a bloody fight. Now the Qua-ha-das hate my heart. They spit on me. They won't forget."

Muddy eyes considered him, impressed but puzzled. "You no like to kill enemies?"

"No. I have to, but I don't like to."

A wistful understanding cropped out in Jim Dan's stare. "You like Delaware, mebbe. No home. Fight ever'body." The puzzled expression crept back. "Broadhat, him say wrong to kill. Love enemies, him say. Be brothers."

"He's right, Jim Dan. Trouble is, takes people a long time to learn how they can be brothers. The white man's been trying now for about two thousand years. Maybe your children, when they grow up, will live in peace. I hope so."

Jim Dan appeared doubtful. "If white man kills white man, how Broadhat's word be true?"

Frank hesitated. "At the agency, you have watched Broadhat look into his medicine book? The black one he calls the Bible?"

The Delaware nodded, intent.

"Well, that's where the agent finds his good words from the Great Medicine Chief. The medicine book is for everybody. All people, not just the white man. When a white man is bad that don't make the medicine book bad."

Silent, Jim Dan reflected on the inconsistencies of the white man.

Frank passed his canteen, a little surprised at himself. It was strange, he thought, how you got to talking sometimes when maybe the end of your life was just four hundred yards away. When whether you lived or died depended on how powerful some greasy buck figured the sacred objects in his medicine pouch to be. Anyway, whatever you'd said was boiled down to the marrow of truth.

The Delaware, having drunk in slow, sparing gulps, returned the canteen. Frank took his and swiped a hand across his mouth, wondering how much longer they'd have to wait. There was, finally, a weighted weariness in him, a glumness, a stringy tightness.

He waited some more and saw the riders forming again. They bunched quickly, in an angry knot, scuffing dust, as if scorning needless, formal palaver, eager to finish these foolish people in the wallow. Frank noticed another difference in the attack this time. Instead of the usual head-on rush, then the splitting off, the Comanches commenced circling far back.

Crawling to the back side, Frank poked his weapon over the rim's edge. On the ground near his right hand he laid a small pile of copper-cased shells. He groaned softly as the circle began to tighten, not unlike a revolving pinwheel. Riders slid from view. The buzz bees swarmed again.

"Shoot the horses!" he called over his shoulder. "Shoot the horses!"

His bullet tumbled a pinto. Hardly had its rider regained his feet, crouching, when two Comanches swept in abreast. Together they reached down and pulled him up behind the off rider. Frank kept firing. Another pony spilled, the Qua-ha-da landing like a cat and charging the wallow, rifle swinging, screeching, eyes wild.

Frank knocked him down only ten yards away.

Jim Dan's threatened yell flung him around. Three shrieking riders were racing straight in. There was a simultaneous roaring in Frank's ears as he and Jim Dan fired.

A pony ran wildly, riderless.

Frank saw surprise shock his Indian's

face, saw his rifle fall like a loose stick as he clutched his pony's long mane with frantic hands and hung on.

In a smear of piebald colors the third pony flashed past, nostrils flaring, the rider's head and shoulders bobbing down at the final instant. Too soon — and Frank, levering in a shell, rearing back and pressing, missed, his snap shot late. But in that fleetness he'd glimpsed reddish hair, the buckskin patch covering one eye, the other pale and staring.

Letting the man go for the wallow's exposed rear, Frank saw that all but one of the remaining warriors had stayed clear of the coup-counting dash, because that's what it was. You joined if you felt strong; you didn't if your medicine was weak. All but one warrior, who ventured in a little way, keeping up a steady chorus of hateful yells and challenging gestures. Now, like a circus rider, he slipped to the far side of his pony. He rode no closer.

Frank watched him, dismissed him, and bent back. Only a few moments had passed. But the piebald was running full speed, turning, out of range, handled skillfully, so that the horse shielded its clinging rider.

Details of the man's face started returning to Frank, belatedly, then sharply, rousing, with a sense of shock. Not that he knew the face, more savage than a Comanche's; he did not. It was the eye patch, the buckskin flap and string. A white man fighting with the Qua-ha-das.

He sat still, aware of an incredible silence. Downed ponies blotted the prairie. The circling and hooting had ceased, while the Indians turned to pick up the unhorsed and the dead farthest out. The buffalo wallow fight was over.

Two horses going off stood out across the distance. The yellow one Jim Dan said was ridden by a Qua-ha-da chief called Black Star, and a piebald, with extra large patches of black and white, bigger than most Indian mustangs.

Jim Dan eased around on his haunches, grinning like a fat badger deep in his hole. "Them Qua-ha-das —" he said and blinked, his hunter's eyes turning serious. "You sick, mebbe? Devil inside belly?"

Frank met his stare without speaking.

"You see ghost, look like."

Frank's sudden rising motion cut off the speech. "They're pulling out," he said, as if Jim Dan had never spoken. "Let's get these horses up."

CHAPTER 2

Fort Hazard was not an outpost in the usual frontier style, only because it lacked a stockade. Otherwise, it filled all the requirements and was, in fact, far larger and stronger than most. The hard-working pony soldiers had hewed and plastered well. Barracks and officers' quarters, chiseled and squared from gray limestone, faced a broad central square. There were white-washed picket fences, graveled walks, even a small steepled church, a general store, children and pets, and the blessed voices of women on the cool porches of an evening. With its orderly rows of buildings, Hazard resembled a prosperous village, neat and prim, laid out by a precise mind. It had a comfortable, well-scrubbed appearance, to the extent that some gossiped discreetly that Major R. M. Vier paid more attention to soap and tin bathtubs than he did to arms and mounts.

Jogging across the empty square, Frank Chesney realized he'd never quite placed this town-looking fort with its lonely surroundings, folds of short-grassed prairie dipping southward, blue-shadowed mountains bulking hard to the west, if, after Colorado, you could call those worn-down hulks mountains. For Hazard in no wise favored the brown walls of Fort Supply, far northwest, or the bleak likes of Fort Griffin, southwest. Yet, in spite of its unfortified look, Hazard was a bastion complete within each stone structure. The pony soldiers had come to stay and the Comanches and Kiowas, seasoned plains fighters who recognized an impossible situation when up against one, prudently had never attacked the fort. Rather, as a balm for warrior prestige, they contented themselves by night horse-stealing forays on the stone quartermaster corral, once believed thief-proof. Else they attacked wood-cutting details sent into the mountains, or harried employees of the Quaker-run Indian agency — unless the most satisfying game of all, raiding the hated Tehannas across Red River, occupied the young men.

Frank halted his horse in front of the commanding officer's headquarters and slid down, tiredly regarding the empty square, the used-up feeling registering that a wiser man would have eaten and slept a few hours before reporting. Instead, he'd parted company from Jim Dan, passed up Isaac Roberts' hospitality at the Indian agency, and gone another four miles under a blistering sun.

Hearing boots rapping off the porch, he turned to see Lieutenant Ed Niles, raw-boned and stringy-muscled, big hands and ungainly feet, striding down the graveled walk with the rolling gait of a cavalryman. He was grinning broadly, an easy-natured man just past his middle twenties, several years Frank's junior.

He said, "Major Vier sent Jim Dan —"

"I don't think much of the order," Frank broke in.

"Found you, didn't he?"

"Sure. About got killed doing it."

"You mean he's shot up?"

"Not that foxy Indian. Just cut up some. He's home with his squaw and kids by now."

Niles looked relieved. He pulled at the light brown mustache strands drooping across his angular, friendly face, a question forming in his tolerant blue eyes.

He said now, "So you bucked into some real trouble?"

"Enough."

Niles' glance was busy, examining, grimly humoring. "You've been on short rations. That's plain." And in impatience: "Well, damn it, what happened?"

Shortly, Frank told him and finished in disgust. "Tell me, what did Vier gain? He knew I was comin' in. A wonder Jim Dan wasn't rubbed out. Why risk a good man?"

"Frank," the lieutenant cautioned, "stone walls have mighty big ears sometimes."

"No sense to that order. I aim to tell Vier so."

For a briefness Frank saw understanding build in Niles' eyes. Niles opened his mouth to speak, and reconsidered. "All right," he said mildly. "All right." Slowly, his expression changed to a mocking severity. "As post adjutant, it's my duty to require a written report."

"From a contract scout? To hell with you, Lieutenant."

"In which case," Niles said, shrugging indifferently, "the order is countermanded."

Both smiled and the lieutenant added, "Look here, Frank. How about some sleep before you see Major Vier?"

"I want to get this over with first. When I do, I'll bed-down for a month. What is it, Ed? What's this hurry-up all about?"

Lieutenant Niles put a forefinger to his chin. "There's a Texas party here — a woman."

"A woman?"

"Yes, and a damned striking one. Been

staying at the hotel. Pow-wowing about every day with the Major. Some with old Isaac at the agency. As to what, don't ask me. The CO hasn't taken his able adjutant into his confidence. I'm in the dark as much as you are."

"Fine listener you are, Ed."

"Oh, I still hear well enough. Trouble is the Major does most of his courting — I mean conferring — horseback." Niles winked and threw Frank a sympathetic look. "Since you're so eager for punishment, come on." He beckoned to a private, who took Frank's mount as they turned up the walk.

"I keep wondering," Niles remarked archly, "whether you found any interesting rock samples in Comanche country."

"Nothing to match Niles' Great Silver Rush in the Wichitas," Frank answered and they laughed together. "Afraid I lost the fever after that."

It was an old joke between them, the product of a passing promoter's claims of hidden wealth in the nearby mountains. Niles, despite Frank's scoffing, had insisted they go prospecting. They had, with completely negative results.

"Was going to try my luck again while you were gone," Niles said, "but Louise turned on the damper."

Frank slowed his stride. "How is she, Ed?"

Niles' pleasant expression clouded, his mouth pulling together in a way that made him appear troubled and puzzled. "Maybe things will change when the baby arrives. Won't be long . . . any day now."

Over the doorway of post headquarters black lettering on a plain oak board announced — TENTH U.S. CAVALRY.

Inside, Niles led off down a grim hallway, bare of any decoration, and turned past a stiff trooper into a waiting room lined with wooden benches. Major Vier's office, just beyond, was closed.

"Wait a minute," Niles said and rapped on the door. "Lieutenant Niles, sir. Mr. Chesney is here. Just rode in."

"Come in. Tell him to wait."

Winking at Frank, Niles stepped in and closed the door.

Frank dropped to a bench, pulled out his pipe and broke tobacco off a dried twist, ground the leaves in the palm of his hand and filled the blackened bowl. He rummaged for his match case, lighted up and dragged in smoke, his whole body relaxed. He smelled of sweat and horses; he was greasy-tired. A minute passed. A drowsiness stole over him. The pipe went out and he didn't bother to relight. He was nodding, eyes half-shuttered, when the door opened and Niles nodded.

Past him, Frank could see Major Vier behind his desk, and Vier's frown as Frank, slouched on the bench, stretched to his feet.

Niles stood aside and Frank entered to confront Vier, who, without rising, said on a curt inflection of satisfaction, "It worked out just as I planned, Mr. Chesney. The Indian found you and you're back early."

"I was coming in anyway."

Major Vier sat thick and heavy at his desk. He had, as usual, the well-tailored look of a careful bachelor dresser, his black mustache trimmed precisely above heavy lips, his blue-jawed face still fresh from his morning shave. He looked efficient and hard, which he was, a man about forty priding himself on physical fitness and attention to detail, never bending to frontier informality.

Meeting his stare, Frank seated himself without invitation and selected a match from the box. When he rasped the yellow head along the sole of his boot, and the sulphurous smell fouled the room, a tiny, almost unseen, glint of displeasure twitched in Vier's stern face. Frank inhaled and blew smoke, thinking, He knows I don't like it.

"This is quite urgent," Major Vier said,

34

rising, a trace of pompousness in his voice, and came stiff-legged around the desk. "Mr. Niles, go to the hotel and escort Miss Wagner over." As he finished, he turned his critical gaze on Frank, pecking, frowning, and, for a moment, Frank saw the major's nose pinching in at the horse and sweat smells.

"Mr. Chesney reported soon as he rode in, sir," Niles said. "No time to brush up for ladies."

"Of course not." Vier's cool, black eyes measured Frank again, swept away. The Major sought a handkerchief and began dabbing his damp brow. He was constantly sweating, it seemed, summer or winter.

Niles went out and Vier, smiling faintly, said in his precise manner, "I suppose you're wondering why, when you were scheduled back, I ordered out another scout to contact you?"

"Hard to make me wonder much any more, Major. I do my job. What the army pays me to do." Frank slouched still lower in the chair. His pipe was dead and he scraped another noisy match.

Vier's nose twitched. "Lieutenant Niles informs me you got yourselves involved in quite a fight."

"Tried to dodge one, Major. Ended up in

a stand. Lucky we got out."

"So . . . under such tight circumstances wouldn't you say it was fortunate the Indian was along?"

"Powerful lucky for me — not him. He killed a Comanche gettin' in to me."

Vier cleared his throat. "I've noticed your curious regard for Indians, Mr. Chesney. A rather uncommon concern for a government-paid scout."

"They're people. Jim Dan's a friend. No call to send him out there, that I can see."

"I'm not in the habit of issuing orders for which there is no call!" Vier bit out. "You can be sure of that!" He circled the desk, brushed invisible lint from a perfectly clean sleeve. "It was necessary to be certain of your safe return, and as speedily as possible."

Frank eyed him, suspicious. Vier's studied show of patience, of tolerance, of explaining — none of it fit.

"When," Frank replied, in a voice like dry wind, "did you start frettin' over my hide? Not since Crazy Heart Butte, I'd say."

"We are not here to discuss Crazy Heart Butte," Vier continued deliberately, unruffled.

"Be mighty sweet music, though, wouldn't it, if I failed to show up sometime? Like you hope?"

36

Vier was ignoring, still in his stiff-legged pacing. "An unusual situation has developed. The army needs your experience. You can render a great service."

"Such as" . . . Frank began dubiously.

Vier, with an air of finality, crossed to his chair and sat, erect, his thick fingers commencing an impatient drumming on the desk.

"Major," Frank said distinctly, "you sent me to locate Qua-ha-da Comanches. Well, I did, and I don't mean just that war party we fought."

Vier looked up without interest.

"You want to hear about it or not?"

Heat colored Vier's smooth features. "Of course — of course. I was coming to that later."

Like hell, Frank decided. You clean forgot it. Now you want something.

But he said, "It's this way. There's a big Comanche camp on Pease River, in the breaks. Biggest I ever saw. All the main bands. Qua-ha-das to boot . . . big sun dance."

He let that sink in for Vier's reaction. There wasn't much, just a waiting stare.

"Major," Frank said, faster, with feeling, "it's the first time Comanches ever sun danced. That means big medicine to an

37

Indian. Bad medicine in this case, Jim Dan says, an' he knows. It just about shapes up to scald everything below here to Fort Concho."

Major Vier blinked. "All this alarm over a mere tribal ceremony?"

"Ceremony?"

"That's how it strikes me."

"This is no squaw jig, Major. A sun dance lasts four days. When it breaks up — and it's over by now — feelings hit a high pitch. War parties go out. I believe word should be passed south. And we'll need to look out here."

Vier pushed back, the obscure smile forming in the corners of his mouth. "Why," he demanded, "are the Comanches just now resorting to the sun dance? Answer me that. I hardly think they needed it in the past as an excuse, say, to go raiding in Texas or Old Mexico."

"The Comanches never been pressed like this before. They're hungry, they're pinched in. Last winter they lost a lot of warriors in Texas. They want revenge. Eye for an eye. On top of that, they're mad at the hide hunters. You can count Kiowas and Cheyennes in on this, too." Frank shook his head. "Looks like a rough year."

"Why worse than any other?"

"Because the army's got a medicine war on its hands. Might have it right here on the reservation. Comanches are mighty practical people, Major. They wouldn't sun dance 'less they figured it'd bring 'em something. Give 'em special powers."

Vier's voice was skeptical. "Special powers?"

"That's right. They pray for power same as a white does when he goes to church. If you believe something works for you — it's strong medicine — why, that's half the battle. Until you're hurt bad, anyway."

Vier said irritably, "Always a big scare, isn't there? If not Comanches, it's Kiowas, Cheyennes, Apaches. Comancheros peddling whisky." He threw up his hands.

"I'm just telling you what I saw, Major. What it means. What the army does is up to you."

"I'm fully aware of my duties, Mr. Chesney. Believe me, I am —"

There came a knock and Frank saw Vier's expression undergo immediate change, his annoyance erased. At his brisk "Come in," Lieutenant Niles opened the door and the brushing rustle of long skirts invaded the bare-walled room.

"Ah." Major Vier was quickly up and around the desk, bowing, smiling.

"Henrietta . . . Miss Wagner, may I present Mr. Frank Chesney. He's the scout I was telling you about."

As Frank stood, it struck him how he must look. Unshaven, long-haired, burned sun-black as an Indian buck, the strong stink upon him. He remembered his manners and inclined his head, studying her through an uneasy wariness which he realized had been growing since Niles first mentioned a woman.

"How do you do, Mr. Chesney. I've been looking forward to seeing you."

Her voice was rich, pleasant to the ear. He took the hand she offered him. Her fingers were like pale, slender tapers, possessed of a surprising firmness for a woman. He dropped his arm and found himself admiring her, reminded of a girl he'd known long ago in Colorado, robust and fair-skinned, working her father's claim like any strong boy. Only this comely young woman before him now was smaller boned; she had the strength but not the coarseness of the mountain girl.

Major Vier was a jack-in-the-box as he beat Niles to a chair and placed it near his desk. "Please be seated, Henrietta."

She lingered a moment longer and Frank's gaze ran against the sweeping judgment of blue eyes, wide set in a fair, rounded face. Her interest was sharply searching, weighing and inspecting, neither condemning nor approving. Like him, he thought, she wants something. She was tall, her body strong and filled out, yet slim-waisted in her longsleeved, high-necked blue traveling suit. Her skin showed an ivory shading that somehow had managed to defy sun and wind, and her mouth lay full and alive above a small, determined chin. She wore a flowered hat well forward on a mass of flax-yellow hair, drawn up in tight curls. She was, he supposed, in her early twenties.

This he saw in one steady glance. But the deepest impression he had was of her will, yes, a resolute will, as she moved to accept Vier's chair. She held something bulky wrapped in a blue scarf.

Seated, she looked up and Frank read the swift possessiveness her smiling thanks produced on Vier, who paused over her another moment before swinging to his desk.

Niles started for the door, but Vier's voice chopped him still. "Better stay, Lieutenant. I think we're all concerned in this matter." The Major's glance trailed over Miss Wagner.

"I'm grateful for your help," she said, her

large eyes for all three.

She's smart, Frank thought. Knows what she's after and how to get it. But I'll take no hand in it.

"Miss Wagner's home is a ranch in the vicinity of Fredericksburg, Texas," Major Vier explained, his old brusqueness surfacing. He paused to regard the girl again.

"A German settlement," she added and there was, it seemed to Frank, a certain calm pride as she said it. "We live way out. It's frontier. But please go on, Major. I didn't mean to interrupt." Suddenly, looking at her, Frank found a dead weariness on her face, a downcast futility for which he was unprepared.

"Some months ago a war party raided through there," Vier continued, his expression severe. "Miss Wagner's parents were killed; her sister, Emily, taken captive. Fortunately for Miss Wagner, she was visiting relatives at the time."

The moment Vier finished, Frank knew what they proposed to ask of him, and a hardening knot of resistance began to form deep down inside him. He looked at her, shocked, feeling sympathy for her and yet not wishing to be drawn within the circle of her hurt.

"It's an old story," he said, an unspoken

understanding sharp in his throat.

"Miss Wagner," Vier said, "has tried the usual ransom methods without success. Offered substantial rewards in the Texas and New Mexico newspapers with descriptions of Miss Emily. Attempted contact with New Mexicans who traffic with the Comanches."

"Comanches?" Frank said. "Could be Kiowas, maybe Apaches."

As if on a prearranged signal, Miss Wagner opened the scarf and handed a worn moccasin across, murmuring, "This was found after the raid. I'm told it's Comanche make."

Frank took it and dropped his gaze, seeing the familiar buckskin upper and the stiff buffalo hide sole, where old sinew had given away; and the distinguishing long fringes, Mexican silver tipping each one, that ran from lace to toe and along the heel's seam, and the strung beads.

"Well?" Vier demanded.

"Comanche," Frank agreed and returned the moccasin. "Could be Qua-ha-da."

"Why do you say Comanche?"

"The long fringes, mainly. That's Comanche style."

"I knew it!" the Major burst out, as if he'd known all along. "Now we're getting somewhere!"

43

Quickening in Henrietta Wagner's face, Frank saw a half dread, half hope. "If I could just be sure, some way, that Emily's alive," she told him.

"How . . . old is Emily?"

"Eleven. Only eleven —" Abruptly she seemed to sense some meaning he'd left unsaid and her eyes flicked to his, narrowing, concerned.

"In one way," he said, "her age gives her a better chance."

Relief eased her a trifle, then color flooded her checks. "You mean — what do you mean? Please, please, don't hold back on me. Tell me what you honestly think. Don't be kind, Mr. Chesney."

"I'm not kind," he replied, harsher than he intended. "If I was, I'd tell you it's no use. Forget her. But I won't, because I'm not kind." He looked carefully at his pipe. "You say she's eleven; that's too young for a wife. If she's alive, there's a chance she's with her captor's family, which is a hard lot any way you look at it. Even for Indian women. Packing wood, water; all the camp work. If she's strong —"

"But she isn't! She's had fever. Never strong — like me. Oh, if it had only been me instead of Emily!"

Frank studied her, seeing how that would

be, and was silent.

"If only Emily's alive!" she persisted.

Embarrassment clamped a stillness on the men. Niles inspected the tips of his boots. Major Vier's jaws bulged in grim outrage. He couldn't, however, Frank noticed, keep his bold stare off Miss Wagner.

"There again," Frank said flatly, "it depends on who captured her. What kind of Indian he is. His temper. If the Tehannas ever killed any members of his family or friends, before he captured Emily. If Emily gave him much trouble on the way back. Delayed the war party."

Observing Miss Wagner's dismay, he thought of the possibilities he had purposely not mentioned. Of raiders who gave their captives away or traded them to other tribes; of white boys tied to the backs of wild horses or yearling buffaloes to test their courage; of girls mistreated, slain if they slowed the march. Of other children adopted into the tribe and loved as deeply as Comanche children. Of neither extreme would he speak.

"Mr. Chesney." Vier's black eyes reflected annoyance. "We're not interested in your suppositions. We're after your strongest opinion, based on your experience among Indians." He took a breath. "You've

45

fought them — you lived among the Utes once, I understand."

Frank, astonished, inquired, "What have the Utes got to do with this, Major?"

"Why, nothing," said Vier, straight-faced. "Nothing. I am speaking of your experience. Your . . . ah, knowledge. Which brings us back to the original question. Do you think there's a chance Emily is still alive?"

Frank lagged with his answer, watching Miss Wagner. He said, "A chance — with luck."

"Very well. We shall proceed on the assumption she is. The next step is ransom. Miss Wagner is prepared to pay and pay well for her sister's release."

Frank steepled his hands and considered them. The thing, the old, smarting thing he found himself dodging, he had now succeeded in putting out of his mind. He would not let it come that close again, to remind, to jog, to haunt and dig at him.

"Isaac Roberts is your man," he said.

"Roberts?" Vier played his wearying scorn around. "Why, he has no contact with the Qua-ha-das. You know that. No Qua-ha-da has ever come to the agency for rations. Never will. Not until the buffalo's gone or the army drives them in."

"Other bands come in," Frank reasoned.

46

"Old Owl's Pena-te-kas. No-ko-nies. Yam-pa-ri-kas. Get Roberts to work through them."

Vier arched up in his chair. "So we can be worked in turn! I tell you they're all in cahoots! I believe that quite firmly. You yourself said you saw other Comanche bands with the Qua-ha-das. Isn't that true?"

"You put all Indians in the same litter," Frank said. "Qua-ha-das take more captives, steal more stock, than the rest of the bands and the Kiowas together. Can, because they're off the reservation."

"Well," snapped Vier, "I want none of Roberts and his double-dealing Indians, I'll tell you that. Even if he could arrange some sort of parley through one of the reservation bands, and I understand he's tried, we couldn't wait that long. We've got to act immediately. Longer we delay contacting the Qua-ha-das, less chance that leaves Miss Wagner's sister."

"I hold out for Roberts," Frank said stubbornly. "Indians trust him."

Vier's glance met Henrietta's, comforting, consoling, and returned to Frank, who could see it shaping as he'd sensed it would. He could see the switch starting in Vier, who now was becoming almost genial again.

47

"Isaac Roberts," the Major said, "is a pious old fool who means well. I grant that. No more. We've got to have a man who not only knows Indians, Mr. Chesney, but one who can find them fast, in a virtually unknown country . . . In short, a man like yourself." He was beaming, for him, as he finished.

"Yes," Henrietta Wagner breathed. Her large eyes were luminous, pleading.

Frank was conscious of a pressure upon him, of a waiting in them all, even in Ed Niles, his friend. Henrietta Wagner's expression was rapt, held in, expectant, fearful he would refuse and hopeful he would not. The resentful thought broke within him: So I'm the big medicine man.

He faced Major Vier, fixing him straight, and some of Frank's feeling slapped into his voice. "Major, that's the quickest way I know to get Emily Wagner murdered. One word from me — just one word — if I ever got close enough to a Qua-ha-da to speak it — would cause her death. The Qua-ha-das want my scalp. They'd take it out on anybody I was tryin' to help." That much is true, he told himself, that much.

Everyone became silent.

Vier looked up. "There's another way," he parried quickly, Frank thought, as if he'd expected a first refusal. "You could lead us to the Qua-ha-da camp. I have authority to take the field whenever the situation warrants. Believe me, the War Department has gone the last pinch of limit with this damnable Quaker Peace Policy!"

Frank's voice was non-committal. "Say we did locate the camp. They'd scatter like quail, and if we crowded them hard, they'd kill their captives first thing. You know what happened on the Washita in 'sixty-eight, when Custer caught the Cheyennes?"

"I was there," Vier clipped.

Frank had the impulse to blurt, Wasn't it back with the wagon train on the Canadian? But he said, with a ruling-out wave of his hand, "Won't work. Old Isaac's your best bet."

He was standing now, not looking at the woman.

Of a sudden she rose and stood between him and the door, almost matching his height. "If —" she struggled, in the most desperate of tones. "If — it's a matter of payment for services . . ."

His face went hot and disgust soured his throat. He inclined his body to brush past her.

"Wait!" she amended, one hand quickly touching him, staying him. "Mr. Chesney.

Please . . . please . . ." and he saw the first tear glitter. "You know what it's like in Indian camps. How dreadful it must be for a child — a little white child! You could help! I know you could!"

He said, "Miss Wagner, I'll have no part in bringing on murder," and again he made a motion to go.

The great wet eyes he was staring into opened wider. "But you wouldn't be! Oh, won't you help her! Just try . . . anything! Don't leave her with those savages!"

"I know this sounds cruel," he heard himself saying, finally, bitterly. "Maybe it is. But why should I help your sister, when one of Chivington's men murdered my wife and my son?"

He cut past her, stepped to the door. Vier's voice was like a club pounding his back. "Chesney! You've got to help!" Frank had a curb on himself before he half turned.

"Help?" he said. "Help who? Is this to save Emily Wagner or round up the Qua-ha-das?" then he went out.

As he rode straight across the parade, he thought of Major Vier that lead-gray morning at Crazy Heart Butte . . .

The sleeping Cheyenne camp pitched along the winding bleakness of the creek. Little Hand and his band of reservation runaways from up north, secure in their belief of refuge here in the Wichitas.

Smoke smell lay strong on the raw, cutting wind. One of the Delaware scouts pointed. A dog barked. A child cried once. Below, in the wintry, steely light, lodges loomed dimly. The stream twisted away into a grayish vastness, the timber lurking dark and dull.

"I'd favor a quick scout below camp before we go in," Frank said to Major Vier. "Creek makes a big bend. Can't tell what's down there from here."

"No need. We've got them."

"Expect there's more Indians downstream, Major. 'Rapahoes. They run with Cheyennes."

"I don't share your overcaution, Mr. Chesney."

Again, the plaintive cry of a child reached them.

"We can't wait!" Vier exclaimed, pounding his McClellan, "Camp's waking up. When we open the attack, you and the Delawares will cut out the pony herd."

Major Vier called his officers, among them Captain Parkhurst and Lieutenants Niles, Allison and Monahan, and gave his orders. The conference broke up and Vier struck immediately, sending two converging columns toward the tipis, while the scouts and Frank rode for the dark mass of the pony herd downstream.

Behind him, Frank heard brisk firing commence, heard the reports scatter as the Cheyennes broke for the only cover left them, the straggling, leafless timber along the frozen stream. Somewhere an Indian woman was wailing over her dead, high, despairing, hating.

Frank took the Delawares to the bunched pony herd, where two half-grown Indian boys loosed arrows, then flogged their ponies down valley. During a bad time spent turning the milling mass of the unruly herd, Frank noticed Lieutenant Monahan leading a detachment in pursuit of fleeing Indians. The bluecoats were bobbing figures in the gray morning haze; they galloped from sight into the lower creek timber.

Frank watched after them with a troubled eye. What was downstream, hidden from view? More Indians? Even now riding to help their brothers, the Cheyennes?

The thought persisted as he helped push the ponies into the foothills east of camp, beyond reach of the Cheyennes, where the Delawares held them. Swinging back, he retracked to the point where he'd last seen Monahan's men entering the timber, marked now by strewn blankets and several dead Indians. He followed the signs of hasty retreat some distance, until he flinched still at the solid rattle of carbines.

Close, he thought. Heavy. He rode faster. He topped a hill and looked down, alarm leaping in him.

Below, in the creek bottom, a clump of dismounted cavalry, surrounded, fought Indians on horseback and Indians crawling through winter-yellowed grass. The murky haze lifted for a space as wind whipped between the hills. Farther down, where the creek banded wide, tipis dotted the valley floor. He could make out swirls of movement, mounted Indians cutting short, quick circles. The Indian signal for *Come on, big fight.*

He slammed his horse around, already estimating how soon Major Vier could bring up the command.

Major Vier, alone in the center of the wrecked and smoking camp, was watching troopers set fire to the remaining buffalo-skin lodges. Off from him in littered piles was heaped all the belongings of an Indian village — blankets, buffalo robes, cooking utensils, beaded clothing and parfleche bags of dried meat — most of it burning, smoke skittering on the wind. He seemed to eye everything in detail, to single it out, it struck Frank as he drummed up.

"Lieutenant Monahan needs help!" Frank called. "He's down valley — hemmed in!"

"Monahan? He's with Parkhurst."

"I saw him chasing Indians that way, Major. I found him. He can't hold out long. Whole lower valley's full of Indians."

Vier displayed a quickening interest. He sent a gauging look in that direction, and then said deliberately, absolutely, "Parkhurst would have reported it if Monahan was cut off."

"But I tell you I saw troopers down there!" Frank's voice sounded flat and angry. "There's time to —"

Vier was turning his horse away. Meaning sprang through Frank, an incredible meaning. Vier wasn't going to send help. That was all.

Frank, too stunned to protest further, watched the Major ride across and with fastidious concern point to a small pile of blankets which the troopers had overlooked burning.

Presently, Recall went out and the command began reforming, straggling in, herding some prisoners. But Lieutenant Monahan and a number of enlisted men were missing. By then there wasn't time to search, for Indians were appearing on the back ridges, rushing up from the lower valley.

Major Vier skirmished as he withdrew to Fort Hazard with his prisoners and captured ponies.

Days later a lone Caddo hunter rode in with confirmation of what the post already knew. He'd found sixteen pony soldiers — dead, scalped, hacked, stripped. The signs indicated they'd fought well, long enough, possibly, for a rescue column to have reached them in time — if Major Vier had known, which he had not, post critics agreed.

Frank had kept the story to himself, realizing few people would believe him if he told it. He'd said nothing, not even to his friend, Ed Niles, not wanting Ed to carry the burden of such a secret. Furthermore, Frank knew the army; it stood by its own to the last. Regrettable. A sad loss, of course. A question of judgment in the field . . . Why risk the entire command in a doubtful situation?

CHAPTER 3

Frank Chesney awakened to a post already going about its morning duties. From the direction of the parade ground somebody shouted commands in an iron voice. Horses traveled hard, stopped; there was the brittle clank of equipment. Nearby, in the sutler's barn-like store, army wives visited over their purchases and the mere sound of their voices filled him with an unaccustomed contentment.

He pushed up, planted his bare feet on the cool dirt of the packed floor and moved lazily to the narrow doorway of his one-room adobe quarters, an unshaven man stripped to the waist, his hard body white below the burned saddle-brown of his neck and face, the folds of his torso muscles lax. Wind rushed around the house. He could smell the sloping prairie, clean and sweet; in another hour the land would be baked and shimmering, brass-bright. He gazed off at the hotel, at the fort's clustered stone buildings . . . and then the morning shifted completely.

He was through at Fort Hazard — had

been the moment he stalked from Major Vier's office. Vier, intolerant and unreasonable when crossed, would not forgive.

Frank turned to the plank table and sat with his blunt hands idle, his head tipped down, remembering the young woman's face, her disappointment, her crushed defeat as he walked out. He regretted that, but he had stated his reasons and they still stood. His feud with the Qua-ha-das, that alone, made him dangerous to Emily Wagner, though the real cause was the ancient hurt he'd ground out.

Thus, he knew he'd be riding again, except no new land beckoned this time. He was weary of mind and body, and he realized he'd left a vital part of himself buried in the high Colorado country.

He sat still and his mind settled backward. Bird Woman . . . doe-eyed, slim as a reed, wanting her son to grow up like a white man. Not forever hungry and driven into the mountains like her mother's Ute people.

He could see Colonel Chivington's volunteers passing along the stream where Frank was placer mining. Men fresh from the slaughterhouse of Cheyenne and Arapaho women and children killed like beeves in the pits on Sand Creek. Men waving scalps at him as they rode by. Varmint hunters, they called themselves. Disorderly men, all bearing the same wild lust. A few, Frank knew by sight; of none was he proud.

Near dark, he entered the canyon; coming up it, he stopped on faltering feet. Where light should have been, he saw just the blurred square of his darkened cabin, the blacker patch of the single window. Something clutched his heart.

He was calling as he ran, then groping inside in cold darkness, calling and fighting a terrible silence; fumbling, lighting a coal oil lantern and wheeling instinctively upon the baby's rocker crib.

It was empty. His eyes edged away, pinned, horrified, on the floor, on the battered pulp of the small shape.

He moved like a wooden man for the off room, aware, as a cold, final voice drummed, of what awaited him before his dreading eyes found it.

Bird Woman lay like a discarded bundle left behind in the ruin of the room, wrecked by a savage struggle. Down on his knees, shaking, he set the lamp and turned her over, his throat choking. She stirred feebly at his touch — moaning, protesting, one warding-off hand lifted.

Gripped in her nail-torn fingers, he saw the greasy cloth eye patch. Only her strewn black hair covered her. He found a blanket.

Within the hour she was gone, passing like a whisper of troubled wind, wandering off. Gone.

He had just the soiled eye patch and her dimming voice, telling him in broken bits . . . Big man . . . soldier . . . strong. Hair like red horse . . . One eye . . . Look for gold first. I no tell . . . Say he know you . . . Watch cabin many times . . .

That was all she told him, but the look of terror on her bruised face branded it upon him. He couldn't place the man. Hundreds of gold-seekers had tramped and milled about the country.

His hunt led Denver way, where Chivington's butchers had returned as short-lived heroes.

A patch-eyed man was noticeable, though the mark made him no easier to catch than the next faceless, anonymous rider. Gradually, by questioning and listening, seldom making a fire in the same place, Frank pieced together a name and a picture.

A drifter named Yeager. Bull-chested. One-eyed. From the ridge country district Frank had prospected . . . Yeager, riding for loot with Chivington's volunteers at Sand

Creek . . . Yeager, recognized in Denver as a deserter and murderer of a Fort Lyon Captain . . . Yeager running southward, pursued by a detail of cavalry . . . Into New Mexico, where traders sent long trains of goods-laden *carretas* into Comanchería . . .

There Frank lost the tracks.

Meanwhile, a man had to have something in his belly, and Fort Union presented the nearest solution. Signing on as a scout and hunter, he rode with a column aiming to stamp out the snake-head of rifle traffic between the pleasant, but "no sabe" New Mexicans and their stock-stealing Indian customers.

Approaching the Valle de las Lágrimas, the Valley of Tears, the cavalrymen caught the Comancheros in camp. It made little difference. Comancheros are merchants, not fighters; they merely shrugged at the unpredictable fortunes of plains trading and offered up not a shot. But the Qua-ha-das, camped farther on, fought viciously, until their camp was in motion, then faded from grasp.

An old Comanchero, tight-lipped until hanged a little while from the tip of a wagon tongue, gasped out, purple-faced, why the Qua-ha-das were ready.

Señors, it was the white man's fault. The

one-eyed gringo working for us . . . He warned the Qua-ha-das. Not us! You must believe! Not only did he warn the Qua-ha-das, he joined them . . . fought on their side. Deserted us . . . which is just as well. We want no more of him. He is *muy malo,* that *hombre!*

Yeager, riding now with the whirlwind people, the Qua-ha-das, could be anywhere within a trackless world that leaped across the Llano and into the Nations, clear to the Washita, and south from the Cimarron to the Rio Grande. Yeager with the Qua-ha-das and Frank taking scouting jobs that drew him in and out of Comanche country. One season he hunted hides, the season he killed the young Qua-ha-da chief. But the buffalo slaughter suited neither him nor his purpose. He returned to the army, in New Mexico and Texas, traveling from one sun-blasted post after another, and his man still eluding him.

By this time the Comanches were locating around the new soldier house north of the Red, and Frank took himself to Fort Hazard. Scouting, at first a necessity for existence, had become a skilled trade, a lonely way of choice which allowed him a solitude he'd grown to like, a shell into which he could crawl and not be concerned

61

with the people outside.

Now, he stood up by the table, an unhappy realization coming to him. In these years he'd learned to live by himself — so long as he kept moving, keyed to the fierce demands of a dangerous living. He'd hired out to Major Vier, abided the man after Crazy Heart Butte, simply because he needed a job while he continued the endless, mechanical searching. On the loose again, he discovered that much of his driving vengeance had dulled, blunted by time and failures and a weariness not alone of the body. Bad, it was, for a man to dwell too long over the tracks he could not remake . . .

He walked suddenly to the doorway, scowling out at nothing in particular. The young woman, he thought, Henrietta Wagner . . . she had proud eyes. Same straight-on look Birdy had. Still, the two were as unlike as warm sunlight and first dusk, one fair skinned and strong, the other dark and slim. But was that all he saw in this determined Tehanna woman?

An hour later, he rode past the hotel, bound for the Indian agency, thinking of old Isaac Roberts.

Most of Isaac's Quaker employees had scurried back to Kansas and Iowa after the first Indian scare last spring, and the agency was still short handed. Almost always there was need of a rider for the crew handling the agency's main cattle herd, grazed for reasons of safety sixty miles east in the Chickasaw Nation until issued in small bunches at the commissary corrals.

Frank let his horse set the gait. He was stalling, for once unwilling to put a place behind him, whereas before any impulse had been excuse enough to ride.

In no hurry, he angled east to catch the shade of the cottonwoods and pecans along Cache creek. He followed this meandering way until Buffalo Quinn's trading store, a low-roofed structure of chinked logs, loomed among the trees.

Frank's approach was quiet as he walked his horse over the spongy footing of the creek bottom. Hearing loud voices, he saw a Comanche stomping from the store, followed closely by Quinn. They halted in the shade of the littered yard, Quinn holding a buffalo robe. He made the sign for friend, but shook his head. The Comanche grunted something low, his finely muscled body stiff.

Quinn's head-shake denied again. Suddenly, strongly, the Comanche jerked the robe from Quinn. With an angry, striding motion, he sprang to his pony's back and tore west at a run. Worry mounted in Quinn's face as he watched the Indian go.

Frank, who had stopped on the rim of the yard, rode ahead now. As he did, Quinn turned with a startled recognition. Frank nodded, riding on. Quinn called in a booming voice.

"Get down, Chesney. Stop and light."

Frank turned his horse reluctantly. He said, "Hello, Quinn," and again lifted reins.

"No hurry, is there?" Frank felt the inspection of bright canny eyes. "Blamed if I ain't glad to see a white man this mornin'."

Buffalo Quinn was impressive in a raffish, loud-talking manner. His tawny hair he wore long, in the General Custer style; the ends of his yellow mustache bending downward like tired wands. He was middle-aged, deep-voiced, big-boned, his gestures grandiose. On his visits to the fort he wore a broad-brimmed hat, a fringed buckskin jacket of Comanche design, and carried a Colt Navy revolver with silver stars embedded in the handle. Even now he fancied a beaded vest, greasy down the front, and knee-length black boots.

He claimed to have hunted buffalo for the railroad crews building across Nebraska; if his listeners lingered after that story, he told of fighting the Cheyenne and Sioux nations, throwing back his head and waving his hand as he did, his voice like a drum. Between drinks and, with a sly wink and lowered tone, he might admit having taken his share of Injun hair, and then some, b'God! He spoke a fair smattering of Comanche, the trade language among the Southwestern plains tribes, and nasal Kiowa, and could manage sign like a full-blood. He traded cheap blankets, knives, pots, tobacco, coffee beans, and showy, worthless geegaws for tanned buffalo robes, deerskins and fast ponies. His store was a loafing place for motley civilian hangers-on, Indians and soldiers, when not off limits.

Frank doubted everything about the man except his shrewdness. He was eternally bragging, he was penny-grasping and unscrupulous and drove a merciless bargain, Indian or white, and yet he was blandly persuasive and his agile mind had the cutting edge of a hatchet.

"Something wrong?" Frank asked.

"Wrong?" Quinn seemed surprised. "No shootin' trouble, friend, if that's what you mean. It's what's got into these Comanch' an' Kioways. Independent, they are. Me, I offer a good trade an' they swell up sore. You saw that Comanch' ride off like a wet hen."

Frank smiled dryly. "Maybe somebody told him prime robes bring three-fifty at Fort Griffin . . . not a dollar."

"Sure," Quinn complained, not batting an eye. "They got a market. Nothin' much here. Time a man hauls to Kansas, an' pays freight, the damned railroads got his poke. That's what hurts the hide business. I offer what I can. Injuns know that." His florid face was smooth as he finished, his voice convincing.

Frank said nothing.

"Like I told you," Quinn went on, "an Injun can be mighty ungrateful at times. Reckon I know the trouble signs, long as I been around 'em. If I wasn't tied down here, with a trade to look out for, I'd offer my services to Major Vier. I sure a-mighty would."

"You figure Vier needs somebody who knows Indians?"

Quinn raised a tactful hand. "Now don't get me wrong, friend. I know you scout for the army. Trouble is, you can't be around all the time, on call night an' day. Vier should know more things." The trader, casting a wary glance about, closed in until he stood at Frank's stirrups. Frank had the returning impression of an actor strolling to the center of a stage to speak his lines.

66

Quinn said importantly, "For instance . . ." and halted for a certain emphasis.

Frank was unimpressed.

"It's this," Quinn said. "That Comanch' you saw. Know what he was after? Well, he wanted me —"

Horse sound drummed across Quinn's talk. Looking up, Frank saw a family of Indians approaching, travois style.

"— to sell him a rifle," Quinn finished. "Might pass it on to the Major."

"You tell him," Frank replied. "I don't scout for Vier any more."

"Since when?"

"Yesterday. Anyway, Indians always want guns. What you say means nothing — unless you sold him a rifle." He said it deliberately, abruptly.

For an instant Quinn had no answer. Then indignation fired into his face. "I turned him down! Why d'you think he rode off mad?"

"He'll be back," Frank predicted, "when he gets enough loot together."

Into the yard rode the Indian family. The buck called to Quinn, who shot Frank another affronted look before turning away.

Passing from the timber, Frank knew he didn't trust the man. Quinn played both sides of the game and the only reason he'd mentioned the rifle was for fear Frank might have overheard the tail-end of the argument in the yard. But Frank hadn't. He'd merely guessed at what he'd seen — guessed right — and it had angered Quinn.

A low adobe building formed on the brown plain, an out-scatter of sheds, a long storehouse, and steam-driven lumber mill. Farther west, dust marked the agency's commissary corrals.

A tall-bodied woman, carrying a fold of clothing over one arm, left the storehouse. She spotted Frank and drew up, tense, watchful while she eyed him. He recognized Martha Roberts, whose advanced years suggested her proper place was home in Iowa enjoying her grandchildren, instead of accompanying her farmer-husband to a far-off land, wild and foreign to all she knew. Despite the heat, she wore a long-sleeved dress of heavy material. Under her bonnet she presented a tired face, framed in plain, even-lipped lines.

"Jim Dan told us," she said kindly. "Is the day well with thee?"

It was, he said, and added, "I want to see Isaac."

Nodding, she indicated the distant corrals. "He's issuing beef."

"Kiowas?"

68

"Kiowas and Comanches," she said. "Old Owl's Pena-te-kas. Some have been gone a long time; now they've come back to us."

A good sign, Frank thought, since he'd found Pena-te-kas in the Qua-ha-da sun dance village. On the other hand, raiders among both tribes often reported for rations, the proud Qua-ha-das excepted, having learned that the puzzling white man was more liberal with food and goods after trouble than before. It paid to raid the hated Tehannas!

Frank left her and jogged west.

Stretched out on the lumpy straw mattress, Henrietta felt the projection of her own depression in this dreary room of the Fort Hazard Hotel. Long ago an enterprising soul had attempted to create an air of elegance here by papering the walls with pages of Harper's Weekly and Leslie's Illustrated Magazine. Full-bosomed beauties, their waists like hourglasses, cowered in maidenly fright before mustachioed villains, or reclined on plush sofas, or stood gazing aslant at stalwart heroes. There was a lithograph of General Grant at Vicksburg, grimly victorious, bearing the accurate tobacco-juice autograph of a passing Southern sympathizer. Once scarlet roses had brightened the shabby carpet's pattern. A cracked pitcher and bowl sat on the bureau; countless boots had scarred much of the iron bedstead's enamel. Strips of calico, long since faded dust-brown, hung like limp rags at the window.

Morning heat filled the room and sharpened all the ancient odors impressed into the dilapidated furnishings.

It wasn't like her to surrender to her feelings, but she had yesterday, briefly. Reuel Vier had called for her early in the evening, as usual, and Henrietta, who'd seen so little of brightness and men's attentions in recent months, had pleaded indisposition. A good part of yesterday's dejection still gripped her. She had explored every possibility now except venture into Indian country herself, which was out of the question for a woman. She asked, silently, What can I do? What?

Lying there in the sticky heat, in her undergarments, she reviewed the meeting. Giving credit where due, she decided that Reuel could have chosen a more opportune time. Mr. Chesney — Frank Chesney — looked a weary man. It lay in his rimmed eyes, in his dead voice, in his slouched manner of moving. Under more favorable circumstances he might have listened — he might yet. She sat up. If she could talk to him alone! It had required a night's sleep for such a thought to occur. She felt roused again by the driving self-will that had brought her this far, and yet to nothing more than a repetition of her previous efforts.

Rising, she stood by the window and gazed out, her shoulders bending a little. It was a moment of heartbreak, stiff, yearning, of near panic. Heat devils danced on the empty prairie under a cloudless sky as bright as crushed glass. Her mind's eye reached out. Far to the south, very far, what had been home was a blackened square of ashes and the fire-scarred ruin of a stone chimney, so like a monument in the naked clearing now. She felt utterly and terribly alone, nearer a bottomless despair than she'd ever been, she on whom others so often fed for strength . . .

A horseman swung into view, heading south. He'd been in sight some seconds, she realized; only now had she noticed. He rode without haste. She paid him scant attention until he passed directly below. A gust of excitement seized her as she stared, recognizing Frank Chesney.

She acted quickly, turning from the window to the center of the room, locked in sudden, clamoring thought. Head lifting, she saw herself in the cracked mirror over the bureau. Intently, with interest, she ran her eyes over the tall, shapely figure: firm breasts under the long chemise, narrow waist and rounded thighs and legs outlined despite the loose garment. My eyes, she thought, look tired. She touched her yellow hair and turned her head to either side, inspecting, critical. All at once, she looked aside, self-conscious, on the verge of shame.

But a stubborn purpose had hold of her. Within moments she was dressing mechanically, her mind steady and clear, a sense of desperation hurrying her. She would try what Reuel had failed to do. She would talk to Chesney as only a woman could. If that didn't work she could do no more.

Dressed, she hurried downstairs to the clerk's desk.

"Get me a saddle horse," she told him.

"Yes, ma'am, but —" He hesitated, a pale, round-shaped man, out of place on the frontier.

"What is it? I ride every day with Major Vier."

"I know, ma'am. That's it. Major Vier left word, when you came down after breakfast, to let him know. He . . ."

"I'll see him when I come back."

The clerk persisted in an uncertain voice.

"He was set on seein' you, soon as you came down."

A quick irritation touched her. "I want the horse saddled now. Do you understand?"

"Yes, ma'am." He was watching her worriedly. "Major Vier won't like the idea — you goin' alone."

"You needn't worry. I'm not going far. Just to the agency."

Frank Chesney was out of sight when she left the hotel, and promptly she put her mount to a gallop. From her rides with Vier, under escort, she knew the country ahead first-hand, including the location of Buffalo Quinn's trading store, which she'd never visited, and the agency, where she'd gone to talk with Isaac Roberts. For some distance she used her horse hard, expecting to see Chesney at any moment. When she came over a rise and saw the agency buildings clumped in the distance, yet no movement between and none west, she turned east to the creek, trotting her horse. If he wasn't at the trading store, then she'd lost him.

Coming through the shadowed timber to Buffalo Quinn's, she noticed people and horses stopped in the yard before the log store. Her excitement rose. Moments later she reined up, her disappointment keen.

These were Indians, a whole family, it seemed, and a long-haired white man.

Her horse fiddled quietly as she bit her lip, watching, pondering her next move. There was only one — to go back the way she'd ridden.

Still, she did not go and as she lingered, the sonorous voice of the white man continued to hold her attention. The voice drew her forward, a movement that attracted his eyes and produced a nod. He was speaking Indian, of which she understood not a word; but he was speaking it well, she thought. He made eloquent use of his hands, gesturing importantly to his trade goods arrayed on a blanket: a gleaming copper cooking pot, a cheap-looking butcher knife polished bright, a bundle of dark, twist tobacco.

A heavy-set Indian woman judged the cooking pot, her dark eyes revealing a shy longing. Her Indian man considered first the tobacco and then the knife. He bent and hefted the knife handle, ran his thumb along the cutting edge. His face indicated nothing, though he was slow putting the knife down.

The white man said something that sounded impressive and urgent. He waited for an answer; none came. Shrugging his shoulders, he started to pick up his goods.

As he moved, the Indian uttered a single, stopping word and turned to his pony. He loosened a woolly bundle and returned, unfolding a tanned buffalo robe of soft brown.

It was a good robe, the white man indicated, yet not enough for the costly goods on the blanket. The Indian hesitated, then stepped to his pony again, this time bringing back a deerskin of muted lemon yellow, soft and pliable in his brown hands.

Henrietta felt an involuntary protest. The beautiful skin was worth many times the cheap trade articles.

Fast, but not too fast, the white man closed the trade, crossing his wrists. He took both robes; the Indians stooped to pick up their purchases. The white man turned, and Henrietta saw his shrewd eyes fasten upon her.

He stepped across, his smile cordial. "Lady," he said and bowed, "I'm Buffalo Quinn. Welcome."

He was, she decided, a vain man who lived by cleverness, scheming and making money where others tired of scheming. He had a smooth face and up close his smile seemed a little fixed. He was over-dressed, with the air of a showman. Yet the man interested her and now she began to understand why she'd stopped.

"You drive a close bargain," she said frankly. "That deerskin is beautiful."

Quinn looked hurt, humbly hurt. "Lady, trade goods are mighty hard to come by, freight an' all. Man couldn't stick if he made no profit." She puzzled him. She could see it in his eyes, boldly upon her, questioning why a lone woman rode this way.

She said, "Those Indians . . . what tribe are they?"

"Kioways."

"You were speaking their language. Using sign, too."

"Indeed I was. Kind of a gift, folks say. Natural. I can jabber with just about any these tribes. Delawares, Caddoes, Comanches —"

"Comanches?"

"Even better'n Kioway. Kioway's hard to ketch on to. Mighty few white men savvy it. First place, you talk through your nose, an' like you're choked on meat. All the same time. Like I said, mighty few white men savvy it." He paused, hooking thumbs in his wide belt, studded with stars of Mexican silver, while he tried to figure her. "Officers bring their wives here sometimes to buy robes, beadwork." He bowed again, indicating his store. "Have yourself a look."

An idea was strong in her mind, deepening. "You might show me a few things," she said.

Buffalo Quinn gave her his hand down from the side saddle and afterward, with a flourish, stood aside for her to enter. As she stepped by him, she got a whiff of sour sweat and grease.

She entered a low-ceilinged room, and the reek of hides and tallow came to her nostrils at once. Robes and other skins were piled on the dirt floor. Quinn had his cheap trade goods carefully behind a formidable plank counter; save for one narrow opening, it ran the room's length.

A slender Mexican boy hovered in the rear and an old Mexican man was hunched on a stool by the door. The boy was watching Quinn, a queer, stiff alertness in his thin features. At Quinn's abrupt motion to go, the boy and the old man hastened out together. Through the door, Henrietta could see a few rundown sheds and a pole corral holding several horses.

She turned and interrupted Quinn's gaze, hungry bright on the lines of her body.

"Lemme show you this here buckskin," he said quickly, and draped it across the counter.

She fingered the rubbed skin, feeling the soft texture a while. "I suppose many bands come here to trade with you?"

"Heap of 'em do," he confided. "Some from mighty far off."

"As far . . . say . . . as the Staked Plains?"

He drew in, scowling. "If you mean Qua-ha-das, no. They just deal with Comancheros."

Annoyance flicked her. No one thought you could contact Qua-ha-das! "You speak Comanche," she said, putting a taunting edge to her voice. "You could trade with them."

He studied her, as if in a new light. He couldn't remember when a young woman as handsome as this one had shown any interest in what he did, and it stroked his vanity. She looked well-fixed, too. He'd learned long ago to spot moneyed people; it was a sense he had. This one had breeding to go with her blonde looks. Nothing cheap about her, nothing like the foul-mouthed women who came up from Texas each post pay day, came with the whisky peddlers and camped in the pecan groves and went off into the brush with the soldiers, two and three at a time. He sized her up, astonished at his own reaction.

"Don't say I couldn't," he said, sounding a confidence he did not feel. "Might if I took a mind to."

"You could find them?"

"Maybe," Quinn back-tracked, "if it was worth my trouble."

An impossible thing kept flickering in her mind. "What do you call worth the trouble, Mr. Quinn?"

"Money, Lady. Hard money." His bargainer's eyes weighed her meaning and its exactness eluded him. "You ain't no officer's wife or you wouldn't be here alone. Maybe you're just travelin' through. Maybe you're from back East. Maybe you got a notion you can trade with Qua-ha-das. That it?" Suddenly it became a huge joke; his coarse laughter rolled over the room.

"I have nothing to sell Indians," she replied decisively, in a way that straightened his face. She had the impulse to tell him of Emily, then decided against it. "I'm surprised, though, that a man like you makes so little of his opportunities."

Quinn cocked an eye at her. "Know what you're talkin' about? Tradin' with Qua-ha-das is risky! Don't like to stretch my luck that far. Thin enough as it is, right here."

"I realize that," she said, smiling. "But you wouldn't be taking chances like most people. You know Indians. I can see that."

He listened, liking how she put it, and said, "Don't aim to brag, but I seen some

79

tight places in my day. Fought the Sioux an' Cheyenne nations up north. Killed buffalo for a livin' right in the heart of Injun country. Where I got my name. Nothin' stopped me. Did as I pleased." She was, he discovered, an avid listener. He went on. "No man around here savvies Injun ways or tricks like me. Frank Chesney may claim to, but he don't," Quinn snapped, recalling their hot words over the rifle.

"Isn't he a scout for the fort?" she inquired innocently.

Quinn's nod was sour. "Sure got somebody fooled. Just because he holed up with a squaw once, he figures he knows the Comanch'."

"He was married, wasn't he?" It meant nothing to her, and yet she was interested.

"Lady" — Quinn winked and she saw the slyness enter his worldly eyes — "I didn't say married. Does a white man marry a squaw? Common talk at the fort."

"I haven't heard it," she said, finding herself defending a man whom she had no intention of defending. "Perhaps someone should tell him that to his face."

Contempt twisted Quinn's mouth. "I speak my mind to any man. If Chesney was here, right now, I'd say the same. Fact, he was just before you rode up. We had a little argument. I sent him hightailin'. Just as well — him an' Vier fell out over somethin'. Chesney's through at the fort. Wouldn't be surprised a-tall if he don't leave the country."

That alarmed her. She had listened too long to this Buffalo Quinn, this braggart. Perhaps, if she hurried, there was yet time to catch up with Frank Chesney if she could learn where he went.

"You must be joking," she said, standing clear of the counter. "I saw no man between here and the fort."

"Chesney didn't go that way. He was headed for the agency."

She moved to the doorway, trying not to hurry, and heard his boots strike the tamped floor as he followed her. "Better buy that deerskin," he said in his overly hearty manner. "Worth twenty times what that Kioway got in trade."

In Henrietta a tiny warning sounded. She was playing her cards poorly. If Frank Chesney had quit the fort as a scout, to whom could she turn? What if Quinn could help? At this point she realized how deeply her desperation ran. There was, she knew, no limit to what she would attempt for Emily.

"It is pretty." As she spoke, she faced

81

Quinn and gave him the full, deliberate interest of her eyes and a smile that flattered him. "Could you . . . could you save it for me?"

"Save it?" Her request was new to him. He spread his feet and canted his head, seeking to assess her real meaning.

"Yes" — her hands were busy in her purse — "for a few days," she said and laid a ten-dollar gold piece on the counter's edge. Not waiting for him to speak, she turned outside and mounted.

She did not look back; to do so would spoil her exit. She left the yard and traveled steadily across the glaring prairie, feeling the slovenry of Quinn's store and of the man himself dropping away, remembering his close, clamping glance on the gold and his frequent stares at her breasts and hips. She took no pride in the deception she'd just practiced. Of course, the pretty buckskin mattered not; Quinn was sharp enough to understand there was something more behind it and too smart to ask at the time. She hoped she'd not have to return there, but she would if necessary — if there was no other way . . .

The prairie ran on and on, broken by the brown dots of the agency buildings. Seeing them lifted her up, made her feel that anything was possible. She was pushing her horse hard once more, her attention fixed ahead, hoping to see a horseman.

Unwarned, she jerked at the outbreak of hoofs behind her — startled, then calmed when she saw the detail of cavalry, Major Vier in front.

Something in the way he rode told her. He halted his escort and cantered up, alone, a solid bulk filling his McClellan saddle, erect. He bore straight upon her, unsmiling.

"Henrietta," he called sharply, "what in the world are you doing out here?"

"Is it that bad? I just decided to ride."

"Ride — this time of day? You said you didn't feel up to it yesterday evening when I called. Now you have to go in the heat — by yourself — while the country swarms with Indians." He drove his reproach at her. She saw an honest concern and she also made another discovery. Reuel Vier was an extremely touchy man, sensitive to any hinted slight, his self-importance always to be reckoned with, man or woman. Her insight stilled her, troubled her. He hadn't changed in the brief time she'd known him. Had she? She was fond of him; he was attentive. But was she just now really beginning to see him?

He said, "Why, if I hadn't known —" and

compressed his lips.

"You knew I'd gone?" She was taken back, in the sudden chafe of resentment. He kept his mouth firm. Nevertheless, she understood abruptly, and she said, "The clerk — he told you."

He sought to shunt it aside with a fling of his gloved hand. "Now, Henrietta, what's wrong if I look out for you?"

"You have no right to spy on me, Reuel."

"Spying? It's anything but that. I'm just concerned for you. My God, Henrietta, if you only knew how helpless you actually are!"

"Not as helpless as you think. I can ride and I ride well. To tell you the truth, Reuel, I much prefer riding astride than side saddle."

"Where were you going?" he asked crisply.

"The agency. Where else?"

His eyes, on her, shifted and returned. "You rode from the creek. Is that the way to the agency?"

"One way . . . and much cooler."

He wasn't satisfied. "If you're determined to ride that far, you may do so under proper escort."

"I think not," she said, seeing instantly how it would be: Reuel Vier and Frank

Chesney at odds again. "We'll go back, Reuel."

But already she was thinking ahead to the evening.

As the plain flattened, Frank could see mounted Indians around the corrals and two riders inside cutting out stock. When a steer darted out, several Indians would haze the animal to open prairie. Hooting and yelling, a buck would knee-guide his pony in close and knock the beast down with arrows. Usually this did not happen until the steer had traveled some distance, for Indians believed meat tasted better if the blood ran hot before killing. Next, the squaws took over, their curved knives flashing as they cut and skinned and quartered.

Amid the fuming dust near the corral gate, Isaac Roberts marked in his tally book. He looked more farmer than Indian agent in his broad hat, awkward on his horse, a bearded man of thick build, with quiet eyes of solemn patience, shaggy brows and a wide, placid mouth. He rode unarmed, as he did everywhere, while around him milled armed and mounted Indians.

Frank recognized only Old Owl of the Pena-te-ka Comanches, a shriveled, wrinkled warrior whose thin hair was white as bleached bone. He sat his pony alongside Roberts. Now and then he gave a spongy cough and spat into the dust. He was stooped, weary in his high-pommeled, raw-hide-covered saddle, thin and aged, but his dark-brown eyes were alert. He held an ash lance like a walking stick, humped over it, as if he sought support from it even in the saddle.

Frank stopped his horse short, intending to ride in when the agent signaled. Otherwise, he'd stay here and watch until the issue broke up, for it was bad manners to interrupt an Indian receiving rations.

There was an air of tautness here which he sensed as he looked around. Some thirty warriors drawing beef for their families. These men looked well fed; they handled themselves with a kind of arrogance, the way a Comanche will around whites when he's listened to war talk and remembered old wrongs. Frank kept watching them. What had he stumbled onto? Did Isaac realize it? Only Old Owl among them seemed friendly.

A pause came, a quietness fell, as the agent motioned his cutting crew out of the corral, still enclosing a small bunch of steers. Roberts' riders jogged out; one got down and started raising and sliding the gate poles into place.

The surrounding Comanches stirred. By the time the last pole slapped home, they were converging on the corral.

Roberts turned to Old Owl, gestured that the issue was finished today, and the Comanche nodded.

Roberts was about to go when an inward crush of riders made him check up. A young Pena-te-ka blocked the way. He was naked to the waist, a knife at his belt, his movements wolf-like and defiant as he pointed to the leftover cattle, as his hands cut signs.

Frank got it. The Comanche wanted more beef. Now! His people were hungry. These cattle were his. He wanted them pronto!

Isaac Roberts considered him, no visible fear showing. He could speak some Comanche words, Frank remembered, a few. But he had no real knack for the sonorous, flowing tongue and its rolling r's. Sometimes Jim Dan acted as interpreter, or one of the Mexican agency employees. Having previously agreed with Old Owl as to the number of steers to be issued, he hadn't foreseen another parley.

He turned his gaze. His two riders, both boys in their early teens, sat frozen. Fear enlarged their eyes and put strange lines in their young faces.

"One of thee speak Comanche?" Roberts inquired calmly.

Both shook their heads. One licked dry lips and swiveled his head, thus noticing Frank. A quick appeal built in the boy's eyes. Roberts, following the latter's stare, saw Frank for the first time. As Roberts discovered him, Frank was walking his horse forward.

He felt a flinch of caution as more Indians crowded up to the corral. A Comanche wheeled in front and Frank lifted his hand in the brother sign. The Indian held ground, his defiance growing.

Frank, slowly, continued to move in.

A voice shrilled in Comanche; it carried authority. Old Owl was speaking. For several counts the Comanche facing Frank did not budge. Finally, though no less threatening, he swung to let Frank through. But as Frank reached the agent's side, the circle thickened.

Indicating the young Pena-te-ka who demanded more beef, Roberts said to Frank, "Tell Standing Bull the steers left in the corral are for the Na-ko-nies and Yam-pa-ri-kas. Surely he doesn't want his brothers to go hungry?"

Frank, eyeing Standing Bull, took his time explaining. If you talked too fast here that would have just one meaning to an Indian — your heart was afraid. After some moments, Frank began speaking slowly in Comanche, in Spanish, throwing them together.

The Comanche looked back narrowly. "Tell Broadhat he lies! The cattle are ours! We did not get enough last time!"

Roberts' reply was blunt, also patient. "True, you did not get enough beef. That was because Indians raided a herd of Tehanna cattle being driven to the agency for the Comanches and Kiowas. One rider was scalped. A boy. Some cattle killed and butchered, much of the meat left to rot, wasted; many cattle stampeded and got lost. Until another herd comes the Pena-te-kas will have to share with their brothers."

"Broadhat lies!"

Without warning, Standing Bull pushed his pony in still closer. Other Indians flanked him.

Frank got ready. He slid his hand low on his thigh, though he made no gesture toward his carbine. The tiniest wrong move could touch this off. There was a chance as long as both sides talked and bluffed.

Glaring at Roberts, Standing Bull drew

his knife and snatched a hair from his pony's mane. Splitting his glance between agent and hair, he flicked the blade once. Half the hair was cleanly gone. He flicked again and there was only a shortened end; this he pinched up between thumb and forefinger, letting the wind whisk off the remnant.

The white men, he signed, could go as swiftly.

Roberts said firmly, "Tell Standing Bull I see his knife is very sharp, and I'm glad. He can let the Pena-te-ka women use it to hasten the skinning."

Standing Bull's response was to glare more fiercely.

More Indians massed in, all displaying weapons of a sort. One buck commenced taking shells from his breech-loading rifle and noisily snapping them back again. Another strung his *bois d'arc* bow and fitted an arrow to the sinew string and sighted along the dogwood shaft, first at Roberts and then at Frank and then at the huddled, drawn-faced boys, and again at Roberts. Another took his butcher knife and whetstone and went to whetting the blade, making a harsh grinding.

"Tell them," Roberts said, his jaw thrusting out, "I am not afraid."

Standing Bull stepped his pony forward.

Less than an arm's length separated Comanche and Quaker. Standing Bull eyed Roberts' square hands, folded over the saddle horn; he eyed the Quaker's face, as though testing each feature singly for some sign of weakness. A scowl roiled the Comanche's brow. He sat another moment. Very deliberately, he leaned in and pressed his hand over the agent's heart, over the heart of this strange white man who never rode armed.

Roberts sat motionless, like a post, refusing to flinch. Beyond a slight tightening of his mouth and a lacework of moisture under his hat brim, he showed them nothing.

All at once, Standing Bull pulled back. He inspected Roberts again, curiously, impressed. Then he turned his pony and was gone toward the skinning grounds. The others, after a pause, followed in silence.

Just Old Owl stayed behind. He had shifted position, Frank saw, posting himself at Roberts' left, to the rear, his parchment hands gripping the ash lance in readiness. His toothless grin was approving.

"Broadhat no scare," he said, touching his own heart.

Roberts appeared to have forgotten he'd outbluffed the young Comanche men. He

91

was worriedly considering the steers left in the corral when the old Pena-te-ka peace chief spoke in soft, hesitant Spanish.

Roberts shook his head at Frank. "What did he say?"

"No Pena-te-kas will steal the cattle. Not tonight. But better issue them by tomorrow. After that, Old Owl can make no promises for the young men."

Roberts nodded in agreement and Old Owl, coughing wearily, headed his pony away.

Gazing after him, Roberts said, "Old Owl won't live much longer, I'm afraid. He used to fight the soldiers. Now he keeps many Comanches out of war. If it wasn't for him and Kicking Bird, who holds three-fourths of the Kiowas in line, we'd have an empty reservation. Neither will Old Owl be pushed or driven. He's a peace chief, but he has pride. He's still a warrior."

Almost brooding, Roberts peered at the hot, white sun and the heat-hammered face of the powdery prairie, so dry that an Indian woman's moccasins raked dust as she loaded beef on a travois, so alien and barren in the eyes of this stubborn, tranquil man whose senses quickened whenever he dwelt wistfully on the black-soiled richness he'd left behind to come here. Still, inhospitable as it was at times, like a desert in summer and early fall, the prairie was a place where his conscience dictated he must be. He had decided that long ago. He must accept it and be content.

Sighing, he said, "I thank thee for thy help, Frank. Thee will eat with us. Thee and the boys."

They talked as they rode along and presently the matter was settled. Besides needing a man to handle the herd problem, Roberts could use someone to assist around the agency. He looked thoughtful when Frank told of his refusal to aid in the search for Emily Wagner.

"A hard thing," Roberts said. "An old story. Texans coming to our agency looking for their taken people. I talked to Miss Wagner about little Emily. It is sad. I asked other bands to carry ransom talk to the Qua-ha-das. They refused. Everyone is afraid of the Qua-ha-das."

"Old Owl's not. He might help. I saw Pena-te-kas in the Qua-ha-da sun dance camp."

"He's man enough. Has a warrior's prestige and a sense of honor; is sympathetic. Except he says what the Qua-ha-das do is their business. We must remember Old Owl is tired and old, like his name. Besides, a sick man. His lungs. The ride would kill him, and a lesser chief wouldn't be heard."

"There's Kicking Bird. He's got a say with the Kiowas."

"Just the Kiowas. If any other band had the little girl, I could hold back their rations 'til they brought her in." Isaac Roberts stared long at the ground, his heavy face solemn. "Meanwhile, the Qua-ha-das live well off Texas cattle and buffalo, and a child's life is at stake."

"That's what I mean," Frank said, and yet his arguments had lacked their former conviction when retold to Isaac, although his feelings, like a tap root growing deeper, hadn't changed. He kept silent, somehow dissatisfied.

They rode a little way and old Isaac said, "Hate is destruction in itself, Frank."

"My family was wiped out by a white man."

"The man deserves punishment," Roberts agreed, to Frank's surprise. "He did a terrible thing."

"You think I'm right?"

Frank felt the placid eyes straight upon him as old Isaac asked, "Thee means going on, hunting the man who wronged thee, or not helping Miss Wagner?"

"Well . . ." Why did he hesitate? "The stayin' out part."

Isaac Roberts strayed his glance across the brown-burned country and back before he put reflective, even words together. "I can't tell thee what thee must do." He trailed off a moment. "What worries me is thy hate; it's hurting thee, Frank."

"I got a right to kill him!"

"No doubt thee will some day."

"Why shouldn't I?"

"It is in thee," the older man said, with gentle compassion. "Thee's hating too hard. Thee's turning away from other people, when they need thee, and it's not like thee. As though God gave thee a great power and thee won't use it."

Frank couldn't anger at him. Neither could he hold to Isaac's calm stare. Frank looked front, thinking how damned uncomfortable old Isaac, in his simple, reasonable way, could make you feel.

They rode on, observing the silence.

A streak of dust boiled like surly smoke this side of the agency. A single horseman in gallop; he closed rapidly, Sergeant Tinsley of M company.

"Major Vier's respects, sir.

Isaac Roberts looked vaguely troubled. "Good day to thee, soldier."

The thrust of his jaw increased as the sergeant handed him a folded paper from his jacket. Roberts scanned it, his mouth working with a ponderous concentration. He hauled in a deep breath, scowling, and the hand holding the message dropped. A kind of perplexed despair sat heavy in his eyes.

His voice was dull and wooden. "A woodcutting detail was wiped out this morning. Major Vier's issued an order . . . All bands camp east of Cache Creek within twenty-four hours, else be driven in." He moved his head from side to side. "Not enough time. Now the innocent will suffer with the guilty."

CHAPTER 4

The sun was low when Frank passed the hotel. He rounded the sutler's store to the pole corral, turned loose his horse for hay and grain, and entered his adobe to find one of Ed Niles' mocking notes ordering him to report for dinner. His first reaction was to refuse, reasoning that he wouldn't be helping his own uncomfortable position by dining a man high on Major Vier's displeasure list. On second thought, he changed his mind. He longed to go; been a long time since he'd visited them. These people were the closest friends he had on the post, along with Jim Dan, and Louise Niles worried him.

He kissed her offered cheek while Ed Niles grinned at them. "Louise," Frank said, "you make a man feel younger."

She was glad to see him, smiling, but as she looked him up and down an unhappiness returned. "You're too lean and overworked," she said. "Oh, I don't know what's worse, being in the army or scouting for it. Either way you're ground under . . . Frank, don't let it smother your life as it has ours. Get out before it's too late."

A shadow clouded her husband's easy grin. "Now, Louise," he said gently.

Louise Niles had large hazel eyes, a sensitive mouth and a round face made almost child-like by the mass of rich auburn hair. She was slim-shouldered, pretty in a fragile, big-eyed way that never failed to touch Frank, as if she were some small girl lost in a strange and frightening land, which he guessed she really was, Ed having brought her here from a well-to-do Philadelphia family. She didn't look well. Heat flushed her face; the big eyes showed lack of sleep. Her mouth was tired at the corners, and the child inside her seemed enormous for her small-boned body. She wasn't the laughing, natural girl of a year ago. There was a bitterness when she spoke.

"You needn't try to correct me, Edward. It's all too true." She left them, then, moving heavily, her weariness breaking through again as she called tiredly to the girl hired to help in the kitchen for the evening.

Niles said, very low, "I haven't told her about you and the Major. She'd just fret some more, be afraid you'd leave. She can't stand to see close friends leave the post, Frank. Still talks about the Fitzpatricks; they've been gone to Fort Richardson six months."

"I shouldn't be here tonight, Ed. It's a bother."

Niles lifted a silencing hand. "You're far better medicine than I am. If you pull out, I might as well resign my commission."

"You won't have to. I'm lined up with Isaac Roberts."

Niles sat up, relieved. He punched Frank's shoulder. A gradual soberness altered his face. "So you know about Vier's order?"

"Isaac told me."

"Well —"

"I don't like it. He's forcing trouble. How can all the bands get east of the Cache in time? Isaac did the best he could. Sent word to the camps."

Niles was watching the kitchen door. He was going to speak when Louise appeared. He waited until she passed to the bedroom, then said regretfully, "Eight men in that wood-cutting detail."

"Kiowas or Comanches?"

"Couldn't tell for sure."

"Comanches, most like. Too much sun dance. They got mean with old Isaac today. Wanted trouble. He bluffed them down."

"Another bad sign, then."

"How's Vier going to handle this?"

"Hostages, I gather," Niles replied

gloomily. "Not that he's said so. I'm just guessing." There was a pause. "How will it be?"

"They'll come in or spook."

"I mean, if we start rounding them up?"

"Like hitting a wasp's nest with a rock. They'll scatter and swarm somebody."

"Like the Crazy Heart fight, maybe?"

"Vier might stir up half a dozen Crazy Hearts before it's over," Frank predicted. "Louise know a campaign's coming up?"

Louise, entering at her heavy, careful walk, brought an end to the conversation. Both men stepped to her side. She had combed her pretty hair and the mellow candle light struck flecks of reddish gold, restoring much of her undeniable charm. Her eyes shone livelier, her well-shaped mouth had a freshened fullness.

Afterward, on the stone porch, Frank said his thanks and goodnight. Louise, he sensed, had lost some of the gaiety she'd displayed during the meal; now she was almost as before. Ed made a tall, thoughtful shape beside her.

"Come back," she told him, stiff and heavy in the half-light. "Promise me, Frank."

He smiled and took her hand and murmured, "Just try and run me off."

"Remember, that's a promise."

He was gone all too quickly for her, his horse a high bulk moving across the moon-bathed square. "He's lonely," she said and watched another moment and turned to the heat-filled parlor. Niles followed. She stood still and kept her back to him, and it was the turned-away stiffness of those small, lovely shoulders that tore into him.

"What is it, Louise?"

She answered without turning her head. "You're still trying to hide things from me, Edward."

"Like what, now?" His voice was gentle. "A good many things happen around an army post. A big one, like this. You wouldn't want to hear them all."

She faced him accusingly. "Those poor men! Killed — murdered in the mountains! Mrs. Sweeney told me this afternoon."

"I was going to tell you, Louise."

He might not have been in the room, so lost and far away did her voice sound, so lifeless and dull. "A campaign . . . there's a campaign coming. You'll be gone. Mrs. Sweeney says —"

"I wish," Niles interrupted wearily, "that woman would stay out of this house. She breeds rumors. If she hears none, she makes up her own."

"She's kind. She means well — and it's the truth, isn't it?"

"We'll know tomorrow." He took her arm; she wrenched away. "Louise," he said, "you're not going to be left alone when the baby comes, no matter what happens. Whether I'm here or not. Now please quit worrying."

She eased her unwieldy body to a chair and reached for a fan on the table. Her weakness appalled him; it pulled him across to her and he regretted his tone of moments ago. "I'll get you a glass of wine," he said.

"No."

"Maybe you'd better get some rest."

"I'm not sleepy." She fluttered the fan while she continued to stare straight before her.

He studied her in a puzzled, hurt exasperation. He was young and his knowledge of women was confined to this one pretty young one, accustomed to every comfort of life and the attentive presence of a generous, spoiling family. The impulse to speak harshly came to him with a powerful surge. His breathing was heavy, his mouth hard. But catching her depression again, it occurred to him that the heat and the nearness of the baby had affected her mind a little, and that such was merely the usual course of things. So he thought the rough, hurting words, thought them only and let them beat and break themselves against the walls of his mind. In the gentlest of voices, he said, "Whatever you want, Louise."

"It's not what I want," she replied. "It's what happens out here to a woman. I know. Look at Eileen Fitzpatrick. Wrinkled, lean, when she left. She was pretty once. Very pretty."

"Still pretty," Niles said.

"I'll be bloated when the baby comes," Louise continued. "I look horrible enough now. Old. My skin is already dry, like leather. I'll look like a homesteader's woman. My hair . . ." She made a helpless gesture.

"Your hair is as pretty as ever. If you could only see it in the light as I can. If you could've seen yourself as you came to the table tonight, in the candle light."

Her mouth and cheeks smoothed; for a moment he thought she was going to smile. Instead, her fixed composure returned, and, hoping to erase that, he stepped over and kissed her on the temple.

The touch of her skin startled him; it was moist, hot. He waited for her to tilt her face to him as she used to. He bent for her kiss and put one arm around her shoulder. She did not stir. Under his hand her body was like putty, without life. He came slowly erect, aware of something he'd never admitted to himself until now.

There was a gap between them, widening these late months, widening steadily, and it wasn't because of the baby, he knew. Louise was sick of army life — the heat, dust, cramped quarters, lack of gaiety, his dreary outlook for promotion. She was unable to view the future as he did; she could not be content. He liked men and his easy-going nature reconciled him to the plodding pace of whatever uncertain prospects lay ahead. He had never quite found himself, he was somewhat unsure; perhaps he'd be fortunate to die a major.

In silence, Louise stood and went like a sleepwalker into their bedroom. He heard the rustlings as she undressed, heard the bed creak.

An hour later she was still awake in the dark room when he lay down on the makeshift cot across from her. The still air was sticky, it made the skin cling to the hot sheets. He was sweating freely.

She stirred and he said, "Louise," and found her hand, trapping it gently. "What is it? Everything? This place? The way we have to live?"

She was flat on her back, staring up at the ceiling, her breathing deep, uneven. The suggestion of a child's wistfulness crept into her tone.

"I keep remembering when we were married back home. You know, I've never seen a church so nice. Not since. And there were so many lovely parties, fun and music we never have anymore. The houses . . . the pretty houses and flowers. You can't even raise a flower garden here. Why couldn't it last, Edward? Why?"

He framed his reply carefully. "I enjoyed those things as much as you did. We rode the cloud as long as we could. Yes, it was wonderful. We had our turn," he said and tightened his hand over hers. "But this is living, too. It'll be better after the baby arrives. Children make a family. You'll see," he assured her.

She was silent so long he thought she'd drifted off to sleep. Then he heard her move and begin uncertainly, "Edward . . ." not completing her words, though he sensed the thought formed clear and strong in her mind.

He turned his perspiring body, hopefully seeking to pierce the gloom around her face. "Want me to get you something? A drink?"

"Never mind."

"I'll fan 'til you fall asleep," he said. "Don't mind."

"No."

He lay back, deeply troubled, wondering how he might yet reach her, what he might say. He kept recalling how close they'd been once; it seemed a long time ago.

"Edward," she said, and the decisiveness he heard alarmed him, "I won't have a child growing up the way we exist here. Soon as the baby can travel . . . I — I want to go home. I want to stay."

He lay still, stunned into dismal silence, and yet he'd seen this coming, he realized now, only he wouldn't let himself admit it. But it was how she'd said it that struck him hardest, as if one of them was already dead to the other.

Taps drifted across the empty, moon-bright square. Glancing back, Frank picked out the single light in the Niles' quarters along Officers' Row. He thought of the two people back there, their youth and their differences, and found no answer. Even Indian women, he thought, want better and they take what comes without complaint.

Reaching his turnoff at the sutler's darkened store, he saw the hotel just beyond, dingy lamplight showing on both floors, and, farther on, the wild, open prairie. On west the mountains, seeming wrongly placed in this rolling prairie vastness, massed like buffalo humps against the sky-line. He rode to the corral through a night as mellow as day, unsaddled and turned to the adobe. He glanced skyward and sensed a tiny, remote calling; nights like this made a man want to stir his stumps and never look behind. He was walking slowly, a kind of rebellion knotting inside him.

"Mr. Chesney."

He froze instantly — and could see nothing. Nothing until, in the twilight shadows under the overhanging porch roof of the adobe, a figure stepped toward him. A woman. The Tehanna woman, her yellow hair like soft gold in this filmy light.

Through a sudden astonishment, he said, "You shouldn't be here. People will —"

"Let them talk." There was defiance in her answer. She had a graceful manner of walking, he saw, in her long skirts. "I have to see you."

"We went over that once," he said, and yet there was sympathy in his tone.

"Please, listen to me. Yesterday was no time to talk. You were worn out. Major Vier was too demanding. I don't blame you the way the proposition was put to you. Like . . .

107

well, like something you had to be coaxed into doing." She wasn't a begging woman; she didn't have to be, he decided.

He looked around. "If you're bound to pow-wow, guess it better be inside." Leading off to the adobe, he knew this was bad. He wouldn't change his mind and she'd just get hurt again. Why talk about it?

Inside, he struck a match and lighted the candle on the table. Turning, he found her quietly behind him in the doorway, and he noted how tall she was. She came in and stood near him; she seemed to stand that near deliberately. He saw the quickening in the blue eyes, the beginning of a deliberateness — he saw it form and settle, then break uncertainly. A ripple passed over him, left him disturbed and unsure.

He pulled out a chair for her and sat himself on the edge of his narrow bed. Resting her hands on her knees, she leaned forward and considered the room with an interested attention.

He said, "Not much. I bunk here when I'm in. It looks it."

"It's cleaner than the hotel."

"You're used to better things." Knowing what was coming, he felt no hurry to reach an unpleasant ending at once. "Any home ranch beats these mangy civilian stops on army posts."

"Our house burned to the ground. But there's still land and cattle. I'm going to have the house built back," she said firmly. "Stone walls three feet thick. This time it will stay. Nothing can destroy it."

"Ranching's a good life. Fits the country. I'd like to try it."

He let talk pass for a spell, content to watch her, admire her. She seemed more natural here than in Major Vier's office, more at ease. She'd changed from the blue traveling suit he remembered to a rose-patterned dress, tight around her strong, smooth body and low over her high, firm breasts in the fashion of the day. Waiting for her to go on, he saw an expression that he couldn't define.

She said, "I was wrong yesterday. I said the wrong thing. About the money. I realized it the moment I said it."

"Not as wrong as you think," he replied, wary, half-smiling. "The army pays me five dollars a day in the field. I work for hire. That's all."

She gave him a straight scrutiny. "I don't believe you."

"You don't have to but it's true. I work only for money." She seemed to seize on a thought. "If so, why did you refuse when I offered to pay you well?"

He saw the trap. He crossed his arms and said, "You heard my reasons; they haven't changed. I can't bring Emily back to you alive. That makes me the wrong man."

"I don't agree."

"You mean you don't understand. One thing, Qua-ha-das want my hair, bad. I killed a Qua-ha-da chief one time."

He saw her determination; if anything, it made her prettier, it accented her well-made features. "If the Qua-ha-das are after you," she reasoned, "why did you scout them this last time?"

"The army'd like to hit the Qua-ha-das, break 'em down, and scouting gives me a chance to look for the man that wiped out my family. White renegade; runs with the Qua-ha-das, I'm pretty sure. Scouting's not like ransom work. Big difference. I'm not tryin' to deal with 'em for something they have and I want. See? If I tried to trade for Emily, they'd make sure I never got her. With an Indian it's slash for slash," he said and struck downward, twice, with his fist. "Maybe I'm the same way." She started to break in, but he spoke first, deliberately making his words cruel and unfeeling. "You won't find any soft spots in me. Don't go lookin' for something not there."

"I know you better," she insisted, shaking her head. "You do have feeling . . . It's there. But you — you're afraid of it. Since that dreadful thing happened to your family."

He kept silent, on guard.

"I'm sorry," she said, coloring, and glanced down at her hands. An earnestness swept into her voice. "I didn't mean to hurt you by bringing it up again."

His jaw firmed. "You didn't. I'm not ashamed I had an Indian wife. Never tried to hide it. Most folks know, I guess." A sensation roughed up inside him. "But I won't take filthy talk because she was Indian. That's what Vier had in mind yesterday, when he beat around the bush. He's got no respect for Indians. Any Indian."

"But —"

"They're all alike to him," Frank went ahead. "Pack of wild animals. Not human. No souls — no hearts. Can't love. All they know is hate, and maybe that's the one thing he's right about. Indian hate for a white man." He shut off, aware he'd been talking at a rapid clip. "My wife was a wonderful woman, Miss Wagner. Our boy — well, he'd be about ten now." He was staring at the floor, the old ache as knotted and big and futile as ever.

Her large eyes were sympathetic when he looked up. "I'm very sorry," she said. "Now I understand why you said what you did, yesterday. Won't you tell me about her?" She was sincere, he saw, truly interested. "Her name? What she was like?"

He wanted to speak, but suddenly the words jammed in his throat. He could not free himself. His chest and throat felt paralyzed.

"Oh!" She leaned as though to touch him, then drew back. "I oughtn't have asked you."

"Her name . . . her name was Bird Woman." There it is, he thought, spoke out.

"It's a very pretty name."

He added nothing.

"Like," she said, musing, "a name you might find in a story. I wish you'd tell me more about her, if you'd like."

"Been a long time."

"Time means nothing. You haven't forgotten her."

He was watching her, fascinated by her frankness and knowledge of him.

"You never will," Henrietta said, "I can see that. I wouldn't like you if you did. You wouldn't be much of a man, either."

He looked at her, half curiously.

"I say that because I'm a woman. I've

never truly loved a man. When I do, it will be forever. I'd want him to feel the same. If something happened to me, my hope would be that he'd never forget me — that he'd remember me with tenderness and gentleness. How could you forget someone you loved, even if you married again? How could anyone? A fine person you'd loved?"

This was unexpected, all the more so coming from a white woman. She swayed him, and presently he was talking naturally. "She was easy to look at. Cheerful. Always cheerful. She liked nice things — she was clean. Slim. Straight. Not very strong. Half Ute, half French . . . We got married Indian fashion, in the mountains. I was a hard-rock miner. Had plenty of money. Paid fifty horses for her. Wasn't a preacher inside five-hundred miles. We didn't need one. The Indian way can be just as binding. She was loyal. Like you, there wasn't any limit to it . . . She wasn't a Christian, but she had faith. Still thought she was going to live, when she was dying."

He stopped all at once, taken by surprise, unable to recall when he'd let himself talk at such lengths about Birdy. He made a blunt, chopping motion and was conscious of a warm embarrassment. Yet, having spoken and retracked the past a little, he felt better

113

inside. It was out of him, at least for the time.

"Now you've heard it," he said.

She sat in a listening attitude, as if he still talked. She rearranged her hands and slowly brought a mingled sympathy and sweet-lipped gravity to bear upon him. "I'm glad you told me," she said, with understanding.

"Afraid that's not helping you," he said, dissatisfied.

"Perhaps I can't be helped."

He was frowning.

"The hotel people will be wondering where I've gone." She rose and idled to the door. There she gazed back and her slow turning motion brought into the dusky light the lines of her smooth body. She said with the frankness which he had come to realize was natural for her, "It's all right. You know what you can do, what you cannot." A belated sliver of emotion twisted and fled across her full mouth. "I have a confession to make. I saw you ride out this morning. I followed. I lost you, came back and waited . . . I came here for one purpose — to make you want to help me. Any way I could. I thought there was nothing I wouldn't do to get that help. Nothing . . . but there is. I've changed my mind."

There was a dead misery showing through

114

as she finished. She lifted her body to stare sightlessly out the door.

He could feel himself changing. But he said, "I'd help if I could. I'm just not the right man. Wish to God I could make you see why."

She half-nodded, head down, and stepped through the doorway.

He stayed motionless, a tide of sympathy coming at him. He stretched out his hand to her in a gesture of helplessness, of under-standing. "Wait," he said.

She walked faster. She was across the porch before he caught her. Involuntarily, he grasped her arm, halted her in the moon-washed yard. He turned her in one fast motion, yet gently. Her head was bowed. Unable to see her face, he had the terrifying fear that she was crying.

He put both arms around her shoulders and drew her to him much as he would to comfort a frightened child, and he felt her sobbing high on his chest. She was strong and yet pliant; there was a faint scent from her hair. For a time, she lay completely against him while he held her, and then she pulled away, her face averted.

His throat felt thick. "Isaac Roberts is the best bet," he said. "If he could find some Indian with prestige willing to talk ransom with the Qua-ha-das —"

He snapped off, eyes narrowing, and suddenly caught her shoulder, gripping so hard she winced with pain. He spun her front with his left hand and reached for her chin with the other. Resisting, she tried to keep her head down. He increased the pressure. He felt her give gradually, heard her quick breathing. Gasping, suddenly she tore loose and he looked down into angry, lovely eyes — eyes that were quite clear.

"You're not crying!" he said, feeling disappointment and disgust. "Put on a powerful act, you did. Fooled me good. Never could stand a woman cryin'. You're mighty foxy — but not foxy enough!"

The bitterness he saw startled him. "Not enough!" she cried. She was trembling, shaking with frustration and hurt. "But I tried! I'm not a coward like you! Dodging so long you're afraid. You don't want to be bothered with people any more. You're afraid — afraid even of me!"

"Afraid?"

"Yes! Afraid you might feel again! Love again! Get hurt again!"

The tears he saw now were real. In a single step, he reached and took her, his arms rough. As he did, suddenly, he heard her explosive breath.

She jerked her head sideways; he straightened her up, rougher than before. He kissed her hard, forcing back her head, his arms pinning her fully against him, the touch of her like a trembling shock running the whole length of him, and the faint-sweet smell of her filling his senses. She made no real resistance, but neither did she respond. Her body, rigid in the beginning, and then almost answering, turned impassive. Her lips, exciting in the first moment, became dull, indifferent.

Baffled, he released her and stepped back. He continued to eye her, jarred by a sharp knowledge. Violence would never bend or break her. She could challenge a man, every last particle of him. But you never knew where one thing ended and another began.

She took a choppy breath, her eyes taunting. "I was wrong. The first way would have worked better on you! I know that now! Oh, damn you!"

She flung him her scorn and turned on her heel.

He watched her, a tall woman in firm stride, graceful even in anger.

He shaved and cooked his breakfast in a thoughtful mood, taking extra long this morning, and walked to the sutler's store, tarried briefly, and started back. Heat from a metal-yellow sky hammered the post in layered, dazzling waves and there was no breeze, the air huddled and oddly still. He strolled to the adobe and sat a while in the shaded doorway, smoking his pipe, not liking the shape of things he saw rising ahead and finding no way he might avoid them. Another night's rest had freshened him, his mind was quick, his senses keen. And he could thank the Tehanna woman for making him take an overdue look at himself, as he'd been and as he now was. He'd lived by one set of rules too long. People, he thought unexpectedly, humbly, were everything.

He came to his feet. He went inside, belted on his revolver, took the Spencer carbine in its saddle boot and walked to the corral, saddled up, and crossed to the hotel.

Inquiring for Miss Wagner, he stirred an irritated grunt from the portly clerk. "She's not in," he said, short and to the point. "Up early and gone."

"Mean she left the post?"

"Not unless she intended to leave her clothes behind, which no woman would do. She rented a horse. Rode off south. Can't say it makes sense to me, her goin' off alone.

But she's got notions of her own, that Miss Wagner."

That she had ridden to the agency Frank had no doubt, so it was with a feeling of relief that he followed south, confident he'd find her in parley with Isaac Roberts.

When the agency came into focus, he sighted horses on travois and dismounted Indians in front of the main building. Children played in the flinty yard and older boys raced ponies on the adjacent flat. Isaac Roberts stood in the center of a group of Indian men, and again Frank was struck by the contrast of a peaceful farmer surrounded by war-like people.

As Frank rode in, the talk was breaking up. Indians moved to their horses.

"Yam-pa-ri-kas," Roberts said. "Small bunch. First to come in."

"Figured Miss Wagner'd have you cornered. Not Indians."

"Miss Wagner? She's not here."

"She rode this way from the hotel, early this morning." Frank glanced to the open prairie and worry began to gnaw in him. He reminded himself that she had a positive streak of independence and therefore a solitary ride wasn't unusual for her; unless she'd ventured west he could see no great cause for alarm. As yet, no Indians had camped east of Cache Creek. He ruled out Buffalo Quinn's store without a second thought, since no self-respecting woman would seek it out, alone, or having run across it during a ride, would stop.

"By any chance," said Roberts, his smile curious, "has Miss Wagner been cornering thee, and thee's changed thy mind?"

Frank considered. "In a way. I been thinking, Isaac, maybe there's a way through the Pena-te-kas, after all. Even if Old Owl's too sick to go, or won't go. Maybe — maybe he can find somebody who will."

Roberts was peering west, squinting, frowning, plainly concerned. "It's Old Owl I'm worried about, Frank. The Pena-te-kas were the first to know of Major Vier's order. Old Owl's camp isn't fifteen miles, due west. His people should be here by now — across the Cache."

"Any sign of No-ko-nies or Kiowas?"

"Not yet, though I'm not worried. They have farther to travel than the Pena-te-kas. Long as the Indians keep moving east, I don't look for trouble. It's the ones that won't budge I'm worried about." Roberts gazed down and his shoulders slumped. "If Major Vier won't crowd too fast — that's the thing. Twenty-four hours isn't enough time.

Frank," he said in an incredulous tone, "Major Vier informs me that four companies of soldiers . . . four companies, mind you; that many — will be posted here by ten o'clock, and Vier himself is taking the field. At that time, they will move out to round up any Indians found west of the Cache . . . I'm going along. There must be no bloodshed on either side." A hopefulness came over the grave, square features. "Thee'll please me much if thee'll go with me. I cannot order thee; there may be fighting."

"All right. Nothing we can do for Miss Wagner today. Man wouldn't get far smoking up peace and ransom to Pena-te-kas while Major Vier charges their camp." Dismounting, Frank realized how unfortunate was the timing of Vier's order. It bothered him and his thinking centered on Henrietta Wagner with a steady insistence. He watched the Yam-pa-ri-kas drag east, and as the sun climbed a band of Kicking Bird's Kiowas pulled in. After much shaking of hands and oratory, Roberts managed to start them eastward again.

"Isaac," Frank said, eyeing the sun, "there's time to make a quick ride along the creek, past Quinn's store, before Vier gets here. If I don't find her, then she's gone back to the hotel, and I'll give up today."

"Quinn's? Why would she go to Quinn's? No place for a lady."

"Where else would she go? Sometimes officers take their wives there for curios."

"She could," Isaac Roberts pondered, "ride east of the creek and circle around to the post."

"Could . . . I won't be satisfied 'til I take a look."

"Thee's worried," Roberts said, himself concerned now. "And she's alone. I don't like that."

Promising to ride after the command if delayed, Frank rode north, toward the post he could not see, before him the dipping prairie vacant and burning to his eyes. He studied the nothingness without letup for two miles or more, his gaze holding until he angled east and the land sloped and he invaded the creek's thick timber.

A hush held here. Buffalo Quinn's yard was empty and the store door was shut, chained securely. A stout wooden shutter, let down from within, closed the single window on this side. Although not familiar with Quinn's habits, he thought this strange, and circling the low log building, he found that the emptiness also included the corral where Quinn kept his Indian trade ponies.

That's it, Frank thought, and then he stopped. Toward the creek sat a square hut made of poles no larger than you'd use to build a calf pen.

Something was in there. He saw no one, but sound had come faintly from inside the hut. Not the brittle, lively sound an animal might make in scurrying, but something dull, just audible, maybe a cough. Crossing over, he looked into a semi-darkness that couldn't begin to conceal the filth — nor the old man on a bed of dirty blankets and brush limbs, cut so long ago the leaves had turned brown. He was Mexican, slight and gray, wizened as dried cowhide, eyes like dingy buttons.

Frank said, "You sick, oldtimer?" and got an uncertain stare in answer. Leaving the saddle, he bent over and discovered the bleeding ear. Dirt on the Mexican's shirt and trousers told plainly that he'd dragged himself here.

"You a packer for Señor Quinn?" Frank asked in Spanish.

A faint glint of feeling leaped into the stare, and passed. The old man's mouth hung open; his face was the color of tallow.

"Did a white woman come here this morning from the fort?"

A vagueness glazed the tired eyes.

"A white woman with yellow hair?"

Frank got no answer; there was no response even in the eyes.

Seeing a tin cup on a table, he took it and hurried to the creek, filled it, and ran back. Inside again, he looked down and stopped still.

The old Mexican was dead. In these last moments, the haggard face and its taut, yellow-muddy skin appeared to have relaxed in a contentment and peace perhaps never found until now.

Isaac Roberts, when told of the dead man in the hut, dispatched a Mexican employee with a spring wagon.

Thereafter, they waited for Major Vier, and the waiting proved short. He came on time, precisely. Four companies, in column of two's, slanted smartly across the prairie, swung into line before the agency and halted.

Major Vier, curt of manner, turned the command over to Adjutant Niles and rode across. He was quick to notice Frank. His singling-out nod was only for the agent.

"I'm going with thee," Roberts said, firm on the point.

"If you don't try to interfere," Vier corrected. "Otherwise, no."

"I want Frank, here, with me. I trust thee's no objections, Major?"

Vier's stare flicked Roberts. "Mr. Chesney is no longer a scout for the army. His services were terminated upon his return."

"That's why I hired him," Roberts replied simply. "He's an employee of the agency now."

The news sat ill with Major Vier and in the pause that followed there lay a definite air of strain. "As you please," he said, contempt for Roberts seeping into his voice. "You may accompany the command if you like. I have my plan. Captain Parkhurst is working northwest of the post."

"An ample force," said Roberts, unusually dry-voiced, and Vier, about to turn his mount, hitched his shoulders sharply. "I told thee that by holding back rations I believed I could force the chiefs to surrender whosoever is guilty. They deserve punishment, I agree. To me that is more just than making everyone pay for the mistakes of a few young men. Whatever is done, thee ought to allow more time. Else we'll have more bloodshed."

"Bloodshed? You think for a minute those Indians hesitated to massacre our wood detail? Of course not. Well, I propose to round up your Indians and drive them in, and those that won't drive the army will make into good Indians. The army's the righteous rod today, believe me. There's your real justice, Roberts."

Roberts bowed his head over his rough, blunt hands, a sadness drifting into his expression. "In the end, mercy will triumph over justice, Major."

"I'll not argue the point," Vier replied, his spurring causing his horse to swerve. "Either attach yourself to the command or stay behind."

Frank, seeing the agent's discouragement, decided he had changed his mind. As the column formed again, however, Isaac Roberts turned his head.

"We'll go with Major Vier," he said.

CHAPTER 5

Henrietta walked rapidly until she rounded the corner of the store. There, quite suddenly, she stopped. As she did, the whole weighted stillness of the night and her failure crushed down upon her. She was alone once more. She had gained nothing. The silver-starred night, warm and close while she waited on the porch, seemed cold and distant, empty of meaning. Wind hissing off the wild prairie had a sibilant rustle. The world around her gave off a dry, dead smell. She stood in dust.

Going slowly on, she reflected with a sharp mixture of irritation and pleasure how he had kissed and held her, his hands more strong than rough. Still, when he'd let her go, she'd found confusion and shame in him for his handling of her. In that moment, she realized, she had begun to know him for the first time. He was lonely, just as she was. But threaded through all this was a new thing — she was willing for him to kiss her. She'd wanted that, she'd needed it, and so had he.

Approaching the hotel, she heard a chair

scrape on the darkened porch. A long-striding man hurried out to meet her. It was Reuel Vier, his quick movements intercepting, impatient.

"If you don't ride alone," he rebuked her, "you go walking alone."

"It's a night for walking. Look at the stars, Reuel."

He ignored the sky and fixed his attention on her, as though seeking a hidden meaning. "Perhaps —" He spoke grudgingly, which told her that the waiting rankled. "Where've you been this long?"

"I just told you," she said, sounding reasonable about it.

"A two-hour walk?" His tone doubted her. He looked back the way she'd come.

"Does it matter? An hour — two hours?"

"It does." He had her arm, turning her away from the hotel, and she sensed his unswerving possession, his suspicion. "I waited here for you," he informed her heavily. "Two hours, Henrietta. Now tell me. What takes you from the hotel like this?"

A rippling resentment stabbed her; she forced it down without speaking. She walked on, collecting her thoughts, tempted to tell him she'd been visiting the sutler's wife, with whom he knew she was acquainted. But her pride took hold. Instead, she paused and deliberately freed her arm, saying, "You're not responsible for me, Reuel," and turned to go back.

He reached her again, quickly, his hand heavy on her wrist. "But I am — that's what I'm trying to tell you." He appeared to wait for her favorable reaction, and when she made no reply, he said in a shortened tone, "You're tired. I'll see you to the hotel. First, however, there's something I propose to make clear to you."

It was coming, as she'd foreseen days ago, and yet she wasn't prepared. When he took her hand, she thought he approached a certain boyishness, a suggestion of humility. In the next instant, it was gone. His expression changed and he was saying in his precise, orderly fashion, "Henrietta, you must have some idea of my intentions by now."

She dropped her gaze.

"I want you to marry me," he said.

"Reuel" — she spoke on impulse, almost sharply — "I can't think of anything like that now. Not 'til Emily's found."

"That may be years — never," he protested, and it came over her how unnecessarily true and unfeeling it was of him to remind her.

"I'd rather not talk about it," she evaded.

"I wouldn't feel right."

"Why go on making life harder for yourself?"

"Don't you see? I would be."

"I don't follow that," he said, displeased.

She made a small motion with her shoulders. "I can't help how I feel. Emily's my obligation." She'd not be pushed; still, she had no wish to hurt him.

He said with authority, as if sensing the change, "Being a major's wife isn't the worst of lives. You'd be the principal woman on the post. People would look up to you. And I won't be a major a great deal longer, I assure you. I have friends higher up. I'm going up in rank. My record's not exactly mill-run. As commanding officer here, I am accorded —"

Her sudden gesture cut him off. "Reuel . . . don't."

He smiled and loomed over her, a wide-bodied man, very sure of himself. A late-coming thought flashed to her that, in his self-confidence, he put first things last — he made no mention of love. He talked of the little things that followed marriage, arranging them neatly before her much as Buffalo Quinn had exhibited his cheap, eye-catching trade goods before the Indian family.

"No man can hold back and expect to impress you," he said, and confidently took her shoulders, bending his head and seeking her mouth. She accepted the formality of his firm kiss and, after a short moment, was the first to draw away. In doing so, she observed his flicker of affront.

She said, "You can't understand about Emily, can you? Why she comes first?"

"My God, Henrietta, don't misjudge me!"

"I'm trying not to. I know it's hard for anyone else to feel as I do, and I don't expect it. But Emily's all I have left — all my family . . . and she's young and helpless." In her straining to be fair to him, she felt herself turn uncertain and dejected.

"I hope you realize I'm doing all I can for you," he reminded. "Didn't I bring Chesney in? Didn't I ask him to lead a search? Of course, I should've known better. These white scouts — they're little more than Indians. Most of them have a string of redskin wives and half-breed children behind them. Unreliable when you really need them. Playing up Indian scares to keep themselves in army pay. Except this time Chesney got fooled." She noted the satisfaction in his voice. "He figured I'd beg him — then raise his pay. Well, he's finished

131

— finished for good. His ability no longer impresses me."

A feeling tapped her. "You said he was the best guide on the post. The only one who knew Qua-ha-das."

"I was wrong. I over-estimated him."

She faced into the night with a fixed despair, feeling entirely alone. She said, "So we're back where we started. Without a competent guide, the army can do nothing."

"There are other guides. I propose to keep looking."

"Where?"

"Perhaps some Texas post can furnish a man." She was silent a long while. If he did mean to encourage her, she decided, little could come of it. "Reuel," she said, "I don't think you can find another man like Chesney — a good one."

"I said I'd look."

"I'm going in," she said suddenly.

"Look here, Henrietta!"

His hand shot out. He had her arm. Again, he glanced in the direction from which she'd walked.

"Reuel! You're hurting me!"

"If you've been talking to Chesney!" he accused. "If he's been feeding you lies about Crazy Heart —"

132

She tore free, so angry that it astonished and frightened her. "Reuel," she said unsteadily, fighting for control, "I want you to take me in — now."

He glared at her. After several more moments, he shrugged and said in his stiff way, "I had no intention of hurting you," which was, she saw, the nearest he could bring himself to apology — if she'd wanted it, which she did not . . .

A great deal later, she lay awake in the heat-filled room. Bits and fragments jostled and drifted across her mind. Reuel Vier and Frank Chesney; she judged the difference between them with a sharpening perception. Each was strong, though moved by far different reasons. In Reuel it amounted to ambition and an inclination to bull over whatever blocked his path; getting there was the thing. In Frank it measured to a swerving from anything that might press old hurts; yet he wasn't cruel, no matter what he'd said. He was very honest and very stubborn. But despite what she saw in him, and what he could be, she had failed to persuade him.

And so a realization deepened. She was like a weary traveler, after finding no clear-cut trail, who turns and sees the distant peak of his destination across glaring wastes, sees it dimly — a way of desperation and the only way left.

Light was still gray when she took the gelding into the clearing and dismounted in front of Buffalo Quinn's store. Smoke coiled from the rock chimney. Bacon smell whetted the air. She tied her horse to a porch post and looked up to find Quinn's furtive face like an unwashed smear at the dirty, fly-specked window. His face vanished and she heard him slide the door bar. There was ever, it struck her, this prying caution about him, which explained, in part, how he managed to get by in a chancy trade.

He handed the door open wide, his flourish grand, too grand, she thought, though the impression was erased by his hearty greeting, "Up kind of early, ain't you?" He eyed her a second, his jaws working on the last of his breakfast.

"A little," she said.

Quinn was dressed the same as yesterday, probably as he had been for a month, save his beaded vest bore fresh grease stains. She noted his shrewdness again, the bold question mark of his glance, the hungry undressing edge of it like a dirty finger tracing the outline of her body. All at once, she

134

wanted to run. She turned, and then, breathing deeply, she brought herself firmly around.

"Did you save it for me?" she asked coolly.

"Give my word, didn't I? Come in." He stood aside.

She hesitated and entered, oppressed once more by the grimy unkemptness. Remembering the slim Mexican boy, she looked around for him. He wasn't in sight. She would have felt more assured were the boy nearby. As it was, now that she had come, she wondered where to start. To find a beginning, she sought additional time by moving gradually along the counter, considering the cheap trade items.

Quinn, stepping behind the counter, drew down the buckskin and spread it out for her inspection. "Nobody can tan up hides like a Kioway," he said.

She studied the soft yellow skin for a pause, and faced up into his greedy eyes and said, "What would you say if I told you I'd changed my mind about the deerskin . . . but for you to keep the money?"

He was surprised. Suspicion sounded in his voice. "You're not fool enough to throw away hard money."

"I'm not. But I can be generous, and

there's more where that came from."

Quinn was a close man, a careful man for all his bluster, and the closeness around his eye corners became a blend of distrust and curiosity. The curiosity got the best of him. He grunted, "What do you want?" and swept the deerskin away.

"I will make it worth your trouble."

"Trouble? What trouble?" Already, as she feared, he was backing off, interested and yet skeptical.

She was cool and direct. "Put me in contact with the Qua-ha-das."

He recoiled a step, his long jaws dropping. "Think I'm loco?" he blurted. "What you fixin' to do? You ain't no Quaker preacher woman, come to save heathen souls. That's a-mighty certain. Don't make sense. Who are you?"

"My name is Henrietta Wagner. My sister was taken captive by the Qua-ha-das in Texas. I'm trying to arrange ransom for her. Does that make sense?"

He wiped greasy palms on his vest. "No, it don't. Not a bit. Plumb crazy. Never been done, I heard tell."

"It can be done," she insisted. A single-mindedness gave her strength; she longed to drive it into him, to forge it into his thinking. "You can help me."

He cleared his throat. "Whyn't you try the fort? Lady, that's soldier business."

She said savagely, "That's the last thing I want — attack the Qua-ha-das. I want her ransomed alive."

"There's the agency," he said, no sympathy in him.

"Isaac Roberts would help if he could. So would Major Vier. But the Qua-ha-das never come in for rations."

Quinn wet his lips. "What about Chesney — this Frank Chesney?"

"I thought," she flung at him, "you said he didn't know Indians?"

"Reckon I did. Maybe he knows enough."

She refused to let him squirm out of it. "Mr. Quinn, you made a claim. A big one. Now stand up to it. You said no man knew Indians better than yourself."

"Some difference," Quinn parried, his florid color heightening, "between knowin' injun ways and what you ask done. A man's got his limits. I know mine. If Ches—"

Henrietta's look silenced him. "He's out of the question. Listen to me," she said, thinking of his conceit. "I came here because I know you can do this. Because you're the only white man that can help me now."

Quinn pulled back a little, his mouth shut tight.

But it beat inside her that he hadn't refused and she waited a moment before she spoke again, murmuring and casual. "Naturally I don't expect you to take me to the Qua-ha-da camp. Even for the gold I'll pay."

Quinn drifted back, like a man on thin ice. His fingers rubbed the counter top. "Lady," he threw in dryly, "you're chuck full of ways to get a man butchered up, ain't you?"

"I said you needn't go to Qua-ha-da country."

He looked amused. "Couldn't if I had the hankerin' — an' I don't!"

"You understand Indians. It shouldn't be hard for you to locate a friendly Comanche, say, one willing to fetch a ransom message to Qua-ha-das."

He flattened his thick hands on the counter and pushed himself erect. She could imagine his careful mind squeezing her words this way and that, for loss or gain.

"Maybe you savvy Comanch' better than me," he sneered, and turned his back and began sorting a pile of gaudy blankets.

She had her instant of defeat, but she knew this man more thoroughly than he was aware. "Old Owl," she said. "You could guide me to his camp. I've heard his name at the fort. He's no hostile."

Quinn's sudden about-face betrayed him. "That all you want?"

"Just that. You guide me there and back."

"Still risky," Quinn weighed, the canny trader in him emerging.

"I said I can be generous," she said, estimating him. "Three hundred in gold?"

"That's cheap."

"It's outrageous."

Quinn chewed his mustache, his expression telling her nothing.

"I won't quibble," she said. "How does four hundred sound?"

"Take me for some stone-headed Injun?" he sneered and made as though to walk off . . .

"Five hundred," Henrietta said before she thought. Quinn pivoted slowly, and by the sly turning of his gaze she knew that he had outbargained her.

"In advance," he said, swinging to her, extending his palm.

Suddenly his cocksureness stung her. "Half when we start. The rest when we return. After I've talked to Old Owl. I won't go a cent higher, Mr. Quinn."

"Lady" — he let go a hearty, mocking laugh and bowed low from the waist — "we're pardners." He stuck out his greasy hand. She took it, striving not to show reluctance. He held longer than necessary; she withdrew coolly. Again his hesitation returned, and she could see the hint of evasion. "Be a couple of days," he said. "Need time to put an outfit together. Pack mule or two. Grub. Blankets."

"We leave this morning," she said, sounding flat, impatient. "As soon as you can saddle up. You don't need pack animals. They'd just hold us back. I'm ready now, and I won't wait another minute, Mr. Quinn. If you know the country like you say, we can be back by evening."

He calculated for so long she feared he was going to refuse after all. He puckered his large mouth, displeased and cranky.

"Those are the terms, Mr. Quinn."

He gave in with a grunt. "All right," he said, grumbling, and strode out the rear door, calling, "Carlos! Carlos!"

She could see him facing the creek. No one appeared and his loud calling kept coming and she felt it each time, tightening her breathing, her throat, in excitement.

Just then, the Mexican boy ran up, like a slim brown shadow afraid of the sunlight. Quinn canted his head, indicating the corral. They passed from sight as the wall of the store hid them.

Carlos Vasquez was fourteen years old,

but his diminutive body, as undersized as a stunted sapling, gave him the elfish appearance of a child. Only his eyes conveyed his age, enormous black eyes older in living than they should have been, mirroring the buried misery all through him, staring out of a haggard face upon a world which Carlos had never found friendly.

Quinn did not speak until they were beyond hearing of Henrietta.

"Saddle two horses. You ride the mustang. We're goin' to Pena-te-ka country."

Carlos' lips were bloodless. Shaking his head, he murmured in protest, "Indios! Indios!" The great eyes bugged; he shuffled his bare feet, ready to run.

Quinn grabbed the boy's arm, rougher than need be. Carlos squirmed to pull away, could not. "Señor Quinn," he protested. "I don't know the way."

"Hell you don't!" Quinn grunted. "Lived amongst 'em one time. 'Fore I took you and old Amado in, give you a good home here with me. You wouldn't want anything bad to happen to him, would you?" Carlos shook his head and Quinn lowered his voice to a persuasive undertone. "We won't look for any Indios. You know the country. We can go around the camps. Idea is to make a big circle out there, an' bring the woman back."

141

Carlos was puzzled.

"The yellow-haired woman you saw in the store yesterday," Quinn filled in. "I'll do all the talkin'. Remember that. Stay away from 'er much as you can. If she asks you where we're headed, anything about directions, you just say we're lookin' for Pena-te-kas; that I know where to go. If you guide us right, now, we won't run into any Indios. If you take us wrong, maybe we will. Savvy me?"

Carlos nodded, but the young-old eyes were troubled.

"Now high-tail it. Saddle up. Take the horses around in front."

As Carlos hurried off, Quinn let the plan run through his mind again. It had crystallized as they bargained in the store and he noted her eagerness. He reviewed it step by step, savoring his own cleverness. Easy, he decided, to cut a wide circle west of the agency, careful to miss any Comanche camps, while he pretended to search for Old Owl. Failing, he would suggest they go out again tomorrow and the next day. The rides would be hot and tiring; discouraged, she'd drop the search after a day or two. Even if she got suspicious and didn't believe his story of failure, there wasn't any way she could get back at him, because it was plain she'd run out her string. She was desperate.

Only one detail worried him — the other half of the money. He shrugged mentally and his agile mind pounced on a possibility. Although the risk of an encounter with Indians appalled him, he might hunt up a small camp and pow-wow with some old Comanche. That would impress her. In conclusion, he banked the notion for the present. He'd think of something; he always had.

Carlos led the saddled horses past. Then a voice spoke behind Quinn. "Señor Quinn, where you take Carlos?"

Quinn slewed around in swift irritation, wondering how much old Amado might have heard.

"I'm busy," Quinn said. "Go on."

Old Amado, who had the annoying habit of slipping up like an Indian and listening to talk, had hobbled up silently from his hut on the creek bank. A shrunken sight he was — his bent, twisted frame suggesting gnarled mesquite, his crinkly skin as stretched and cracked as weathered rawhide between cheekbones and jaw. He was ragged and barefoot, a defiant scarecrow with burning eyes.

"Where you take Carlos?" he persevered and sought to square his narrow shoulders, to straighten his slight body.

Quinn ignored him and stepped on a pace. Amado, his quickness surprising for one so old, lurched and hung on Quinn's arm. Quinn started to fling him off. Just in time, he remembered the woman might be watching from the doorway and he lowered his arm and muttered, wheeling behind an adobe shed, "Come over here, if you got to talk."

Amado limped across and Quinn turned on him angrily, "By God, you ever gonna learn! Don't cross me. Get back to your shack. I'm in a hurry."

"Carlos is afraid of Indios. I heard you say —"

Quinn's glare silenced him. Without Carlos the plan wouldn't work. Carlos knew the Pena-te-ka country; Quinn did not.

"Shut up!" Quinn ordered. "Carlos works for me. Understand? Otherwise, you'd be out on the prairie. Starvin' — no shelter. Carlos goes where I say. He's hired to me."

Amado raised veined hands in protest. "But you pay nothing —"

Quinn whacked him across the face, a quick, savage swing. The noise of the blow cracked the quiet. Amado was driven against the adobe wall like a bundle of loose rags, but he did not go down. He stood there, wobbling, swaying.

Somehow the sight infuriated Quinn. He stepped in, propelled by a sudden desire to smash this bothersome old man's spirit once and forever. At the last moment, though, Quinn hesitated. Instead of striking Amado, he clutched the rags of his shirt and shook him.

"You old fool — you nosey old fool!"

Quinn shoved suddenly and stopped, expecting the old man to fall. Amado slammed against the wall, bounced and lost his balance, his arms reaching loosely. He grabbed at the uneven adobe bricks and caught, half-righted himself. An almost forgotten sense of dignity, bolstered by a sick man's hatred, a sick man's desperation, seemed to sustain Amado.

"Carlos fears Comanches. They will capture him again. You will not take him!"

Amado's voice was a screech, rising dangerously. Another moment and he might bring the woman.

Quinn hesitated no longer. He smashed his doubled fist to Amado's head, all his weight behind the long, looping blow, high alongside Amado's ear and temple.

Amado reeled, falling. He landed on his back; he lay very still.

Quinn, gazing down, felt a twist of fear.

He had struck Amado before, but never this hard. Quinn glanced frantically behind him. But Carlos had led the horses on. He'd be in front of the store, waiting, waiting because he was afraid to disobey.

A low moaning turned Quinn. Amado was alive. All Quinn's indifference surged back. The old Mex looked kind of strange, though. Not stirring much. But he was alive. Leave him be. Next time he'd know better, maybe. Learn him, b'God!

Quinn left him. By the time he reached the store door, he had completely forgotten Amado. He was thinking of the gold again.

Quinn rode armed, a carbine slung under one leg and a six-shooter, inlaid silver stars in its handle, belted across his thick middle. He looked impressive, filling the saddle on a racy-looking sorrel, his hair sweeping out under his sweat-brimmed hat. Henrietta noticed one change, however, in his manner. He had lost a great deal of his garrulousness. When he spoke, it was briefly and curtly to Carlos as the two rode in advance.

After a while, she thought their progress unusually slow, in contrast to the beginning, when Quinn had set a brisk southward course from the store, wasting neither time nor words. But when they shifted west, and the agency lay unseen to the north, tucked behind a fold of bald prairie, Quinn settled to a walk. The country was open and rolling and she could see a long way. West and northwest, it began to bristle and belly up to the sky, rough, bleak to the eye. Somewhere in there, she thought, they'd find Old Owl's camp near a creek or spring. Considering the bare surroundings, she wondered why Quinn paused often to squint and study, when a riding man could see as well as a halted one. She made no complaint, thinking he'd whip up soon. When an hour had passed and Quinn's pace was unchanged, she called him back and suggested they ride faster.

"Reckon this does seem a mite slow," he agreed, amiable, nodding. "But we got to be careful — and certain."

"Certain?"

"I mean where we come into them hills you see. Just right to hit Old Owl's camp." He tugged on his chin, his mouth pursed. "Was last spring, late, when I visited the chief in his lodge. Country don't look the same in summer, she's so dried up. Not that I don't savvy it. We keep on like we're headed."

"I thought Indians moved around a lot," she said.

He nodded. "Comanch' are nervous buggers."

"You expect Old Owl's camp in the same place?"

"Foolish if I did. No white man can figure that. Maybe he's moved three-four times since last spring. Maybe he ain't. Could be he's gone for buff'lo. Got meat hungry. Just have to see."

He was both sure and unsure, which was neither.

She said, "I understand Old Owl stays on the reservation, draws rations."

"Most times. Just depends. Never can tell about a Comanch'. He's where he can fill his belly."

Rejoining Carlos, Quinn resumed the plodding pace. For the first time today, Henrietta realized how slim were their chances of locating a shifting Indian camp. The fine feeling of anticipation with which she'd started the ride, and which had increased as she sighted the low arches of the hills, began to ebb a little. This vast sunshot, lonesome land did that, she thought. It made you feel small, it shrank the mind and clutched the heart and made you doubt.

Wearily, the early morning wore itself out with a scalding slowness. At length, Quinn led them into yellow-grassed hills. Here, he halted and looked off and pondered. She saw nothing, no movement as they bent southwest. Later, they watered in a shallow, elm-lined creek and ate dried meat and cold bread. Quinn put his back to a lightning-shattered cottonwood and rested. Carlos tended the horses, a mute, drawn-faced boy yet to speak a single word to Henrietta. He was, she decided, too sober and grave for his years. She offered him a friendly look as she walked over to Quinn, removing her hat and shaking out her long hair.

"How far's the camp?" she asked.

"Four miles, I judge. Maybe five." She was conscious of his eyes roving over her, up and down, as he spoke.

She pretended not to notice. "Which way?"

"On southwest."

She gazed in that direction, where the hills flattened and gave the illusion of losing themselves and beyond them dwelled the suggestion of a still greater prairie world, still flatter. Westward a notch cleaved the low, folding hills.

"Mr. Quinn," she said uncertainly, "won't we be getting back to open country that way?"

Annoyance entered his eyes. "Always figured a fox knows his own hole best."

149

Henrietta had spoken naturally, out of the common-sense knowledge of a ranch woman. She saw more heat shade into Quinn's fleshy cheeks and it fastened in her mind that she was on the edge of quarreling with the only person who had offered services that might lead her to Emily. True, for a price; but she was willing to pay for results and she acknowledged there was some risk to the venture. Quinn was a loud-talking man, rough, a self-fond braggart, vain around women, but she would be eternally grateful if he succeeded where others refused or were incapable. She rebuked herself. Why, they'd hardly started and here she was doubting him! She'd hired Quinn for his knowledge. She must respect it; at least give him the chance to prove himself right or wrong.

"I'm just saying how the country looks to me," she said reasonably. "Not much wood or water for an Indian camp. But you understand these Indians. I don't."

"You got a right to your opinion," Quinn said, as agreeable as she. He heaved to his feet, confident again, unruffled. He studied her some moments. "Big country, this is — she's wide open. Why, you could hide an army behind one long hill. Remember that if we don't raise Old Owl's camp by dark.

150

Like I said at the store, what we need is a small pack outfit. Save time. No goin' in 'til we have to. I'll rustle up some mules tomorrow, if we don't connect today."

True. She admitted that now, downcast; she'd hurried him before he had time to make full preparations. She nodded in agreement.

"Don't you fret none," he assured her. She saw his little gleam of hunger break through. He lifted his hand to pat her shoulder, but she twisted aside, suddenly, deeply angered.

"Mr. Quinn!" she told him straight. "Keep your hands to yourself!'

"No harm meant; no harm," he replied, easy-like, as if it mattered not, and idled away.

She watched him mount, anger and disgust gathered in her throat. Going to her horse, she noticed Carlos scanning the country. He was alert, tense and fearful, it struck her of a sudden, of something out there which he could not see. Quinn's curt call stirred Carlos. He mounted immediately, and Henrietta, her eyes on his too-old face, saw him slide his gaze away from hers.

"Carlos," she said on impulse, sorry for him, "ride with me a while."

Carlos fixed his eyes ahead. He reined by,

151

in silence, and rode over to Quinn.

He's afraid, she thought. Afraid.

Now Quinn demonstrated his first decisiveness of the day. He struck southwest into an up-and-down, rolling country, wind-blown and empty. He rode at a trot, without letup, as if to make up for time lost, as if he knew where to go. Presently, he came to a sloping flat that dropped to another summer-dry creek. He stopped and looked back and forth, searching the emptiness.

"Damn the luck," she heard his grumble. "Cleared out. Camp's cold. Well, I might a'knowed it." Something in her face made him touchy. He jabbed a finger, pointing at the slope. "Look for yourself."

Weather and time had faded the signs, but she could still make out the blanched patches where tipis had stood, the blackened holes of long-dead campfires dug in the center of the lodge circles. This camping ground was old, very old. She found it hard to believe Indians had lived here in recent months.

"Old Owl camped here last spring?" she asked sharply.

"He did." Authority rang in Quinn's voice. "His lodge was right 'bout there."

"What're you going to do now?"

152

"Take a peek from that high knoll. Carlos, you come along."

His order impressed her as unnecessary, Quinn always keeping the boy as close as his shadow. She knew her reaction showed, for Quinn grunted over his shoulder, "He's got eyes a heap better'n me."

She rode after them. Quinn, in front, climbed to the crest. Carlos hesitated at the foot of the knoll. She rode up to him.

"Carlos."

He kicked his pony's flanks. But she was expecting such a move and quickly jumped her mount in front of him.

"Please talk to me," she said. "Don't be afraid."

His eyes tore off her to Quinn on the hill and returned, sighting her hesitantly. Up close his thinness shocked her, angered her; the brown eyes enormous in the pinched wedge of face.

"Señorita," he said, "I am not afraid of you. You are kind."

"Something's bothering you, Carlos. Is it Señor Quinn? Or Indians?"

"Indios," he replied instantly, and she wondered if she'd provided him a ready answer, until he said, "I was a Comanche captive one time. With my papa."

A sudden sympathy engulfed her, then an

153

arresting thought. "Qua-ha-das took my little sister. That's why I'm here — to find a Pena-te-ka who'll talk to the Qua-ha-das. Did the Qua-ha-das capture you?"

"Pena-te-kas," he answered, drawing it out as an Indian would.

"Oh," she said, let down. "Did relatives pay ransom for you?"

He shook his head and a hidden liveliness twinkled up through his gravity. "One night it was storming bad. We stole ponies. My papa, he is very old and sick, here." Carlos tapped his skinny chest and fell sober again. "Next day, we found Señor Quinn's store."

"You work for him?"

"Yes."

She said slowly, thoughtfully, "He . . . knew you ran away from the Indians?"

Carlos looked up, giving no reply, but his dark eyes glinted.

"What would the Pena-te-kas do," she kept on, "if they found you out here?"

Fear flew into his face. "Take me back!"

"Quinn knew this? Yet he made you come along?"

Fright and the wish to speak fought in Carlos' face. His mouth twisted, worked. He swallowed and looked up hill. Before he could bring himself to answer, Henrietta saw Quinn urging his horse to join them.

By afternoon, she knew the day had become hopeless. Quinn hadn't found a single Indian, though he was moving constantly, turning them, crawling up empty draws, between long slopes, until she had no idea where they were in relation to the fort and she felt like calling for him to stop. Glazed heat smote the vacant land. Wind was a steady fire-breath fanning out of the southwest, off even more sun-hammered stretches.

Dust gritted against Henrietta's skin. Her throat felt dry. Easing her body in the saddle, she recalled Carlos' face as Quinn rode down hill.

Carlos feared Indians. He hadn't lied about that as she'd first thought. But he was terribly afraid of Quinn, who'd forced Carlos to accompany him into a land which held only frightening memories of the past. She tried to guess what else Quinn might have done to Carlos, what other cruelty he might have inflicted. The boy — the child, she thought — looked hungry. She felt a rising indignation and was certain of one stand. She wouldn't allow Quinn to bring Carlos, if they rode out again tomorrow.

Carlos stopped his horse in the spare shade of a shallow creek, more branch than creek, its water shrunken to a stagnant hole here and there. She heard Quinn's instant order, "Carlos! Come on!"

Perhaps Carlos hadn't heard. He put his Indian pony through the willows and down the bank to the first pool. Henrietta did likewise and saw Quinn's unconsenting look.

"We can water later," he said, louder.

"I want to rest a while," she told him. She watered her animal and, afterward, rode out and dismounted in the shade, Carlos following and getting down at the same time.

"Long way yet," complained Quinn, who hadn't left his saddle. He walked his horse a little way and glanced back. "Carlos, you aim to hunt shade all day?"

"No, señor. My cinch is loose."

Carlos took interminably. He pulled at his saddle blanket; he set his saddle straight. He'd dismounted near a broken cottonwood, with his horse between himself and Quinn. Once, twice, Henrietta saw Carlos set his glance on the cottonwood. When he looked a third time, and back to her, with meaning, she felt a tap of recognition — obscure at first and then sharp. Turning slowly, she scanned the creek and the jumbled country off west. There was a break in the line of hills, a notch.

The feeling of having been here before grew, until she had no doubts. She overcame the hot urge to speak out and gathered herself a moment while she watched Carlos finish cinching and ride toward Quinn, who was moving off.

"Mr. Quinn!"

At her call, he stopped his horse and came around. His eyes, she thought, sought to avoid hers. There was no patience left in her now, only a wrathy conviction.

"You've been circling!" She paced straight to him. He got his mouth open, just barely, when she wheeled and pointed. "That old cottonwood! Lightning-struck! I remember it — and this creek! We stopped here around noon. You've been circling — leading me back and forth!"

Fury shaking her, she tensed for Quinn's denial. But he was smiling in his amused fashion, yet not quite mocking nor denying.

"Sure, it's the same creek," he said. "I leaned right agin' that busted cottonwood. Rested here 'fore we turned south. We looked over everything down there, so we've come back. Had to come north — this way. No call swingin' west this late in the day. Call it circle if you mind to."

"But you tried not to stop here!" she flared.

"Long way to go." He was mildly turning aside her complaints. "Can water plenty

157

places on up. Be sundown 'fore you know it. Better travel fast long as we can see."

He was convincing, he was logical — almost. Thinking back on the futile day, she recalled the continual shifting of direction. The awful heat and the riding had wearied her, and she had brooded over Emily in this raw emptiness. At times she hadn't paid particular attention to the land, which had a sameness, a monotony. Much of their traveling might have been aimless wandering. Or was it a calculated wandering? It had taken Carlos to point out the landmark tree. She should have been more alert. A self-guilt lashed her. Once more her suspicion welled up.

"I don't believe you," she told Quinn.

He rolled his shoulders. "Can't help it. That's how she is."

"I'm going back to the fort."

"We're headed that way."

She was contemptuous. "I'm going to tell you something, Mr. Quinn. I don't believe you're familiar with this part of the country. Not at all. I think you forced Carlos to come so you'd have a guide."

"You think! Let me talk, woman. There's only one way, if we make the fort by dark. North — like we're headed. Go into the mountains — come out west of the fort."

"Why not northeast?"

"Been that way once, comin' out. Got to keep lookin'." Buffalo Quinn threw back his head. "I don't beat around the bush. Ain't my style. I'm fixin' to earn all that money. If Old Owl's on the reservation, I'll find him. An' if you don't think I know where I'm headed, go out there. Look for yourself. You say I'm wrong, I'll go however you say."

Firmly leading her horse, she left the timber and walked up slope, in the open, until she could view the country rolling off in all directions, shimmering, endless. Straight east, she reasoned, would bring them in some miles below the agency. The most direct route to the fort lay north, and a little east, for the fort was close to the mountains.

"I guess it's north," she said finally to Quinn, a rod behind.

"I'm right. You see now?"

"I hope you're right, Mr. Quinn. I hope you are."

He said no more and rode on.

Suddenly, this unavailing day crashed around her, leaving her trembling. She was still shaking when she rose to the saddle and fell in behind. It took effort, but she forced herself to concentrate on the newness ahead and what it might hold. From experience she'd learned that any hope, however small, was enough to draw you on and on. Except, she thought, you have to have something. Something.

Far north the hills peaked bolder. Quinn kept to footing paralleling the creek. Several times he paused to ponder and squint at the dazzling distances.

Henrietta was unimpressed; she could see for herself and she knew the way home. Her gelding, without an easy gait and used to casual rides in the fort's vicinity, had given out by early afternoon; thus, his plodding trot set the pace for the party. Sun-glare knifed under Henrietta's small hat. She breathed scuffings of gritty dust, kicked up from the brittle, yellow-brown grass. In all, she realized the utter waste of the day.

When the creek bent westward, Quinn halted. "Last water 'tween here an' the fort," he announced.

Across the creek, north, Henrietta saw, stretched sweeping slopes, patched here and there, in the low places, with scrub oak and mesquite.

Before long, the horses filled and it was time to go. Quinn rode up the low bank and, unexpectedly, stepped down. "Goin' to rest a spell," he said, and rumped himself down in a shady spot. "Carlos, you scoot up ahead and keep a sharp lookout. Sabe?"

Carlos hesitated.

"Vamoose!" Quinn bawled and Carlos went.

Henrietta stayed in the saddle, resenting Quinn's tone. Tired as she was, something told her not to dismount.

"Ain't you gettin' down?" Quinn suggested.

She measured him, distrusting him. "A while back, you couldn't stop long enough for water."

"Last water's here," he said and eased to his feet, taking tentative, deliberate steps toward her. As he halted at the head of her horse, his eyes dirtying her, she got once again the full, dismaying effect of the man's squalor. "Missed our Injuns today, looks like," he added. "No need hurryin' now. Take our time."

"I want to get back before dark."

"We'll make it. No hurry."

"Well, then," she answered, "if there's no hurry, we should look around some more."

"Throw us late."

"Mr. Quinn," she demanded, "just why are you delaying?"

His eyes moved over her. "Nice an' shady here. I figured we'd kinda get acquainted better. You an' me."

Henrietta felt astonishment, then a sweeping anger. "How dare you say that!"

"You got me all wrong," he said in his sly, humble tone. "I don't mean no harm, now."

"It's perfectly clear what you mean!" In the instant, she shortened reins. "I'm riding on. Our bargain's off!"

She cracked the reins across the gelding's withers, but Quinn was much too quick for her. He held the bridle bit. Henrietta kept whipping, but Quinn merely led the dancing animal in a tight circle. He stopped.

"Don't go gettin' high an' mighty on a man!" he said, sharper, and scrubbed his whiskered chin reminiscently. "Women better'n you been snugged up to Buffalo Quinn. Been glad to, b'God!"

"Let go that bit!" With her warning, Henrietta switched her slashing to the greasy forest of Quinn's face, now at Quinn's fending arm.

He yelled in pain. "I'll fetch you down offa there!" he swore and ducked in and up, reaching, grabbing high.

She whirled the gelding, reined it against Quinn, the blow more brushing than solid; but it knocked him to his knees. She lashed the passive beast under her, turning north through mesquite at a heavy-footed run, searching for Carlos and not sighting him.

She was in the open when she heard Quinn rushing up behind. She looked over her shoulder and saw him coming fast, gaining with each jump of the sorrel. She glanced ahead, and this time she spied Carlos in the distance. He was riding back, in a fogging violent run.

Quinn caught up first. Running his horse alongside, he clamped onto the bridle and forced her gelding to a swerving stop.

"Lady," he sang out in a changed voice, "you got me wrong! We'll ride back tomorrow. Look this country out good!"

"You're fired, Quinn! Get away from me!"

He was, she saw furiously, again in the role of the friendly Indian trader, wheedling, sly, hypocritical.

Quinn held to the bridle.

"Señor Quinn! Señor Quinn!"

It was Carlos yelling and pointing behind him.

"Hear them — the guns!"

CHAPTER 6

Major Vier took his command west from the agency, past the commissary corrals, into the first knuckled stand of hills, and there he halted and called his company commanders together.

"Mr. Allison," he ordered, "you will proceed southwest with Company D, rounding up any Indians you see and starting them toward the agency. If they resist, you will pitch into them and send me word at once. If you encounter no Indians, you will halt where the first creek makes a big hook west. Remain there until the rest of the command joins you. Meanwhile, we will be clearing the country to your right, in the direction of Camp Radziminski."

Lieutenant Allison, showing eagerness, pulled his men out and the column stirred forward. Major Vier ordered extra flankers spread wide, and Frank saw Sergeant Tinsley swing out with Company M's detail.

Isaac Roberts, jogging beside Frank, shook his head as the troopers rode by. "One day we preach peace to the Indians;

the next we send soldiers to bring them in. Many innocents pay for the few guilty. Is it any wonder, in Indian eyes, heathen as they are, that the white man puzzles them?"

The leather-creaking column, in alternate walk and trot, was a dusty snake pulling itself through sun-punished nothingness. Frank watched flankers top distant ridges and drop from sight, only to appear again farther on, dipping, climbing.

Deep into the afternoon, having completed one leg of his sweep, Major Vier shifted from southwest to southeast, with nothing yet caught in his pincering movement. In some vexation, he drew rein in front of Roberts. Lieutenant Nibs looked ill at ease.

"We're in the heart of Pena-te-ka country, Mr. Roberts," said Vier, both puzzled and cross. "Any idea where they're hiding?"

Roberts shifted his bulky frame. "Not hiding, Major. Running. As for where an Indian might be . . . well, I never found one yet where I expected to find him."

"They're around here somewhere," Vier insisted.

"I can't tell thee because I don't know." Roberts rubbed his massive hands a moment and, looking up, put the question silently to Frank.

Frank waited, glancing at Vier and back to Roberts, who nodded and said, "Maybe thee knows."

"Main camp's likely on Lieutenant Allison's line of march," Frank said. "If Allison keeps on southwest."

Vier said coldly, "You might have volunteered that before we started, Mr. Chesney."

"Nobody asked me, Major."

"Hardly necessary, I think, in view of the unusual circumstances. On the other hand, I shouldn't expect a guide to offer pertinent information when he's not drawing army pay."

Frank felt the sudden sting of anger over his face, and it threw him stiffer in the saddle, but he held on to his temper.

Having said it, Major Vier tossed his arm and the wide-flung march continued. He was, Frank thought, an extra hard-headed man to deal with, cold-jawed like a horse that refused to be turned from hole or gully.

There was no indication of Comanches, no smoke raveling the clear, hot sky, no swift, tell-tale movement, no fresh sign scratching the baked earth. The wear of the ride pressed in, hotter, heavier. The smell of dust was everywhere, a fine coating of talcum on cavalry jackets, troopers so many taciturn lumps.

Frank rode with his legs loose, his body relaxed, having learned years ago not to fight discomforts he couldn't change. From habit he tracked his gaze to the ridge ahead, and drew in, searching in an arc from left to right, probing every rise and mesquite clump. It was then he remembered Henrietta's face, surprised how his mind, retaining the details of her features and movements, cast them again minutely. He remembered how graceful she was, and the softness of her yellow hair under lamplight. She was considerable woman; of that he had no doubt.

At three-thirty they paused for water in a grove of rustling cottonwoods and elms. Frank saw at once what the greenest man among them couldn't miss — the unshod hoofmarks everywhere, the recent camp signs, the litter and leavings of a big camp and the scratches of travois poles bearing southeast.

"Pulled out early today," Frank told Roberts. "Good-sized camp, Isaac."

Roberts was scanning the direction which the Indians had taken, his heavy concern questioning. "Thee thinks they're moving to the Cache?" He tried to sound hopeful, but his own doubt came through.

"They wouldn't go roundabout."

"S'ppose not. Not an Indian's way." The bewilderment of a stranger to violence got into Roberts. He said, unconvinced, "I can't believe Major Vier will attack them."

"You heard his order to Lieutenant Allison."

"Yes — yes. But the women and children?" He shook his head with a lack of comprehension.

"Won't make any difference," Frank said, twisting it off, bitter. "Never has, much. Didn't at Sand Creek."

Old Isaac, remembering, looked at Frank and there was the misery of sympathy in his expression.

Frank said, "Chivington's volunteers took a hundred scalps back to Denver. Like a big circus coming to town. Men wavin' bloody hair at the crowd, and the crowd liking it. Hair ripped off squaws, kids — if there was any left after the brave Indian fighters blew out their brains."

Isaac Roberts lowered his eyes.

"That wasn't all. They brought in three little Indian kids; showed 'em off between acts at the opera house. Everybody had one hell of a time. Some sight. Made a man proud he was white."

168

"To think," Roberts said, "that Christians did that."

"Let's say white men. But you know, Isaac, most settlers said it was good. Figured Sand Creek was a needed thing, good for that part of Indian country . . . Be a lesson to the Indians. And it was, in a way. A wild animal will dodge you just so long, but when you hurt him he'll come at you. Not long after that, the Cheyennes caught a party of white men traveling east. Chivington's men. The Cheyennes cut 'em up into little chunks . . . Another time, I found what was left of an emigrant train on the Butterfield Trail. Just south of Flat Top mountain, in Texas. Kiowas and Comanches had rubbed 'em out. Long time before I slept easy again." Frank looked across at Major Vier. "No, women an' children never stopped any fight I heard of. Never stopped it on either side. And remember these yellow-legs had friends in the woodcutting detail."

Major Vier, Lieutenant Niles riding at his elbow, was cutting his horse back and forth over the trampled ground, a controlled excitement in his brisk reining. He checked and raised his gaze, his mouth forming a curt order, and Niles cantered back, laying a call across the wind that

169

swept the companies to saddle.

Vier took the point. He stepped up the march.

About an hour onward, an approaching streak of dust ruffled the blank land. One horseman closed rapidly in focus and by his headlong run Frank knew there was trouble. The trooper rushed up to the column and stopped, the traced pattern of dusty sweat on his crimson face. His voice was hoarse, dry-tight.

"Lieutenant Allison's respects, sir. We jumped a big bunch. He says come quick."

"How far?" Vier demanded, rising in his stirrups.

"Ten miles. Maybe twelve. The lieutenant had to withdraw, sir."

"Mr. Allison didn't reach the creek?"

"No, sir. He's makin' a stand. 'Bout two miles this side."

Major Vier acted immediately, a bold, rash eagerness straining in him, an impatience nagging him. He spoke a swift order to the trumpeter and Recall blasted the yellow slopes, retrieving the flankers. Vier did not wait for them to rejoin before he moved off; they would have to catch up.

They traveled alternately at sharp trot and hard gallop. Vier appeared to ride with his mind closed to all save the Indians somewhere in front of him. He rode doggedly, pressing, as if fearful that these Indians might yet escape him.

It was late afternoon when Frank heard the first dim banging of carbine fire. There'd be a flurry of shots, a weighted silence, and then the banging again. It was uneven, irresolute, ominous on the wind. When the messenger from Allison's company pointed to a long stringer of ridge, Major Vier threw his flankers left and right, exactly, and took the rise in a horse-grunting rush. The firing was very close now. Vier halted on top.

A mile away Indians swerved their nimble ponies in dust mist so thick it was hard to tell the size of the forces boiling there. Something glittered in the center of that rapid, smoky swarm — glittered like sunlight on lances. Off to the west of the Indians, on a stubby finger of hill, dismounted cavalry crouched in an irregular line, and huddled behind them, darkly, stood little knots of horse-holders. Black powder-smoke puffed on the hillside as kneeling troopers fired into the dirty haze.

As Frank watched, there was a stir on the hill. Men turning and pointing. Carbine fire slackened, then quickened. Some troopers began waving hats, throwing them into the air, their throaty cheering muffled by distance but nevertheless strongly coming.

At the same time, the Comanches had spotted Major Vier's command. Frank glimpsed Indian ponies drawing off. In an interval of moments, they were stringing south, fading toward a gap that led between bald, stretching slopes.

Major Vier stood in his stirrups and shouted, "Left into line — gallop!"

Sets of fours angled out like a fan on the ridge top and formed a broad attack line. Galloping, they dropped down the long grade of the short-grassed slope with sergeants yelling, "Close up — close up!"

For a surging time there was just the thudding racket of heavy horses, the leather slaps and the jingles of cavalry going hell-bent.

But Major Vier was too late. Halfway to Allison's hill he slowed down. His Indians were slipping away through the gap, beyond catching, their agile ponies already melting in the hazy distance.

CHAPTER 7

Henrietta saw everything through a stunned silence. Quinn holding her bridle; Quinn slung half about in the saddle . . . Carlos' haunted face; Carlos out of breath and pointing, excitement like a fever shaking him.

"Guns!" he said over again.

His voice laid a hushed stillness around them. Henrietta picked up sounds. Distant, popping sounds — ragged, cracking on the endless wind, unmistakable.

But her anger was still there. Her stiff immobility broke. She yanked hard on the reins, so suddenly Quinn lost his grip. He jerked with the movement of her horse, but made no effort to grab the bridle again. He was very still. He appeared to have forgotten her. He cocked his head to listen, as though he wasn't certain or didn't believe his own ears, though she could hear the gunfire distinctly.

"Yeh — guns," Quinn said needlessly, swallowing, his voice high in his throat. He ignored Henrietta, had eyes only for the boy. "Carlos," he said in something of his old sharp tone of command, "you see 'em? Get close enough? What —"

Carlos sat frozen, robbed of speech. Henrietta saw him struggle to talk.

A short series of cracks rent the wind, heavier, nearer than before, swelling in volume.

"Speak up!" Quinn said.

"Yonder!" Carlos got out.

He pointed north again, where the sounds came from and the slopes swept aside and left a broad gap, where a smoky haze was mounting the sky and moving streamers of high, angry dust roiled.

In that dust, Henrietta saw, emerging these past few moments, horse movement was plainly visible.

"Injuns!" Quinn blurted. He sounded sick, as if it couldn't be Indians. "Headed in on us," Quinn said uncertainly. "Somebody's stirred 'em up."

His raffish face was sickly pale, yellowish, the skin mottled. His eyes strayed, jerking, and she caught his longing to run.

"Quinn!" she called. "You're armed! Stay with us!"

Then, violently, Quinn was bringing his horse around, the brightness of raw fear bulging his eyes. For a second she thought he meant for them to ride together.

174

But he cried, "I'm gettin' outa here!"

"Quinn — wait!"

He was digging spurs as she called, lumping out the sorrel, blindly, going east toward a low, bald ridge.

She called to Carlos and reined after Quinn. Her gelding was maddening to handle, slow to answer, to turn, and when she lashed him brutally, the only response was a broken lope.

Carlos had swung with her. He stayed beside her, though every drop of blood seemed drained from his face. He stuck doggedly, holding up his faster mustang.

A killing anger soared as she saw Quinn's intent. He wasn't slowing down for them, not even concerned to see whether they followed. Above all, she knew a blazing contempt, stronger than the anger, which lent her a certain clarity. She set eyes on the gap and distinguished Indians in some detail, phantoms riding in a pall of gray dust. Many ponies in motion. Ponies dragging travois. The quick jerkiness of people fleeing, in bunches, singly. A whole Indian village, it looked.

It pounded in her that she wasn't going right nor nearly fast enough. She was close to panic. She wrenched and glanced south, sighting the covering timber along the creek and was tempted. But that won't do, she thought. They're headed that way.

"Señorita! Señorita! Look!"

She found Carlos making frantic gestures. His lips quivered as he pointed at the easterly ridge. "Indios! Indios!"

She saw only Quinn. Quinn — damn him! — running his fleet sorrel up the ridge. Once over it, he'd be safe.

Next, in a sinking sensation, she spotted riders farther north. Bodies shining like greased statues. Indians sweeping south along the bare rim of the rise, cutting across Quinn's path.

She watched Quinn pull up. He saw his danger, too, but not in time. Sawing on the reins, he fought the sorrel's head around and swapped directions and got off a wild shot with his pistol, the single pop making a futile sound. The Indians slackened not a bit; they came faster with the dipping grade.

Spurring, raking flanks, Quinn had the sorrel in a slamming run. For a little while he ran untouched, neither widening the distance nor losing ground; holding his own.

Henrietta, on held breath, discovered herself hoping for him, unconsciously urging speed to his horse.

Whooping hideously, the Indians seemed to burst down the slope, recklessly racing sure-footed ponies, gaining on Quinn.

Quinn's horse stumbled oddly, lurched, and she saw a puff of dirty smoke bloom behind Quinn and heard the crack of a rifle. Then Quinn's horse was breaking down, losing speed, and Quinn was pitching forward, over the sorrel's pumping head, grotesque and graceless as he fell. He hit and lost his showman's hat and rolled like a spinning log, his long tawny hair spilling out, beckoning to the shrilling Comanches.

It was done within moments, suddenly.

Quinn weaved to his feet and stood there swaying. He'd lost his pistol. His hands hung half-raised. His horse was down, floundering. Quinn was pitiful to watch, and to Henrietta's mind came a wounded coyote and a pack of baying hounds. Except Quinn wasn't fighting; he was cowering now as the ponies charged for him, rooted. And yet, when the lead pony plunged within the final yards, Quinn tried to wheel and run. Swarming riders hid him. Henrietta saw the down-striking arms and heard the terrible screeching, saw the last savage snarl of motion around Quinn.

Sickened, frightened, she twisted her head away. She'd pointed the gelding south in sluggish gallop, watching over her shoulder as she ran. Carlos began drawing in front on the mustang. When he pulled in, lagging for her, she yelled, "The brush — go on — to the brush!"

He was fright itself. Eyes enormous. Mouth bloodless. Yet he held back for her. Henrietta's gelding gained on the mustang, with a frightful slowness drew even.

"Go on!" she cried.

Carlos continued to delay.

Leaning out of the saddle, abruptly, she started slashing her reins across the rump of Carlos' mustang, slashing and yelling. The startled animal broke away.

She felt relief and then a white terror as she fell rapidly behind, alerted to a new drumming. Even before she glanced backward, she knew she couldn't outrun them. She whipped to see — found them closer than she'd judged, a whooping knot of half-naked, painted men on incredibly fast ponies.

She flung about, seeing Carlos going south like the wind.

An instinct seized. She cut her gelding away, deliberately westward where there was no escape, and, turning, saw the Comanches veering to follow her. Even so, there was little time left her. Her gelding was finished.

At the last, when she turned the trembling animal so that she might face them, it was as if she turned to die.

CHAPTER 8

Lieutenant Allison, looking well blown, cantered out to meet Major Vier's command. The dreadful day was smeared in haggard strain on his sun-scorched cheeks and jaws, in his dead-weary, inflamed eyes. In the matter of a few hours, since eagerly leaving the main column west of the agency, he had turned much thinner and older.

"Old Owl's band, sir," Allison reported. "Close to three hundred Indians. When we approached for a parley, some young bucks dashed out. Had a fight before we knew it. No chance to talk or turn 'em east."

"Yet you let them get away? Lost them?" Vier's voice carried a stiff reprimand.

Allison flushed through his sun-beaten coloring. "Sir," he faltered, surprised, stumped for the explaining words, "they pitched a big rearguard at us so the village could take off. When they went to caving in our flanks, I withdrew to the hill. Deemed it unwise to try to follow the main band, even after the hostiles in front of us thinned out. We've wounded, sir, and three dead. In my opinion their casualties —"

"It isn't necessary to reconstruct any further, Mr. Allison. Evident what happened here." Major Vier turned his back on the Lieutenant. It was a deliberate thing. "Mr. Niles, take companies H and M and scout beyond that gap. I'll follow shortly, in case these hostiles have any lingering taste to fight. Which I doubt!"

Curtly motioning Allison to accompany him, Major Vier rode forward to examine the hill position.

As Niles drew out the two companies, Frank was waiting for his beckoning nod and soon got it. He looked at Isaac Roberts as he started off, old Isaac quite still, a witness to Allison's hill, dejectedly considering the flattened shapes. Comanches as well as troopers. In Isaac's face regret and a sad acceptance sat dully, heavily, maybe the end of a dream. These were not the red men of William Penn's peaceful time, yielding to brotherly love and mercy and sharing. These were savage and proud, unforgiving, hard-dying, hard-used by the white man — not to be led, not to be driven. Likewise, it was contrary to reason to expect soldiers to have the patience and understanding kindness of a Penn.

Niles moved his companies rapidly and was inside the gap when he said, "Frank, we're chasing heat devils," said it on an inflection of irony, which was unlike him.

"Tail-end of a storm. Think we can catch it?"

Niles was downcast. "Not a chance, today. And we're not fixed for a long chase." He rode in silence for a full minute. "However, I look for Major Vier to call out the entire regiment. Better get set for a long campaign."

"Me? I won't be in it. Vier wouldn't take me if I crawled in and begged."

"Did today, didn't he?" Niles replied curiously. "Doesn't it strike you as a little unusual that he permitted you to come along? Does me. Don't count on being left out, that is, if you want to go. I know him pretty well, Frank. A strange man at times."

"Damned strange. I don't want any part of him."

Both fell silent. Niles looked morose as he posted flankers to the east and west, ordering them to prowl the ridges. He took the companies down the powder-dry floor of the prairie between the slopes, riding in silence for several minutes.

It came out of him suddenly, with a sharpening bitterness. "Frank, I'm thinking seriously of resigning my commission. To hell with all this!"

Frank sat up in the saddle, staring at him. He let his surprise settle a bit and said, "You figure you want that?"

"Hell, no!" Niles said passionately. "Except I've got a family to think about. Louise hates all this. Can't say as I blame her too much." He swept his hand in an angry circle. "I've thought it out pretty well. We can move to St. Louis. I have business connections there. Considerable change for me, but I can get used to it, I guess."

Frank held his tongue. It wasn't right, it wouldn't work. But he'd never say a word to Ed.

A trooper called to Niles and Frank saw flankers bunching on the east ridge, crowding up to something on the ground. One man wheeled clear after a pause and flung up an arm, beckoning again and again.

When Niles and Frank galloped over, a recruit was leaning over the off side of his horse, retching.

Frank rode between two men and looked down and felt his own stomach kick. He forced his eyes downward again; not until then did he recognize Buffalo Quinn.

Quinn was sprawled on his back, expertly scalped, his body pin-cushioned with arrows, hacked, gashed. His gunbelt was gone. His forehead and face had a wrinkled, slipped-down look, for the Comanche lifting his scalp, no doubt prizing the tawny hair, had slashed out an extra large patch.

"What," Niles asked softly, "was Quinn doing 'way out here from his store? He never went among the camps to my knowledge."

The answer wasn't here, Frank realized. He rode out, starting a deliberate circle over the area, and returned presently, shaking his head.

"Tracks don't say much. Too many horses along this ridge today."

"Little odd, too, isn't it?" Niles questioned. "Along here. So much travel on a ridge?"

"Except today," Frank said. "Been Indians everywhere. They'd ride the ridges for a look around." Frank turned his head, studying the close-in ground, trying to piece together Quinn's final moments. "Quinn wouldn't know about Major Vier's round-up order. If he did, he wouldn't been here. Whatever it was, he had strong reasons comin' out here. Lieutenant Allison had things stirred up good. Comanches on the move, south. Quinn ran right into 'em."

"Maybe some Indian recognized him," a trooper spoke up dryly. "Quinn sure took a heap of hide when he traded."

Assigning a detail to take care of Quinn's body, Lieutenant Niles hastened the companies forward in fast-fading light. Purple shadows blackened the western slopes; evening's first haze had fallen.

Backward, Frank could see the dark mass of the command in motion. Allison was starting his dead and wounded homeward and Major Vier was trailing through the gap.

Mesquite cluttered Niles' advance and when the land pitched downward to a creek bed, he reined in and sized up the broad Indian trail beating southwest.

"They got a big start on us," Niles said. "Be full dark in another hour. My guess is Major Vier will give chase quick as we can draw rations and Parkhurst rejoins." There was, Frank noted, a heaviness, a foreign glumness in Ed. "Frank, this campaign's been in the wind since last spring. Just waiting for an incident to touch it off. We got two now; one on each side." Ed Niles glanced behind; the nearest trooper was out of earshot. He said, "You know, six months ago I'd have looked forward to such a campaign. Taking the field. Now I dread it. Makes a man wonder if he's got it in him. If he's worth a damn for anything."

"You've caught on fast, Ed. Don't worry."

"Fast? Well, I wonder. If that had been me on that hill instead of Allison, what'd be the story? Wiped out?"

"Like hell."

"I'm not so sure. Allison was in a tough situation. Could have lost every man. He fought very well, I thought." Niles' angular face darkened, "It's like looking into a black cave that winds through a mountain and wondering what's on the other side. If it really goes through. If there's a way out."

"Every man wonders that before an Indian fight, when his wife's about to have her first baby. You're too good an officer to give in to it. You won't feel like this when the campaign's over."

"When the campaign's over, I'm through."

This was the extent of their scout, and the jangling trot of Major Vier's men approaching from the rear was audible. Niles swung his horse, and then turned back and came to a standstill, his attention fixed. Frank was watching also, where a mesquite had moved. He saw the thicket quiver again, part, and, haltingly, a brown, elf-like face and shoulders appear.

At the same moment, a trooper flung up

his carbine. Niles yelled, "Hold your fire!"

As the trooper lowered his weapon, a scrawny boy stepped from the thicket. He was undersized, barefoot, his tattered flannel shirt gaping on bony ribs, and in his great, bugging eyes the pale glaze of terror still lurked. He ventured a cautious step, another and another, while his eyes flitted over them. Then he froze.

Frank motioned him farther. "Come out. Don't be afraid. The Indians are gone." He dropped to the ground, as did Niles; in accord they waited for the boy to come nearer, as if sensing that one sudden step forward might turn him running.

He seemed more assured. He approached on slow feet, still cautious, still disbelieving a little. He came on and stopped in front of them, and as he did the stiff, animal vigilance quit the thin body. Suddenly he was sobbing, sobbing, Frank saw, with relief. Tears made tracks down the gaunt cheeks. The boy raised a brushing knuckle across his face.

Frank gazed at him, touched. He slipped an arm around his shoulders, and when the gusty crying ceased, he spoke gently. "Guess you ran away from the Pena-te-kas?"

He got a negative head-shake.

"How'd you get here?"

187

Raising his hand, the boy made a vague motion that meant nothing.

"Your name? What's your name?"

"Carlos — Carlos Vasquez."

"That's a good name. Maybe you live around the fort or agency?"

"No, señor. Señor Quinn's store. My papa is there. We work for Señor Quinn."

It came back to Frank. The old Mexican on the floor of the hut, dying like a fly. He said nothing.

"You know my papa?" The great eyes brightened, then dulled. "I don't know you."

"I saw your papa one time at Quinn's store," Frank evaded and looked aside, hearing Vier's commanding voice and horses thudding up from behind. He felt a tug on his arm and he turned again to the boy. Carlos' face was tightly drawn.

His words gushed out. "Indios — the yellow-haired woman —" The rest of it stuck in his throat.

"Yellow-haired woman?" Frank crouched down, feeling a coldness clutching his stomach.

"Indios — Indios took her away! She whipped my pony — made me run off. I didn't want to. I hid in the mesquite."

"Who, boy? Who? What woman?"

"I don't know her name."

188

Frank said sharply, "Did she live at the hotel, by the fort? Think hard."

Carlos screwed up his face. "I don't know. She came to the store. She was kind to me . . . she was pretty."

Frank changed his tone. "She rode out here with you and Quinn?"

"Yes! Señor Quinn said he'd guide her, but he went around the camps —"

"Camps? What camps?"

"Pena-te-kas. I remember now! She was looking for a Pena-te-ka — to talk to the Qua-ha-das about her little sister."

Silence took hold, ran on. Frank stood, a heaviness dragging at him, and saw his own shock matched by Niles' stunned look.

"My God," the lieutenant said. His voice broke. "Miss Wagner . . . caught in this."

Frank groaned and was motionless, the thrust of the thing driving deeper and deeper. He felt shaken up, physically sick. Slowly, grimly, he turned to face Major Vier, who had proceeded in close.

"Sir," Niles was explaining in a pushed-out strain, "Pena-te-kas took Miss Wagner. We found Quinn on the ridge. He —"

"I heard," Vier silenced him.

Frank said, "Major, you'll have to pull out tonight."

"Tonight?"

189

"Tomorrow's too late. You'll lose 'em."

"That's impossible," Vier said.

"If you want her back alive, you'll go tonight."

Vier's face was a mask of concentration, of speculation. He stirred his solid shoulders and passed a hand over his trimmed black mustache.

"Forced march, Major. Each man better take extra salt. We'll eat horse meat before we're through."

The Major's dark stare was like a file. "You've changed your tune," he said, pointedly malicious.

"So I have. But we're wasting time."

"Oh, we're going after them," Major Vier said. "And remember this. You make one move that doesn't ring right and I'll order you shot. Strike out on your own — leave us — I'll have you hunted down all over the southwest!" He craned his head forward. "You're responsible for this. When you refused to help Miss Wagner, she took matters in her own hands. Remember that. You're responsible!"

Frank took it, though there was a churning in him, swift and hot. He looked carefully at Vier, wanting to tear the man from his saddle. But it was no time for anger. Frank fought it down, controlled it.

"I trust that's clear," Vier said and whirled his horse.

Frank hadn't moved. As he sought his own horse, he heard Major Vier's voice shaking the command into motion; it reformed and commenced trailing through thickening twilight for Fort Hazard.

CHAPTER 9

When the last officer had hurried from the adjutant's office, Lieutenant Ed Niles turned on heavy feet down the gloomy hallway, leaving the lamp burning weakly behind him, for he'd be returning shortly. Lists and reminders snarled in his head, struggled for last-minute attention with the chore still before him that he dreaded more than anything in his life.

There wasn't much time. As soon as he could following dismissal, he'd gone to his quarters and told Louise, afterward eaten his dull-tasting supper while she watched him in accusing silence, and returned to speed up preparations for the long march. There was ammunition to be drawn, guns inspected, dry rations and grain issued each man, fresh horses brought up and saddle gear made ready. Thinking of the horses, he dwelt on the irony of a laden trooper, restricted to a single mount, trying to catch an Indian with a dozen backs to switch to. A fight was strong on the wind, a big fight. Major Vier was moving out tonight.

Hurrying across the moon-drenched

parade ground, he was aware of the rising hum of war. From the stables the hammers of the blacksmiths crashed rhythmically, breaking the normal night-quiet of a sleeping post, pounding and shaping new cherry-red shoes on anvils.

Troopers ran briskly here and there. Niles could hear murmuring voices. Lights gleamed in all the family quarters and barracks. Enlisted men, in cramped, laborious styles, would be penning last wills or simply telling which friends were to get what keepsakes or valuables, and where to mail other belongings. All these acts were routine preceding a campaign, but by now every man knew that Lieutenant Allison's company had been roughly handled and that Major Vier would pursue to the finish. The Texas woman's capture furnished another active conversation piece. Too bad. Too bad. Fine looking woman, too. Made a fine figure horseback.

Niles went across the porch into the front room and stopped still, struck by the lamplit emptiness, a man turned uncertain in his own home. His eyes searched the room. A jolting thought shocked him. Gone? He called quickly, "Louise — Louise," and when there came no answer, he stepped at once to the bedroom.

Louise Niles made a dim, swollen shape in the shadowed room. Despite the lack of light, her small pallid face formed a blur that stood out and had its instant effect upon him. Thought of her alone and waiting bent him downward. He kissed her damp, hot cheek.

"Louise," he said, "you all right?" and stood over her.

Her mouth was set. "Did you expect me to be all right?" she responded, speaking straight to the ceiling. "Did you, Edward?"

He sat on the edge of the cot across from her, and discovered that he had nothing to say. He was bone-tired and jerked tight, with a sense of helpless failure so far as Louise was concerned. Nothing he might say, he was aware, could change her tonight. She kept the silence and, at last, he stood and said, "You rest. I want some coffee."

Going to the kitchen, he brought coffee pot and cup to the front room. There, for several minutes, he sipped and hopefully watched the bedroom doorway. When, directly, he heard her stirring on the bed, his heart jumped. His easy-going nature surged. She was coming to him; they'd talk and the world would be made right before he left her.

An interval passed, as if she might be sitting on the edge of her bed.

"Louise," he called quietly.

Then he saw her, dimly at first, walking heavily. She came into the room. Before he could go across to her, she reached a chair and sat. Her settled expression warned him. He returned to his seat, pushed the coffee cup back from the table's edge.

He said quietly, "Other men are telling their wives and children goodbye tonight. My father did it many times. It's part of our lives."

"Your father was killed at Manassas," she replied tonelessly. "Your mother died of a broken heart."

"A good many men besides my father were killed in the war," he said, "and a good many women suffered. My mother was older. You're young." He considered the faded carpet pattern and heard the restless stirrings outside. Horses traveled by on the parade. Somebody gave a command, the man's voice like an ax chopping the night apart. The hammers were striking again, a constant, ringing resonance. He heard voices in the yard next door, subdued, earnest. From this room he could fathom every changing tone and mood of this post which he knew so well. It was the only life he'd known or desired to know. He felt a deeper sense of fleeting time; he looked up and said, without argument, "You want me to leave the army. The only thing I'm fitted for. It's a hard thing."

"I want *now*, Edward! *Now!* For us . . . our lives. So we can live as civilized people are supposed to." Her intensity had drawn her forward, upright, stiff; now she sat back slowly and stared at her hands in her lap.

"We're marching in an hour," he said after a little while, hoping it sounded routine, as he took a silver-cased watch from his pocket and glanced at it. "I doubt that we'll encounter any Indians. Allison flushed them today. They'll keep traveling, and we'll be hard put to catch up."

"What," she reasoned, "if the Indians stop? Quit running and decide to fight?"

"Then there'll be a fight. But I don't look for it."

She was accusing, thoroughly wretched. "Regardless, you won't be here when the baby comes."

"Maybe I will. Maybe this will be over in a week." Conviction wasn't in his voice.

"Few days — a week — a month. It doesn't matter, I suppose. No, because the time's near. I feel it, and you won't be here," she repeated darkly.

"I promise you'll not be left alone when

the time comes," he assured her. "I reminded Doctor Murdock again tonight. Thank God he's not going with us. You'll be in familiar hands. He's been your doctor from the start."

"You don't seem to understand, Edward," she brooded in her wearying way. "I'm not afraid to have a child."

"Then what is it?" He was sharp, without intending to be. "For God's sake what is it?"

"As if you didn't know," she told him, and waved an encompassing hand. "This post — this terrible place! Always the fear that some calamity is about to happen." She shook her head back and forth, a wholly rejecting motion. "I want a house of my own, where my children can grow up and feel safe. I want to get up in the morning knowing that the pretty things I saw last night in my parlor will be there still. Be there as long as I live. I want to grow old in such a place, Edward. I want my husband with me. My family. My friends."

Unconsciously, he was moving toward her, pulled by the utter bleakness of her face, feeling a sadness for her. Halfway across something halted him, a sudden, tiny gesture of her uplifting hand that anchored him still.

"Louise," he said, "army life isn't an easy

bed. True enough. But we'll never find better people. I know. Why, there isn't a man or woman on this post that wouldn't die for you. I swear it!" He smiled and dropped his tone, speaking more gently. "If I am gone when the baby comes, you can get word to me. Major Vier's having dispatch details follow us at intervals. You'll think differently when I come back."

"When you come back?" She was regarding him with the strangest expression he'd ever seen from her. "When you come back, I won't be here, Edward. Nor the baby. I thought I'd made that plain. I'm . . . I'm going home."

"Louise! You can't mean that!"

But she did, he saw.

It was there — resolute in the hazel eyes, firm in the tilt of her chin, embedded in the tautness of her distended body. It clouded her undeniable prettiness and he saw her in a hurting light, saw the petulance of a spoiled child and the consuming discontent.

He started to speak, then closed his lips. He drew a trembling hand across his eyes. His words died, for there were no words, and suddenly, where once a wonderful tenderness and faith had lived, there was nothing to hold them together. Not even the child. And he glimpsed also his loneliness as it was going to be, the deepest loneliness of all, that of one who has known love and lost it for all time. It was gone as irrevocably as the dead men on Allison's bloody hill.

CHAPTER 10

The weariness of the march pressed in upon their jaded nerves, and along the horse-snuffling column a trooper spoke wistfully of cool steins in a St. Louis beer garden and was growled off to silence. There was no beginning and no limiting border to this gray-yellow world of striking sunlight and burning wind, no trees since they'd forded the low-banked, sand-choked channel of the North Fork of the Red, fringed with lofty cottonwoods and stubborn willows. There was nothing to relieve the monotony of a lonely land, where poor, thin buffalo grass browned on prairie that rolled in long sweepings like a gently restless sea.

By noon the second day the Comanche trail changed directions, bearing northwest in a broad, trampled scarring of many pony prints and lodge-pole scratchings. Jim Dan and Frank dogged after it in silence, except for a few words when they would slip to the ground to examine the signs or talk with Major Vier, leading his eight companies of cavalry. Sometimes the Delaware or Frank would sheer off from the march and ride far ahead.

Away to the northwest, the column made dry camp late the sixth night. No fires, no trumpet signals. Men lay on their blankets in the light of a great Comanche moon, yellow as half-candle glow.

Frank hunted up Ed Niles, squatted on his heels and filled his pipe. Beyond them, sentries walked their rounds. The cropping of some four hundred horses grazing the short grass rubbed across the clear night.

"March resumes at four o'clock," Niles said. He was slumped on the edge of his bedroll, hands clasped in front of his knees, turned taciturn and indrawn by his reflections.

"We're closing the gap," Frank said. "Sign's fresh. They won't look for us to come this far, this soon. Cavalry seldom moves this fast."

"Major Vier means business."

"Colonel Mackenzie made the last swing through here couple years back. I was with him. Fall of 'Seventy-Two. Came up from Camp Cooper. We scouted deep into Qua-ha-da country. Learned a heap. There was a big fight on McClellan Creek. Took over a hundred prisoners."

"Mackenzie impress you?"

"He did. A fine soldier."

"You should have stayed put, Frank."

"I got restless."

"You mean it was getting too peaceful at Cooper?"

"Maybe so."

"Or too far from the man you're after?"

"Guess that's it."

"Well, you asked for it, coming to Hazard. When do you think we'll catch our Pena-te-kas?"

"Late tomorrow. Next day. If they don't scatter on us." Niles' voice took on a hopeful interest. "We could wind this up in two days? Be on our way home?"

"Hard to say, Ed. Wouldn't bet on it."

Niles was gazing at the star-littered sky. "Yes, I believe we'll catch them. No doubt in my mind. You know, Frank, I've a queer feeling about this campaign, and I don't like it." There was no bitterness in what he said, more of a groping bewilderment, a reaching out. "I'm not superstitious; never was. But it's . . . it's like sensing you're moving toward something, maybe circling a little as you go. A detour here and there. A side road. But you're going that way just the same. You feel it. It's out there."

Frank liked Ed Niles more than any man he'd ever known, and with that knowing came sympathy and understanding. He said, "You're too young for that kind of talk."

"I feel two hundred years old tonight."

"Natural. We all do."

Niles dropped his gaze. "I must sound like an old man who's been staring into too many campfires."

"Grab some sleep," Frank suggested, rising. "It'll look better tomorrow."

Bootsteps aproached and an orderly halted in front of Frank. "Major wants you."

Frank traded glances with Ed, deliberately knocked out his pipe and followed the trooper to the dim cone of Major Vier's tent, the lone tent in the command. It stood apart, in the center of the bivouac. Frank pulled up at the entrance, almost bumping Captain Parkhurst coming out.

Parkhurst, second in command to Major Vier, had served faithfully but without fame in the War, a ruddy-faced veteran whose mane of white hair made him appear older than he was. He was heavy of frame, thick jowled, and he fought Indians in the hammering, bludgeoning style of a Grant, successful as long as you could come to grips with them. Parkhurst's greeting was gruff as he paced on. The orderly vanished.

Stepping in, Frank felt a guardedness take

stand within him. Major Vier, at his desk, was erectly examining a map by sallow candlelight. His revolver hung behind him, the burnished black leather holster gleaming. He sat motionless, holding that precise position even after Frank had stood there several moments, holding it, Frank understood, just long enough so a man might feel ignored or humbled.

"Well, Major —" Frank broke in.

Only then Vier glanced up, as if deeply engrossed. "Godforsaken country," he said, tapping the map with a forefinger. Even out here, Frank saw, he had the over-groomed air, the faint but perceptible pompousness; the long nose and heavy lips pinched in a trifle, in the manner of a person smelling something distasteful. His blue jaws glistened from the shave he'd had within the hour. Perspiration laced his forehead; now he pressed a handkerchief, dabbing. His black eyes strayed over the desk and he flicked his hand at something unseen to Frank. Still, he looked hard and capable of following a plan, a man unchanged by his surroundings.

"It won't get any better," Frank predicted.

"Water's going to be a problem."

"Comanches find it. We can."

"You seem rather confident, Mr. Chesney. Ordinarily, I hear only the gloomy side from you."

"Just the facts, Major. Happens I know where most these water holes are."

"I expect you to. In addition, we'll need meat before the week's out, if we're gone that long."

"There's buffalo, horsemeat."

Vier turned his hand, palm upward, and studied the tips of his fingers. Frank, sensing the circling drift of their conversation, wondered why he'd been called here. Not to talk about water and meat.

"Sit down," Vier said in rare congeniality.

"I'll stand."

Annoyance altered the dark, constant stare. "Look," Vier said, "I want to talk, I've dismissed my orderly. Perhaps I can offer you a drink of Kentucky whisky from my saddlebags?"

"No, thanks."

"Don't you drink?"

"Depends."

"You mean — with your friends?"

"Good a way as any to put it, Major."

Major Vier stiffened, "You make no effort to hide your dislike for me, do you?"

"Why should I? You — you'd like to get me killed, wouldn't you? Thinking up a rescue party for little Emily Wagner was a smart try. Covered your tracks mighty slick. Had me fooled for a while."

Vier snapped to his feet. "You can't forget Crazy Heart Butte, can you?"

"No. Or that I'm the only man besides you who knows what really happened. That makes me dangerous to you, Major."

"I trust," countered Vier, his smile thin, "you won't let your emotions interfere with your duties as scout."

"You getting worried?"

Hands locked behind him, Vier made a sharp turn in the cramped space. He stopped, his eyes penetrating and hostile.

"Has it ever occurred to you that I had to make a fateful choice that day? It was the lives of Monahan's detachment or the rest of the command. We had to get out. There wasn't time."

"You could've tried."

"With the whole lower valley swarming with Indians? You reported that fact to me. Remember?"

"I did, and there was time — then."

Vier was amused. "Since you're so positive about something beyond my control, who haven't you whispered it around the post?"

"Who'd believe me?"

"No one, of course." Vier was smiling and yet he wasn't smiling.

"Maybe I should have talked," Frank said slowly.

"You waited too long."

"Guess roundabout talk's not my way. I'd rather face a man. Tell him. Like now. Let's be honest, Major. I never had much use for you. None after Crazy Heart. You none for me. But you need me to guide your yellowlegs."

"I'm of the opinion it isn't quite that simple." Vier's mouth curled in a mysterious, lip-twisting smile; triumph polished his blunt gaze. He was himself again, confident, commanding.

Frank watched him warily.

"I know what happened in Colorado," Vier said, distinct to the syllable.

Frank's mind leaped to Vier's remarks in his headquarters that afternoon about Utes, as though he knew a secret and couldn't keep it to himself. "I don't see the connection," Frank said.

"You shall, presently. I sent to Fort Lyon — Denver — Fort Union — and around for a report on you."

"Report?" A feeling began tapping in Frank.

"Precisely. An army report. Took some

time. I learned you're fairly well known as a scout."

"Come out from behind the bush, Major."

Vier smiled as only he could smile, putting a tilt to his mouth. "You were a placer miner, working the country between Sand Creek and Denver. Chivington's volunteers went through. One of them, an army deserter named Yeager, raped and murdered your Ute wife. Also, killed your son. You've been hunting Yeager ever since." His voice had a pitiless resonance, all the coldness of an official report.

"What about it?" Frank bit. "Lot of people know."

"All the details?"

"But I don't see —"

Major Vier's gaze was a ramming thing. "Well, if you think you're going to lead my command into a trap because you hate all white men, you're wrong!"

Frank's jaw fell; then he felt a violence pouring into the pit of his belly.

"You may be interested to know," Vier went on, with something like relish, "that I requested the report immediately after Crazy Heart Butte. As early as then, I noticed your peculiar concern for the color of copper skin. I'm not at all convinced the

208

last-minute scout you suggested wasn't to warn the Cheyennes! Nor that the Valle de las Lágrimas Qua-ha-das weren't warned by you!"

"You bastard," Frank said. "You filthy bastard!" His hands came up. Major Vier, as if anticipating, was an instant faster, his swiftness unexpected and skilled.

There wasn't time to dodge. Frank saw the blurred arc of Vier's fist, and felt a sharp explosion of pain alongside his jaw. He felt himself smashed backward, and floundering. He got his feet under him and lurched in, throwing a wobbly right. His knuckles slammed bone. He heard Vier's sudden grunt. But Vier's first blow still dazed him. Although he saw the next punch coming, he couldn't duck in time. Vier closed with the quick movements of a trained boxer. Frank tried to raise his arms, to bend his body away, and was knocked to his knees.

Feeling raced in him, a murderous feeling. Blood tasted like brine. His lips were bleeding. He pushed up, careened forward and stopped flat-footed, catching the dark shine of Vier's revolver.

Vier spoke between his teeth. "Another step and I'll shoot you down. I will! I swear it!"

Frank froze, his hands dropping. In Vier's unrelenting face, he read the nervous glitter of fear and the will to kill. "Pull that trigger," Frank breathed, "who'll guide you?"

"Your mangy Delaware friend."

Frank nodded. "My friend. He'll lead you plumb to hell."

Vier cocked his head a notch. "I think not. He won't get the chance. Because you're going to finish what you started, Mr. Chesney. You will because of your absurd interest in Miss Wagner. Otherwise, why'd you suddenly decide to come? Impossible, of course. You . . . a man like you . . . thinking about a woman of her refinement. Her family." Vier's upper lip curled; temper massed in his glistening face. "Oh, I was waiting for her that night at the hotel. She was late. I saw her come from the direction of your quarters. She pleaded with you, didn't she? There in your fine 'dobe house. You refused, again. She turned to Quinn. I'm afraid you changed too late." Vier's fisted hand whitened around the revolver butt. "Now get out!"

Frank's hands were knots hanging at his sides. He longed, he hungered to get at Vier. He hesitated, his eyes on the revolver, and dismissed the urge. He went slowly to the doorway and looked back.

"Major," he said, "we're both where we can't pull out. There'll come a settlin' up time, though, when this is over, if Comanches don't beat me to you. That uniform won't save your hide. You think it will, but it won't."

"Get out!"

Frank lingered. "Think it over, Major. Tonight . . . when Monahan's butchered boys come riding by and you can't sleep."

Going out under the stars, he stalked to his bedroll, took off his boots and felt of his jaw where Vier had struck him twice, the striking skill of a clever boxer. At the beginning, Frank realized, even after Crazy Heart Butte, he'd only detested the man. Now he hated Vier, every part of him, hated strong enough to destroy and not regret. A terrible hate. Not only for what Vier had done to him but to his own command.

He stretched out and presently he forgot about Vier.

Her face formed in his mind, clear-cut, vivid. He could see the mass of soft yellow hair curled under the strange, flowered hat and the large expressive eyes, the full mouth that had been tender and giving, he thought, for a fleetness. Her face often sober when she ought to have been smiling.

He remembered her cleanness, the faint scent of her hair. He felt the substance of her, warm and firm. Where was she now? In some greasy buck's tipi? Was she, he brooded, even alive?

He groaned aloud, at war with himself, miserable and guilty. Vier had accused him of causing Henrietta's plight, and there was, he admitted, some truth in that which he wouldn't deny. She'd not become reckless until he refused to help her a second time. Right as he believed himself at the time, it hurt to know he'd pointed her toward Quinn; though it was Vier who'd given her the foolish notion a man might kite off to Qua-ha-da country for her.

He turned on his blanket, able to summon just one solacing reminder. Old Owl led, or did lead, the Pena-te-ka band they pursued. He was a reasonable chief, far-sighted, wise, ahead of his time. Once a great warrior, he'd quit raiding after losing all his sons. Though still hating the white man, he knew war was a one-way road to destruction for the Indian. Thus, a captive woman might fare better in his camp. Depending, Frank checked himself, on how much authority the young men had seized. Hadn't they attacked Lieutenant Allison? Fought him to a standstill? All this, when

Old Owl wanted peace?

All around Frank, everywhere, save for the muttering of an exhausted trooper turning in his sleep or the brushing movements of the grazing horses, the prairie lay still and lonely. He noted these muted sounds and the quietness had its lulling effect on him. After a while he realized that he was praying silently for her, clumsy, awkward, agony-wrung phrases he hadn't said since Birdy died in his arms.

He slept then.

He was dreaming. He could mark her clearly in the moon-wash outside his 'dobe. She was scornful, mocking him because he wouldn't go to the Qua-ha-das, when across the night drove an erupting sound. Horses, then whoops and shots.

He jerked upright, listening, awake at once. But the sounds of his dreaming persisted. They were, he realized, still about him; off over there. Whooping and shooting. He flung off the blanket and rammed into his boots, hearing horses in violent action, hammering the prairie sod, rolling to his right. Bullets whanged through the camp. The shots seemed wild, at random. Troopers were piling out. Everyone was bawling orders. First, faint daylight pecked the sky.

He dodged a scrambling trooper and, swinging the Spencer, ran toward the hammering horse racket, somewhat lessened now. A few carbines rattled on the edge of the bivouac. Ducked low, running, he came upon two sentries kneeling with carbines leveled.

Powdersmoke fouled the air. Far out, where the troopers watched, he could see a dark clump rushing away. It faded from sight as he looked. A faint hoof rumble drifted back.

A trooper heaved his relief. "Came all at once! Right at us — turned an' ran past."

"They make a cut for the horses?" Frank asked.

"Never stopped. Kept going. Just raisin' hell. Kinda funny for Comanches, though."

It was. Yelling and firing their guns, Frank thought, making a fuss and rushing on with nothing to show for their trouble. Passing up a grab for the horses, when if there was anything a Comanche loved, and doted on, it was stealing cavalry mounts. That Major Vier had his horses hobbled and well-guarded made little difference. Funny. Like the trooper said. The way Comanches didn't behave.

He ran it through his mind as he walked to the milling camp. Major Vier, irksome and sleepy, was bawling at Parkhurst and Niles, the three of them outside Vier's tent.

"They're gone," Frank said.

"Gone?" Vier echoed. "Don't tell me they just fired into the camp and rode on?"

"Way it looks. Didn't slip in on the pickets, either, and they passed up the horses."

Vier and Parkhurst exchanged glances. Niles watched the Major, as if expecting an order. Vier turned on Frank, an acid edge in his tone. "So now they know they're being followed."

"Knew it all along, Major. Now they're saying come on."

"We're doing that," came the amused reply. "There's only one trail."

"Is now. Could be they aim to draw us off somewhere." Frank was certain of it as they rode after the war party's wake under grayish light, the fresh prints avoiding the main trail of the village, cutting south, a hoof-gouged trace that read like an open invitation to follow. Frank, hauling up, shook his head at Vier.

"Pull us off is what they want. So we'll take after 'em. Let the village go."

Vier's voice crackled. "You don't have to draw pictures on a slate for me, Mr. Chesney. I've fought enough Indians to

215

know Miss Wagner isn't with this small war party. Return to the main trail," he ordered.

They swung back. Visible on Vier's left cheekbone was a bluish knot. Frank saw Niles notice it and wisely shift his glance, offering no comment.

Two hours after sunup the wide pattern splintered, fanning out on half a dozen different trails in an arc roughly west to northeast. Frank had been expecting the break-up, even earlier. He waited and frowned over the hoof marks, aware of the need of Jim Dan's judgment, but the Delaware was off on one of his solitary prowls.

"Now what?" Vier muttered, when the regiment closed up.

"Sign's bustin' up."

Delays always irked the Major. He spurred to the front, alone, going over each new off-shoot, his stern handling of the reins sending his horse dancing, throwing its head. Frank didn't follow, knowing the man would believe nothing until he'd seen for himself.

Major Vier had his look and returned, out of humor, to be joined by Captain Parkhurst and Adjutant Niles.

"I suppose," Vier inquired of Frank, "we'll be delayed while you ponder over which trail to take?"

"Tough pick," Frank admitted and gestured at the scarred ground. "Old trick, Major. These trails will break up into smaller parties. Later on, they'll come together again. They got a rendezvous somewhere."

"If they're all headed for the same place," Parkhurst asked in his throaty growl, "what difference it make what trail we take?"

"Time's no matter to an Indian," Frank said. "His belly's his clock. Pick the wrong trail, we could wander all over creation. No telling when they'll rendezvous."

Major Vier pointed. "Northeast looks logical to me. It's also the heaviest trail."

"Major," Frank said, eyes on the tracks, "I'd say you're right except for one thing. Northeast is away from Qua-ha-da country. They'll take a white captive, a white woman, straight to Qua-ha-das as they can. Far as they can get away from white settlements or army posts."

Vier's stare was cornering. "Are you trying to tell me you can look at horse tracks and tell whether a white woman rode that way?"

"Indian don't think like a white man," Frank said, striving to hold his voice down. "Big part of the time he lets you see what he wants you to see. Runs when you're primed

217

for a fight. Fights when you figure he'll run; when you don't expect trouble. He lets you find a big track so you'll be fool enough to chase him . . . That's how that northeast fork strikes me. Look here," he called, riding a distance and pointing down. "This trail runs northwest. You notice it's the smallest bunch. They're traveling light. Fifteen lodges, say; not over twenty. Shapes to me they don't want us to follow. But," he said, "I want to."

"Any particular reason?" Vier queried, his attitude doubting.

"Hunch. One hell of a big hunch."

Still doubting, Vier turned to Parkhurst. "It's my policy to give every staff officer an opportunity to state his views. What's it going to be, Captain? Northeast or northwest?" He was seeking to appear tolerant, and failing. He was, Frank knew, asking for opinions and yet unable to hide the driving wish that he expected them to agree with his own.

Parkhurst skirted a quick answer. He had no desire to lock horns with his superior; nevertheless, in him existed a hard core of honesty, which probably accounted for his still being a gray-haired captain while twenty years Vier's senior.

"I'm not familiar with the country, sir.

Mr. Chesney is. He and Jim Dan. No one else in the command is, to my knowledge. We know we can't cover all trails; that's out of the question. It's apparent they hope to confuse us. I'd risk northwest, sir.

As Parkhurst finished, Frank saw Vier's moist face go flush. Vier mopped with a bandana. He said, his voice staccato, "You, Mr. Niles?"

"I realize it's a question of experience and knowledge of the country and Indians, sir. Maybe the trick is to think like an Indian. Imagine what we'd do in their situation." Niles paused, but his voice was calm. "I'm willing to try northwest, Major."

Vier's framed expression changed not at all, but the slight springing up of his chin betrayed his pique. "Gentlemen," he said, "I bow to your opinions. I wonder if I shouldn't include them in my report — in the event we return empty-handed."

That was all. He wheeled and arm-waved the regiment forward, northwest.

At one o'clock, Jim Dan returned from scout. He rested his weight on his hands across the pommel before reporting. "Pony tracks come in — bunch up," he said, bringing his outspread fingers together like two fans.

"What kind of tracks?" Frank said.

219

Pointing to the trail the command rode upon, the Delaware said, "Same tracks. No pony shoe."

"You mean more unshod tracks come in on this trail?" Vier questioned, highly elated, and when Jim Dan nodded in agreement he retorted to Parkhurst, "I rather expected this to happen. Every damned trail is converging. Sooner, I recall, than I was told to expect. Gentlemen, I'm afraid you've given the hostiles credit for military skill and deception they do not possess. No Indian's that smart."

He regarded his officers, awaiting their reaction. There was a period of silence, Vier's presence like a wind blowing coldly against Frank. The silence went on a stretch.

Parkhurst broke it. "How many lodges on this trail?" he asked Jim Dan.

"Fifty. Mebbe sixty."

"In that case," Parkhurst said, "not all the Pena-te-kas are joining this band. Just part."

Vier discounted that line of reasoning to address Jim Dan. "Did you say fifty or sixty lodges? It's got to be one or the other. No maybe to it."

The Indian's response was bewilderment. He looked to Frank for understanding, and grunted in Comanche.

"He counted the lodgepole marks," Frank spoke up. "Not easy, where they run together."

"Why didn't he say that?" Vier answered and ended the parley. Thereafter, he hurried the column to his own straining, restless pace and threw out additional flankers.

As the stifling day wore on, the face of the land gradually changed. Eroded buttes, spaced like sentinels, and rounded knobs replaced the groundswell of the endless prairie. Footing tilted upward amid scattered mesquite and prickly pear. It was dry, merciless and brutal, like a land passed over by fire and since forgotten; yet there was the vague promise of water because the flatness was broken.

Dropping back to ride beside Ed Niles, Frank said, "Qua-ha-da country. Edge of it. Now you can say you've seen it."

"The devil's backbone," Niles commented. "Bad place to get caught. We're in for something, and I'm ready to get it over."

"Sometimes marching is harder than fighting."

"This is — that and the not knowing."

"Years from now," Frank said, "we'll look back on this and find some good. It'll seem easier. We won't remember the heat and the dust. We'll just remember how young we used to be. The good men we rode with."

Niles sobered. "Hope you're right."

Frank and Jim Dan paired off from the plodding column to scout ahead, where the trail led away into a naked country with no shelter except its own shattered hulks. Several miles on, with the serpentine file of the regiment out of sight, they capped a ridge and stopped. The Delaware pointed and Frank saw a lone tipi pitched close to a narrow branch, its trickle of water casting a spangled sheen in the westering sun.

They rode downgrade and slow-walked their horses to the lodge, hearing nothing and finding no movement. The flap of the skin lodge was open, flung back, wide. Looking in, Frank saw a blanket-wrapped shape on the ground. Jim Dan muttered. They rode nearer.

This was the burial of a warrior, his face overlaid with vermillion, his eyes sealed with red clay. Beside him lay his possessions. Frank noticed a lance, bow and quiver, trinkets.

Jim Dan was down like a cat and inside the gloomy place. He took a swift look and faced around and stood over the warrior, his alert black eyes darting. He stooped suddenly and Frank saw the dull gleam of metal in his lifting hand, and as Jim Dan left the tipi he snatched something off a lodgepole. Outside, eyes glittering, he grinned and displayed a shiny revolver. In the other hand, he dangled a long scalp. It reeked, even from where Frank was.

"My friend," Jim Dan said, stuffing the scalp in his saddlebag, "Ingen go fast. Hurry. Pony soldiers close. No time bury warrior." As if the situation struck him as improper, Jim Dan indicated the pitching land, where a natural cave or crevice or rocky wash might be, where Comanches preferred to rest their dead. He shook his head. His hands spoke, gesturing high. Better, he said, for a warrior's body to face the rising sun. This was bad.

"Let me see the revolver," Frank said.

He felt a vague familiarity as Jim Dan obligingly handed him the showy handgun, then gathering recognition as he turned it over and found silver stars on both sides of the walnut stock and a ship battle scene engraved on the round cylinder.

"Buffalo Quinn's fancy Navy Colt," he said and fell into deep thought, working out the story aloud. "This Comanche counted coup on Quinn, took his revolver. Maybe Quinn wounded him first, or maybe the Comanche took it and rode back to fight Allison's men some more. Got wounded there. When he died on the trail, his people left him here with his weapons. Wasn't time, like you say, to bury him right."

Frank was reining off as he finished. "Jim Dan, the white woman's with this band. Come on."

To Frank's astonishment, Major Vier showed no belief in the revolver. "You say it's Quinn's? How do you know?"

"The silver stars, Major. Quinn's Navy Colt had 'em. This is thirty-six caliber. Same as his."

"Navy Colts aren't too unusual out here, and I've seen stars before on revolver butts."

"But Quinn's been the only civilian with one around the fort. He showed it off. Major, this Colt means we're trailing the right band. Same that killed Quinn — that took Miss Wagner."

"I'm not so sure."

Frank pitched him a straight-on look. "Don't matter now, long as we keep moving. Jim Dan says we're so close on their tail they didn't have time to bury that warrior."

Jim Dan's abrupt motions drew all eyes. The Delaware, who'd listened in silence to the exchange, was digging inside his saddle-bag. He came up with a mass of long hair. Intent on the argument over the Colt's meaning, Frank had forgotten the scalp, which he saw now was dirty yellow in hue and of unusual length. A white man's. He stared hard, in comprehension.

Jim Dan, with ceremony, offered the tawny trophy to Major Vier, who recoiled. His mouth clamped. His nostrils pinched. Anger jerked him.

"Throw that damn thing away!"

"You look," Jim Dan urged, undaunted, offering again, his button-black eyes wise and the ghost of a grin playing around his mouth corners. "Find in tipi. Buffalo Quinn's hair."

Vier flung the vile hunk another stare and wheeled his horse, but he argued no more. At his sharp command, the halted regiment unlimbered like a stiff arm in the blazing afternoon sunlight and proceeded at a trot.

They filed past the lone tipi, filled canteens and watered horses, and passed on into a motionless, silent country. Yet so recent was the sign that Frank had the feeling Indians might be just over the next rim of land. Jim Dan was constantly on the prowl, now on the flank, now bobbing ahead, now out of sight. He appeared again, a quarter-mile in advance. He began riding forward and backward, in short dashes, up and down the side of a squatty butte.

"He's found something," Frank informed Major Vier. "He wants us to hurry up."

Vier struck out in a gallop. As they approached, Jim Dan signalled dismount and pointed to the butte's crest. They dismounted and climbed, stiff-legged, with Parkhurst grunting every step, through clinging mesquite and over slabs of gray-red rock like flame to the hand's touch.

"Stay down," Frank said at the top and scanned the humped distance, stretching, unfolding. Glare made his eyes smart. He blinked and peered again, an excitement pounding high in his chest.

He said, "There they are, Major."

CHAPTER 11

Major Vier, on one knee, raised his glasses. After a lengthy watchfulness, he lowered them and shook his head. "I see no Indians."

"Sight farther out," Frank said.

Vier tried again. "No, I see nothing."

"There's brown haze far out."

Vier peered once more, and suddenly he set the glasses tighter to his eyes. "I see haze."

"That's it," Frank said. "Dust smoke from horses."

Vier hunched his head forward and watched for another minute. An aggressiveness flowed through him as he handed the glasses to Captain Parkhurst, exclaiming, "Take a good look. We're going after them!"

The dog-tired Parkhurst had his look, his expression extremely thoughtful, while Vier, watching, naked-eyed fidgeted over the delay.

"Not moving very fast," Parkhurst observed and passed the glasses to Lieutenant Niles.

"Tired running," Vier replied in his positive fashion. "Captain, you and Mr. Niles go halt the column. Notify all company commanders to come forward. I'll be down after another looksee."

When they'd gone, Vier lifted his glasses and studied the distance. "We can handle them without much trouble," he said, elated, still looking.

A thought Frank didn't like came weaving in his mind. "Major," he said, as Vier cased his glasses, "go crowding 'em you know what can happen to her."

Vier tensed; a shot of violent color hit his face. "You talk as though I want something to happen. I trust you know I'm going to make Miss Wagner my wife?"

"Her chances are slim enough without piling into 'em."

"Well, I'm in command. I propose to act in whatever manner the situation dictates."

"One thing, you got enough men to back these Pena-te-kas down, if you'll do it."

"Exactly how," the Major inquired acidly, "would you suggest I go about it? Though, perhaps, as a man who's lived with Indians, you have some plan?"

"Show off your full force," Frank said. "Give them a good look. Then send in a few men to talk."

"Someone, say, like yourself?"

"Not me. You're the pony soldier chief. You'd have to do the talking. I'll go along as interpreter."

"I'm afraid you don't place much trust in me, Mr. Chesney." The tone was malicious. "For that matter, I doubt whether you trust anyone the way you scout. Usually alone. If not alone, with your Delaware friend. Never a white man."

Frank's smile was wry. "Oh, I wouldn't say that, Major. I trust you, when I can keep you in sight. Eye-ball close. I always feel better that way, in case you get sidetracked and start counting dead Indians."

Their glances locked, clashed. But Major Vier was the first to go downhill.

The land widened and the chopped trail, rising, lurched across shaly footing that clacked on iron shoes as Vier fast-trotted his command. Troopers, cursing and sweating, had trouble with stumbling horses. The faster march kindled a dense pall that touched off fits of coughing and sneezing. When the squall of brown haze they followed became distinct, and then disclosed moving horses, Major Vier halted, reformed the regiment into three parallel squadrons of fours and, on the quick, hastened onward again.

Frank watched Vier constantly, somehow

unsure about him, recalling Vier's sparse orders to his commanders before leaving the lookout butte . . . Keep your files closed up. Look to your equipment.

It wasn't enough, Frank thought, on the edge of a fight. It was almost as if Major Vier had barely cracked the door on his intentions to the men under him. Parkhurst, for one, had seemed to delay for more instructions, and not getting them, he'd shown uncertainty and a troubled red face.

Ahead, the Indian cavalcade was angling off sharply, a wiggling earthworm, squirming for the easier, faster traveling between two widely separated buttes.

Vier closed the gap in a rushing gallop. His surge threw the Indians into a milling stop, not yet running or scattering. Settling dust exposed a churning confusion. Riders raced back from the front. Yet, in that disorder, one group of horsemen began forming. It was to this point, toward the Pena-te-ka rear, that riders gathered.

Now Major Vier stood high in his stirrups and flung up his hand, halting his three columns. He swiveled his head to roar at Parkhurst with the right-hand squadron. Frank, on the left, near Niles, caught only the tail-end of the order on the whipping wind. "— head them off — drive them in —" and was as startled as Parkhurst looked.

"Drive them?" Parkhurst called back, taken off guard. "Looks like they're going to talk, Major." He was riding toward Vier.

"Talk!" Vier's voice was a hurled rock. "They've had a week to talk! Captain — you have your orders. Head them off!"

A deeper coloring stole over Parkhurst's ruddy features. He whirled his horse.

Vier bawled, "On the left into line!" and the other two squadrons wheeled, deploying for attack.

Frank, hemmed in by this fanning movement, gave ground while he watched the Pena-te-kas, as yet no warriors bunched to fight. The band was still drawn back, milling strangely, as if puzzled what to do next. He thought of Henrietta somewhere among them, watching, hoping, more fearful than ever now of the wild people surrounding her. He had a brief mental picture of the attack. It left him scared of what might happen — would happen! — if Vier attacked, and he knew that nothing was going to stop it.

He was conscious, suddenly, that he was spurring, rushing past Niles and coming across Vier's advance, blocking his progress. He leaned toward Vier. "Pile into 'em they'll kill her!"

Vier gestured him violently aside. Haste was upon him. He spurred to go around, but Frank jumped his horse in unison and Vier was headed again. Behind them troopers came swinging in, and the Major and Frank, stopped dead, were breaking the line, causing horses to bump. From the tail of his eye Frank saw Parkhurst leading out his squadron, though not rapidly.

"God-damnit!" Vier thundered. "You're holding us up!"

Frank saw the gaping line, heard non-coms and officers yelling. He himself was yelling at Vier, "Parkhurst's right! Look! They're ready to talk!"

"Get out of the way!"

Troopers barged in, trying to swing fully around. Frank attempted to hold fast, to shout again at Vier, but felt his horse buffeted hard as others came against him and the line kept straightening. In the swerving and colliding, he was separated from the Major, bumped frontward. Then the scrambling ceased and the command stood in position. Captain Parkhurst was going slowly off at a lagging trot, looking over his shoulder.

Major Vier twisted to glance along his wide line. Sweat coursed freely down his dark face. His arm shot up, then he hesitated.

Out on the plain, brittle-bright sunlight poured yellow glare on spurts of dust where a frantic conference was ending. A gap appeared among the Indian horsemen and three ponies broke running, the center rider holding high his lance so the cavalrymen could see the fluttering white rag. They rode straight for the command.

Parkhurst, spying the riders, shouted something lost on the wind and stopped short.

Major Vier sat fixed. His arm dropped slowly, by degrees, without signal. "Tell Parkhurst never mind," he snapped at Niles.

Rushing on, the Indians raced within a few yards of Vier. Of a sudden, when it seemed they'd crash him, they set their ponies. Dust boiled. Haunched ponies reared high. It was a pretty piece of riding, cut fine, Comanche style. The man with the lance swayed weakly; a companion reached out and steadied him. With impassive dignity, the lance-carrier settled himself and rode forward, halting directly across from Major Vier. With deliberate emphasis, he laid his ash weapon across his saddle and raised his palm, the sign for peace. A keen face, shriveled as ancient leather, met Vier's stare. It was Old Owl.

He spoke in Comanche. When Vier shook

his head, Old Owl tried again, in broken Spanish. Vier turned to Frank, calling out in exasperation, "What's he saying?"

Frank reined over. "He wants peace. Says just women and children, few old men in his band. They want no fight. He's come to smoke. Talk."

"Tell him to surrender the white woman or we'll rub out his band." Vier was contemptuous.

Old Owl coughed. He said gravely, before Frank could relay the ultimatum, "I am sick and old. My lungs are bleeding. I am old but I came here to help my people. My heart is on the ground." He broke off, as if he had failed already, as if he had more to tell these pony soldiers but dared not. It was a time-consuming speech, brief as it was, underscored by signs, slowed by Old Owl's pauses for breath.

"What's he bellyaching about now?" Vier asked.

"He's old and sick," Frank said, wondering when Vier would learn patience with Indians. "He's going to tell us something, but he's afraid we'll hurt his people. He says his people are not to blame. Looks bad, Major."

Vier could wait no longer. "You tell him —"

"Let him talk, Major."

The old Pena-te-ka, so lean and used up the meat seemed smoked on his bones, began speaking earnestly through taut lips. "I want you to have mercy on my people. You did not give us enough time to surrender on the reservation. You pushed us. One sleep was not enough. Some of my people were out hunting. Do not kill our children as you did some of the Cheyenne children in the Crazy Heart Butte fight. If you have to kill somebody, kill me. I am a chief. I am old and will not live long." He had to cough again; he spat blood, swallowed; pain cut across the eroded face. He seemed reluctant to tell the rest, and in the proud eyes Frank saw a reflection of his own dread. Old Owl continued, "Only our young men fought the pony soldiers. Our young men took the yellow-haired woman."

"She's in your camp now?" Frank said quickly.

Old Owl looked agitated. In alarm, his eyes went to Vier. "You marched fast," Old Owl said. "The young men got afraid pony soldiers would catch them; they took her away."

"Left camp?"

"Yes."

"When?"

"One sleep back."

"Where did they take her?" Frank did not recognize his own voice.

"Long way." Old Owl pointed northwest. "Qua-ha-da country. Standing Bull took her. Will trade her as slave to Black Star. Now Standing Bull and the other young men will fight with the Qua-ha-das. Their bones will be left on the prairie."

Frank told Major Vier, who scoffed, "He's lying to save his own neck."

"Don't think so," Frank said. "He didn't have to tell us about her. He could blame other bands. No, I think he hopes we'll get her back. What worries him is you'll blame the people with him. That's why he's on the run."

"I do blame them. Mr. Niles, send Captain Parkhurst over. We're going to search this filthy pack for Miss Wagner."

Old Owl offered no protest, other than to push his dislike at the Major. "You call me a liar. I am weak. You are strong. It is not enough for you that Broadhat took my word on the reservation. If you are going to kill us, shoot us in the hearts. Kill me first. Quick."

"Remind him," Vier responded, "that I know he understands white man's words while he pretends not to."

After flanking Parkhurst around to head off any rush to the northwest, Vier, his other

236

two squadrons still in a straight line, proceeded toward the Pena-te-kas.

"My friend," Frank said, riding abreast of Old Owl, "did the young men hurt the yellow-haired woman? Did they, any of them, drag her into a tipi? Into the brush? Did Standing Bull?"

Old Owl traveled a space in silence. "Some of us," he replied softly, "have not forgotten Broadhat's black medicine book. His brother talk. The hard road talk."

"You couldn't control Standing Bull's young warriors when they fought the soldiers on the hill," Frank said. "How could you protect a white woman?"

"Standing Bull's heart is bad. That is true. He has listened to bad war talk. But even a foolish young man like him does not make a woman crazy before he trades her to an important chief. Black Star wouldn't buy a crazy woman."

"Nothing bad has happened to her?"

Old Owl showed Frank his unflinching gaze. "I have told you. Nothing bad happened in my camp. What will happen later, I do not know."

"Will Black Star buy her?"

"He is rich. He owns many horses."

"Also many wives. Maybe he has enough wives to feed. If he won't buy her, what will

237

happen to her? Tell me."

"Bloody Knife," Old Owl said, "you ask me things that you can answer as well."

Major Vier posted his force and directed the search personally, starting at the head of the trail-weary Pena-te-kas as Old Owl called quieting words. Solemn-eyed old people stared back, on guard, half-grown boys and girls and women with babies. A sternness lay in Vier's face, in the ramrod stiffness of his back as he finished. There was no white woman.

"What are you going to do with my people?" Old Owl asked through Frank.

"Tell him they will be returned under guard to the fort," Vier said. "Not to the agency. Not to be fed and pampered like children who've run away from home. They will be punished."

Old Owl's voice came high, shrill. "We have done nothing! No crime! We did not fight the soldiers!"

"It's a crime to leave the reservation without permission," Vier said, uncompromising. "You have committed a crime. Broken the white man's law."

Old Owl was downcast. The long flight and his tense parley with Vier had exhausted him. He looked more dead than

238

alive as he clung to his rawhide saddle, more stooped, discouraged; the mahogany skin stretched over mere bones, the burning, fever-filled black eyes like dull coals. He was coughing more; his breathing sounded soggy. It hurt Frank to watch the old man.

"My heart cries for my people," Old Owl said. "How will you punish them?"

"There are many ways," Vier said, harsh and purposely vague.

Old Owl's alarm increased. "What will you do?"

Vier left his intention dangling a little longer, and then he spoke, bartering, "If you help me, perhaps nothing bad will happen to your people."

Hope bolstered the parchment face.

"Nothing bad," Vier said, playing on the words, "if you take me to the Qua-ha-das."

Old Owl's face was long again.

"I want the yellow-haired woman," Vier said. "I will pay ransom for her. You tell Black Star. Otherwise, your people will be punished hard."

"Show me money," Old Owl said.

Something in Frank's face matching the Pena-te-ka's distrust stirred Vier. "I don't do anything half-cocked," he declared and twisted and unstrapped the flap of one saddlebag hanging alongside the cantle. He came up, thrusting a bundle of greenbacks in Frank's face. "This proof enough? A thousand dollars!"

Vier was wiser than Frank had thought. Vier wasn't depending entirely on force. Frank nodded and said, "We don't want to forget little Emily Wagner. Qua-ha-das took her, too. We ought to ransom her as well."

"I haven't forgotten," Vier said hastily. "Of course. Tell him."

Frank explained about Emily and saw that sight of the money had impressed Old Owl. Yet he was slow coming around to an answer. "I am old," he evaded.

"You are old," Vier said. "Therefore, you know Qua-ha-da country better than a young man. You are also a Pena-te-ka chief and therefore can talk to a Qua-ha-da chief."

"I cannot ride far. I am sick." Withered fingers touched the shrunken chest.

Major Vier lost patience. "Do you want your people punished hard? I have the power to send the old men and boys to jail in the hot country. Far away. You'll never see them again."

The Pena-te-ka's veined hands spoke an eloquent protest. "Their spirits would die, I know. One time you soldiers sent a Kiowa chief to Texas; put him in jail, where he could not see the sky or the prairie. His spirit got sick. He longed to see his people again and eat buffalo meat. But you soldiers kept him holed up like a coyote in a cave. He killed himself, and that is bad."

Vier was unmoved. "Take your choice. You are in a position to benefit your people. Are you a chief or a begging woman?"

"I will not take you to the Qua-ha-da camp so you can kill them. They are Comanches like me. My brothers."

"You can tell Black Star I will meet him with one company of my men," Vier said, ready with his answer. "Just fifty men. Not a big bunch. Black Star can bring the same number of warriors and the two white captives. That way he has nothing to fear from me. Rest of my pony soldiers will stay here, guarding your people. When you come back from Black Star's village, they can go free."

Old Owl gazed off, weakening. "What of my people if Black Star won't give up the woman?"

"They still go free," Vier answered. "You have my word of honor."

Old Owl looked to Frank for strength, and Frank said in a loud voice, "We have all heard the pony soldiers' chief give his word."

"I am sick," Old Owl said, giving in, "but

I will go. I will take the white man by the hand and guide him to a place. But when I tell you to make the smoke camp and wait, you must camp there and wait. Wait while I ride to Black Star's camp."

Major Vier approved with a nod.

Suddenly, Old Owl was coughing, stringing blood to the dusty earth, and Frank told Vier, "I'm going with Old Owl when he leaves the smoke camp. He'll never make it alone. I'm not fool enough to ride into Black Star's village with him. But I'll see he gets there."

CHAPTER 12

Around noon the next day, Old Owl entered a shallow canyon marked by vermilion walls and stands of stubby cedar; it twisted and shoved and wandered and fooled, at last revealing its kept secret of a spring trickling from a break in the western wall of red rock, a watering place that only an Indian would know or a roving buffalo hunter, if no greenhorn, might suspect and find.

To the southeast, Old Owl signed Frank, there was no water this time of year.

The Pena-te-ka, traveling steadily west since early morning, now led them south into heat-clutched country which shone like rubbed brass. Before dusk, he halted and the troopers drew up behind, fifty of them, some walking beside footsore horses.

Nobody understood until the old Pena-te-ka pointed at the ground and brought his hands together in the sign for lodge or camp.

It was a gloomy place where ghosts might walk in daylight, a desolate place of cruel arroyos and bald ridges and battlement buttes, and yet, surprisingly, in places, overlaid with a mat of curly buffalo grass. It suggested an awesome vastness and loneliness, and a certain warning, Frank recognized, for by now they had penetrated far into Qua-ha-da country. He squinted at the remote land, glazy and heat-stroked in all directions, empty of life. But in this broken, tumbling country, in the breaks, Comanches found wood and water, game and refuge. Nothing he'd seen all day looked familiar. The sun dance village, broken up long ago, he placed farther south and east.

"Camp here," Old Owl announced, his briefness that of a sick man. "This will be the smoke camp. The pony soldiers will stay here."

For the first time since leaving the main command behind under Captain Parkhurst, guarding the Pena-te-ka band, Major Vier showed a difference of opinion.

"Ask him," Vier directed Frank, "why he has to pick this God-forsaken place? Can't he camp us near water? Where is the damn water, anyway?"

"Qua-ha-das call this the Fat Grass. Ponies get fat here. There's a spring quarter-mile east, but it's no good for defense. We're better off here, he says. More open. Black Star's village is some distance yet. He won't say where. Just west. Gets rougher that way. Whole damn country's upside down. Because this is an old Qua-ha-da camping ground, Old Owl figures we got a better chance to pow-wow if Black Star knows the place. He won't expect any trouble here."

"Trouble?"

"Well, ambush. Indians always look out for ambush. Get pretty goosey when they parley."

Frank expected Vier to question the matter further. But, in place of argument, Vier swung out to order bivouac, and Frank eyed him with a good deal of puzzlement. Ever since Old Owl had agreed to lead the company here, the Major's attitude had switched from cold hostility to a curious co-operation. An instance was Frank's decision to accompany Old Owl within range of Black Star's village. Vier, though reluctant at first, and distrustful of Frank, had agreed without wrangling. It was, Frank thought, going over Vier's change, a damned sudden about-face.

Looking off, he saw a sort of low basin, a shattered basin, about a mile across, sur-rounded by eroded remnants of redstone ridges and buttes. Considering the heaved-up nature of the land, he guessed the basin and its washes provided as suitable a parley ground as might be found in these sullen stretches, better than most, because there was pony grass on the east side, away from the arroyos, and water.

Horse-watering details went out and returned, reporting a sweet spring instead of alkaline, as expected. Grumbling troopers fell to cold rations. Evening's haze dropped like a thrown purple blanket, swiftly, laying down a high-plains coolness.

Old Owl had hobbled his pony and camped apart from the white men, a pathetic, forlorn figure squatting on his buffalo robe, head sunk on his chest. Noticing that he ate nothing and asked for no food, Frank took him hardtack. Old Owl accepted the army bread, but did not eat.

"Better eat," Frank urged. "You can't ride on an empty belly."

The Pena-te-ka shook his head. There was, Frank saw, a terrible exhaustion in him; it was bowing him down, breaking him. When Frank moved away, the old man beckoned him back.

"Bloody Knife," he said, his slow words knowing and flat, "you must not think much of your life. The Qua-ha-das will kill you, if you go with me as you say."

"If they get the chance," Frank nodded. "I don't intend to let that happen. When we get close to camp, I'll drop out while you make your smoke talk. When I see you and the ransom party heading for the Fat Grass, I'll pull out."

Old Owl did not look hopeful. "I am very weak. That is the only reason I let you ride with me." He looked up at Frank. "It will take much talk."

"You have seen the ransom money in the saddlebags of the pony soldiers' chief," Frank said. "You can tell Black Star how large the bundle is."

"Black Star hates the whites."

"But he likes to trade. He sells to the Comancheros. Is he a man of honor, or does he speak with the forked tongue?"

"No," came the unhesitating reply. "He has honor. If my talk falls to the ground, it will because of his hate. Or if the Red One tells him the ransom is bad." Coughing suddenly, Old Owl hacked out the spell and afterward lay flat on his back.

Frank's mind strayed off to the buffalo wallow fight and the one-eyed white man. "He's no chief," Frank said. "No white man can be a chief."

"His medicine is strong. He is a great fighter. He has killed white men. His own people. For that reason, Black Star listens to him sometimes. But the Red One has a bad

247

heart. He is bad for my Qua-ha-da brothers."

"Where did he come from?"

"One of the soldier houses. 'Way off. He killed a brother soldier. He boasts of that deed, something no Comanche would do. His heart is bad," Old Owl reminded, and made the throwing away sign. "Many Qua-ha-das fear him."

Frank turned still and thoughtful. In these past days, since the Pena-te-ka trouble, he'd forgotten Yeager. Forgotten after coming so close to killing the man during the wallow stand. Yeager — and Frank had no doubt the Red One was Yeager — had had to kill to impress the skeptical Qua-ha-das. Be crueler than the wild people sheltering him. Bloodier than the wildest young men. What renegade whites Frank had found on the frontier were as vicious as any bad Indian; more dangerous, in fact, because of their superior knowledge of white ways and weapons. Not only did they pass on the vices and diseases of their own race, but they acted like sparks to dry powder, always mouthing war.

He felt a cold fear lock his thoughts. How would a runaway deserter and murderer, hating his own kind, take out that hate on a pretty white woman?

There was just one answer. It stirred his steps. Going off, he murmured to the Pena-te-ka, "I know that white man. I have fought him."

The Indian's voice was a worn-out sigh. "You should have killed him. Now maybe you will have to fight him again."

Frank went on, in a slow-paced, slouching walk. He wasn't prepared for the stocky shape materializing at his flank without sound.

"Jim Dan," Frank said, "some day you'll get a bullet coming up on me like that." It was too dark to tell, but he knew the Dela-ware would be grinning, pleased at having approached unobserved.

They stood a moment. Jim Dan drifted in until Frank saw the gleaming, triumphant eyes.

"Old Owl mighty sick Ingen. You need Jim Dan go 'long, huh?"

Frank grinned at him, watching the half-sad wistfulness of this lost-tribe wanderer, kicked around by Indians and whites alike; this unimpressive looking man of indeterminate age, who lived like a tenant farmer on the reservation in his 'dobe squirming with kids and hunting dogs, but who, once on scout, became a plains Indian possessed of a great natural dignity and honor, plus all the courage and skills needed for survival.

"Aim to lose your hair?" Frank goaded him and started past.

Jim Dan blocked him gently. "You need Jim Dan."

"Major Vier aims to keep one scout here."

"Me go. You see."

"See, hell," Frank said with understanding. "You stay here. Take off against orders, you'll lose your pay."

Jim Dan coaxed. "Mebbe big fight."

"You wouldn't last two minutes," Frank retorted, grinning more broadly. "You can't fight. And who'd want your hair? Looks mighty poor to me."

In answer, Jim Dan swept off his hat and scuffed up his hair, ruffled it vigorously. It was thick and straight, black as night. "Plenty hair. Damn betcha."

"Sorry, Jim Dan."

The Delaware looked puzzled and hurt. Then, all at once, his eyes were gleaming again. "Buffalo wallow time. You — me." He was pleading earnestly. "Jim Dan fight good, huh? Kill them Qua-ha-das."

Frank shook his head. "Not this time. Forget it."

Jim Dan stepped aside, saying no more, and Frank walked ahead. Over his shoulder, he saw the Delaware still standing in the same spot. He hadn't moved when Frank proceeded to his own bedroll. He eased down at once and drew off his boots, lay back and saw the bedded glitter of the stars. Full dark fell. With it came the pungency of a lost and brutal land riding the restless wind, a wind that called and talked. However, it had no claim on him tonight. It was always this time when he seemed to recall her, when the camp was quiet, when he found himself on his blanket and nothing much gained during the day and another sunup slimming her chances.

A man approached.

"Frank."

Ed Niles. High-shouldered, shank-bodied against the skylight. Frank sensed a hesitancy in Ed's movements and silence.

"Come down."

Niles dropped to the blanket. His voice was grave. "Know what you're getting into tomorrow?"

"Yeh."

"Hell of a chance to take. I know Old Owl's ailing, but why can't he go in alone? They won't bother him."

"Not sure he'd even get there. He's in bad shape, Ed. Just hope he holds together 'til we locate that Qua-ha-da village."

"So that's it?"

"Part of it. I don't want him passin' out before we know. If he makes it, so much the better. He's still our best bet."

"Hasn't he given you any idea where it is?"

"Not a hint. He's still a Comanche. Afraid Vier might take pony soldiers in there. Old Owl's going to protect the Qua-ha-das as much as he can. Brothers, he calls 'em. Looks like you boys wait here on your tokus."

Niles said, bitter wonder tracing his words, "Major doesn't seem to mind waiting. Everything's fine."

"Honey and pie, if you like vinegar pie. I don't. When a man switches that much, look out. What you think, Ed?"

Loyalty, had deep roots within Ed Niles. To Frank's knowledge, he had never criticized his commanding officer beyond a light reference. Niles was mute so long Frank decided he wasn't going to comment. Then, low: "Watch him, Frank."

Across the night slipped a new sound, an outcry, mournful, shivering to the blood. Part wail, part chant.

Niles asked nervously, "Old Owl?"

"Crying for strength," Frank said.

"Death song, maybe?"

"Well, he knows he can't last long."

252

They listened, not talking, and presently, when the high, wild crying ceased, Niles spoke in a musing tone, "How many days now? Eight? Nine? I've lost count. Whatever it is, Louise has had the baby by now. Her time was close when I left. I wonder how they are?"

"She and the post women will manage."

"I'd like to know. I'd like to see the baby's face. Just once."

"You'll see him grow up."

Niles watched the sky a considerable time. He turned his head and said, "Frank, I need a favor."

"All right."

Niles leaned in and Frank felt rounded metal cool in his hand. "Your watch?"

"If anything happens, see that Louise gets it, will you?"

His premonitory tone startled Frank. "Hell's fire, Ed, don't hump up. Don't get any crazy notions."

"I'm not. But you keep it for me."

Frank shook his head. "Me? I'm the last man you better leave it with, where I'm going. Here, take it back." He reached across to force it on Niles, but Niles, rising quickly, stood and moved beyond Frank.

"Goodnight," Niles called, going as he spoke, cheerful again. "Good luck tomorrow."

★ ★ ★

Saddled up and breakfasted before first dawn, Frank led his animal across where Old Owl struggled weakly with gear he could scarcely lift. Frank saddled for him, gave him a hand to the saddle and mounted.

"Mr. Chesney." A chopping voice, arresting, unmistakable.

Frank reined in, primed for trouble. Was he going to have a round with Vier at the last minute?

"It's customary for a scout to report before he leaves," Major Vier snapped.

"We went over everything once."

"Correct. We did — but there's been a change in orders, in addition to your job of seeing that Old Owl reaches the Qua-ha-da village. However, I can't tell you in front of Old Owl. I haven't forgotten how well he understands English." Shrugging, Frank swung across and Major Vier said, "If Old Owl and a Qua-ha-da party haven't started back six hours after he gets there, you are to report to me at once with location of the village. Leaves me no recourse but to bring Parkhurst up for attack."

"What if Old Owl comes out alone? If Black Star won't talk?"

"Makes no difference. You're to ride here fast as you can. However, I'm rather hopeful we'll have a ransom parley. I feel that the presence of a mere fifty cavalrymen here will coax the mighty Black Star out of his den. He should feel fairly safe facing our little handful."

Vier finished on so amiable a note that Frank, gauging the man once more, felt unsure again. Frank muttered, "We'll see," and rejoined Old Owl. They swung east to the spring, watered, and came back past the camp.

An almost formless darkness enveloped them. And for a long time, Old Owl seemed to guide them more by feel, by instinct; when daylight broke, he hastened the pace. Soon the sun smote stronger and the coolness vanished and heat pressed like a hot hand on Frank's back as Old Owl bore northwest, never varying that general direction once he took it. There was an air of hurrying desperation about the old Pena-te-ka, a humped doggedness, a grim concentration.

Twice he reeled in the saddle and Frank caught him. Old Owl's face was grayish, pasty. He seldom coughed any more, as though he had not the strength; and when he did, it came as a soggy racking of exhaustion. For all that, he refused to rest and would go on whenever Frank stopped for him.

After a time, Frank paused in a small, wooded canyon, and was prepared when Old Owl didn't slacken. He caught the bridle, announcing, "We rest here. Get down."

Old Owl made no protest. He slid to the ground, started for the shade of a cottonwood and buckled, slowly folding, settling like a falling leaf, Frank got under the bony shoulders and helped him across, appalled at the old man's slightness, his shortness of breath.

"Old Owl," Frank said when the Pena-te-ka lay flat, "you're mighty weak. Time you told me where the Qua-ha-da camp is."

Although the Indian's voice sounded dim and strengthless, there was resolution underlying it. "No. You bring soldiers."

"If you die before we get there," Frank said, cruel because he had to be, "I won't know where the Qua-ha-da camp is. Then I can't find the white woman."

"My brothers mean more to me than a white woman."

"She's suffered many hurts by the Qua-ha-das," Frank said, watching the sink and rise of the old man's breathing. "Qua-ha-das killed her mother and father. Stole her little sister. You have listened to Broadhat's talk out of the medicine book about broth-

256

erly love. You believed him because Broadhat's tongue is straight. Now the white woman never hurt your people. Help her. Tell me."

Defiance whetted the Indian's eyes.

"You're too sick to keep on without rest," Frank told him flatly. "You'll die if you don't stop."

"No. We go."

Old Owl attempted to rise, but Frank pressed him back down. So they stayed there half an hour or more, Old Owl resting with his eyes closed.

They rode steadily after that, Old Owl going at a trot, clinging to his rawhide perch.

Shattered buttes thrust up around them, and there was always the wild-fire sun that smoked a man's hide and threw glare under his hat brim. Once, Frank spotted buffalo, a dark mass to the northeast. They came to a sandy creek and Old Owl stuck on its meandering course, never stopping. Sometime before noon they reached a point on the stream between rocky hills, where hackberry, oak and ash grew among the cottonwoods. Thus, the country took on a brighter prospect.

"Let's rest," Frank said and expected refusal.

To his surprise, Old Owl agreed. He started sliding from the saddle, clinging, hanging. Before Frank could reach him, Old Owl collapsed under his pony's feet. When Frank carried him out of the sun and laid him down in the shade, Old Owl tried to speak and could not, his open mouth working, as quivering as a birdling's.

Fear and pity mingled in Frank. He acted quickly. Striding, he took Old Owl's skin water-pouch from the saddle and trickled water into the gaping mouth.

"The village," Frank said, intentionally harsh. "Is it on down the stream? You've got to tell me, Old Owl!"

He saw the old man's struggle and struggled with him, and saw, at the last, his desire to communicate. Seeing the pulsing mouth stir, Frank leaned down to listen. He heard merely a throaty gasping, the struggling, then nothing; and when Frank straightened and looked down, Old Owl was fading, appearing to grow smaller against the sandy earth. He was dying like something thin and wasted, used up, long weary, like something very old returning, and longing for it, to the Indian's Grandmother Earth.

He was dead when Frank got up heavily, touched in a way he hadn't expected; for he'd known all morning that Old Owl was going to die before they could reach the village. He walked to the horses and scanned the unfamiliar surroundings. Where was the village? On down the stream? He fumbled the puzzle in his mind, and decided to follow the water course. First —

He was turning in reluctance to the duty ahead of him, when horse scuffle broke as a distant tapping. He whirled toward the sound, looking back trail through scattering timber.

He saw a single rider coming, making no pretense of cover. The rider waved, heel-kicking his mount, and Frank recognized the stocky figure in white man's ill-fitting clothing. There was no mistaking the broad, gleaming face.

Jim Dan was grinning, proud of himself as he rode up.

"So you sneaked away?" Frank said. "Well, I'm damned glad to see you."

Jim Dan's grin dropped. "Old Owl?"

"Dead. Just a minute ago. Other side the horses, under the trees. Come on. We'll bury him in the rocks."

It was Jim Dan who chose the place, a rocky crevice on a hillside across the stream. Together they lugged Old Owl into it and sat him upright in order that he might properly face the climbing sun of a morning, and began covering his grave with rocks. It was hot, slow work under a blazing sun. They ran out of suitable rocks nearby and found some farther around the hill and carried them over, stacking them thickly against prowling varmints.

At almost the same moment, without a word between them, both men quit. A bothersome quiet had moved in.

Frank had no notice beyond a queer feeling that they weren't alone. But by then there wasn't time to act. Already, close, ringing them, he saw coppery shapes rising from the hillside. His carbine and Jim Dan's were steps away, set against the hill during the grave filling. Jim Dan stood like a post.

Frank breathed, short, quick. Behind him there was the click of a cocked hammer. He was sweating, but his back felt cold. He was thinking dismally of their horses, across the branch in the timber, as he turned carefully and gave the peace sign.

His glance bumped into the rifle-holder, a stern, pot-bellied, bandy-legged Comanche of middle age, horribly scarred along one jaw. He appeared more curious than angered, his stare shifting alternately from the two men to the grave. It was the grave, Frank realized, the question of it, that had momentarily stayed trigger fingers.

"Friends," Frank greeted in Comanche, again raising his palm in the sign. "We are burying our friend, Old Owl, chief of the Pena-te-kas."

He'd said it, the only words he knew that might stop them. And now he waited out the terrible moment, watching the ring of faces. Faces like eagles. Qua-ha-das.

Hearing Comanche talk brought a grunt of surprise from Scar Jaw, at whose nod a dozen young Qua-ha-das, armed with a few old rifles, bows and arrows, clubs and lances, bunched in menacingly, snatching for sidearms, knives and carbines.

Jim Dan growled his protest. Frank said tightly, between his teeth, "Let 'em go."

"Friends?" Scar Jaw snorted. He had a crafty look. "Maybe you killed Old Owl?"

"Would we kill him," Frank said, "and bury him like a Comanche? Not take his hair?"

Still distrustful, Scar Jaw crossed to the unfinished burial and looked in. He looked for a long time, up and down, across and back. He was glowering when he turned as if he must impress the young men. He wore no coup feathers and was, Frank decided then, an Indian of minor importance; a good deal of paw and beller to him, and just ambitious enough to be dangerous. A turkey-cock strut got into Scar Jaw's puffed-out walk as he stepped closer to Frank.

"Why you come to my country?" he demanded, almost shouting. "Lying white man. Delaware dog!"

Frank said, "To see Black Star, your chief Old Owl was going to make big smoke talk for us, but he got sick and died."

"Smoke talk?" Scar Jaw was suspicious. "You are scouts bringing soldiers!"

Frank repeated the peace sign. "No soldiers. You can go back over our trail and see there are no pony soldier tracks."

"Who are you? What do you want?" Scar Jaw's hands were nervous on his rifle, which he kept pointing at Jim Dan and then Frank.

"You're a famous warrior," Frank said. "I can see that. But only Black Star can hear our talk."

Two Qua-ha-das started wrangling loudly over Jim Dan's pistol. Another Indian joined the dispute, jerking at the weapon.

"No doubt these foolish young men claim to be warriors," Frank complained to Scar Jaw. "Yet they act like boys not old enough to watch a pony herd. Wasting much time. Our time. Make them behave like warriors. Then take us to Black Star's camp."

Scar Jaw, flattered, spoke sharply and was ignored. Grunting, striding, angry, he tore the revolver free with an appropriative air, jammed it inside his waistband, against his enormous belly, and imperiously commanded by gesture for his prisoners to go downhill. "We won't kill you here," he jeered. "By the grave of a brother."

Side by side, Jim Dan and Frank waded into the shallow creek while the Indians shouted and taunted them. Now more Indians, all mounted, left the timber and rode yelling into the water, churning it, spraying it, making straight for the prisoners to goad them.

One rider, a boy, deliberately bumped his pony against Frank, knocking him off balance. Frank felt a ripping anger. This was more uncertain than the first discovery on the hill, the beginning of a provoking game. If he struck back, he'd be killed instantly. So would Jim Dan.

Frank regained his feet and went on. He was ridden down again; the yelling got louder. He got up and climbed the low bank. Looking behind, he saw several young men shoving Jim Dan. The Delaware showed no anger, no expression whatever, as he got up each time and edged toward the bank.

Now the Indians pushed their prisoners into the timber. There, under the trees,

Frank saw the meat-laden pack animals and understood how it had happened. Scar Jaw and his bunch, returning from a buffalo hunt, had found the three horses. After that it was fairly simple to capture two men piling rock with their backs turned.

The yelling rose to a frenzy. Qua-ha-das rode around the prisoners, whooping and pointing their weapons. Frank felt his mind pulling tighter. He had to fight off the impulse to cringe and duck. Jim Dan's face was steeled; he was ready to die.

"We're going to kill you now!" Scar Jaw howled, waving his rifle.

There came a quick crying of approval.

Frank was clawing for a way out. He gambled without thinking. He made himself as scornful as any Qua-ha-da. "Do you know who I am?"

"Lying white man!" screeched Scar Jaw and got a chorus of clamoring whoops. Scar Jaw howled the words again, liking the sound. Never had he received a high-ranking warrior's attention. Today, for the first time in his uneventful life, he was looked to and admired. Not a mere hunter.

"You — a Qua-ha-da," Frank cried, cold all over, "and you don't know what the Qua-ha-das call me!"

Scar Jaw blinked. This white man was

spoiling the occasion.

"Your people call me Bloody Knife," Frank said, shouting to be heard. He heard a muttering of interest, and caught Jim Dan's look of warning. "Your people will honor you when you bring Bloody Knife in as captive."

Inch by inch, the Qua-ha-da lowered his rifle, doubt and hunger for glory etched like acid in the ugly face. "I think you lie. How do I know you are Bloody Knife?"

"Take me to Black Star. He knows. He's fought me."

Scar Jaw was beginning to believe. He waved the young men back. "I have heard of Bloody Knife," he conceded. "It would be a great honor to take Bloody Knife's hair."

"No Qua-ha-da has ever whipped Bloody Knife in a fight or captured him," Frank called out, so all might hear. "You and your young hunters are the first to take him. You are great warriors to make Bloody Knife prisoner without a fight. That's a greater honor."

Scar Jaw puffed. His burning eyes said he was already visioning the triumphant return to camp. He cried suddenly, "My friends, give them back their horses!" and the young men, impressed and excited, moved to obey. They led out the horses.

As Frank mounted, Scar Jaw leaped his pony hard by. His voice was ominous.

"When you meet Black Star, your heart will be sorry."

CHAPTER 13

In less than an hour's ride, Frank heard the distant barking of dogs. And when Scar Jaw checked his hunters on a ridge crest, Frank saw the camp spread out below, closer than he had any notion it might be. A great camp, larger than Frank had ever seen, lodge after lodge set without particular order in open timber on both sides of the shallow creek which Old Owl had chosen to follow. Smoke-browned lodges as far as the eye could strain, bending as the stream bent, spiking the big sky.

Scar Jaw ordered a boy ahead with the news, and quickly, ever guarding his newly found position of prominence, he placed his captives in the center and galloped his party hard for the village, having left a few boys behind to bring in the pack animals.

A horde of lanky, clamoring, spiteful curs rushed out to meet them. Several mounted Indians could be seen. There was movement around the tipis, though no perceptible excitement. A man of no war reputation like Scar Jaw had to prove his story before his doubting people would believe him. Some of the puffed-up expectancy seemed to leave Scar Jaw when he saw the lack of welcome. Nevertheless, he maintained a stiff trot, even inside the village, and he called, persistently, to attract attention.

"We've captured Bloody Knife! Hear me! We've captured Bloody Knife!"

A coldness ran up and down Frank's backbone as they rode farther into camp. He was sorry for Jim Dan, dragged into this because of friendship. More people stirred, women and children watching with the men. Frank looked for her in that glitter of wide-boned faces. He looked, though knowing he'd not catch sight of her here, in the open.

When well inside the village, Scar Jaw halted at the door of a tipi much larger than those strung in a circle around it.

A stocky, smooth-muscled Indian in his thirties came outside, naked to his waist. His black, scornful eyes lashed Scar Jaw for bringing strangers here, dismissed him. Scar Jaw launched a rambling story in which he figured prominently, using pompous gestures to stress his part in the capture of Bloody Knife. The other Comanche ignored him and took in the prisoners, and Frank's mind whipped to the buffalo wallow fight and the Qua-ha-da in the buffalo-horn headdress swerving his yellow mustang. He was looking at Black Star, the principal Qua-ha-da chief, a conspicuous black star tattooed on his thick chest around an old battle scar. Jim Dan had said that Star alone had stolen and sold thousands of Texas cattle to the New Mexicans; that loot and captives interested him more than warpath glory, though he had many honors.

Uninvited, Frank dismounted and walked within a pace of the Qua-ha-da. Up close, Black Star looked older. His lips were thin, his keen, copper-bright face made hawkish by an aquiline nose. He fancied earrings of long Mexican shells. A band of copper wire protected his left wrist from bow-string slaps. He looked older, but there was a litheness, a quickness, a physical power in him that Frank sensed. A first-coup eagle feather, straight up on the back of his head, showed where he stood as a fighter.

Black Star stared. His sign was abrupt. "You are fools. What do you want?"

"My friend and I carry big talk," Frank replied with his hands. "Chiefs talk. Not for the whole village to hear."

Black eyes raked Frank up and down, and slid to Jim Dan, still mounted, and returned. In that flashing appraisal, there seethed a gleaming feeling that drove deeper than a Comanche's mere hatred for all white men. He seemed to hesitate. Next, curtly, he was motioning Frank and Jim Dan to follow him inside his lodge. Jim Dan came down from the saddle.

Frank blinked in the smoky gloom of a rich lodge, its war trophies revealed in the half-light let under the rolled-up edges of tanned buffalo skins. Star grunted a command and two squaws, heads down, slipped toward the door. Frank knotted. He kept his head straight, while his eyes flicked over them as they went by him.

One glance told. Dark, high-cheeked faces and cropped hair, black, coarse.

Black Star sat at the rear of the lodge, cross-legged, facing the entrance. To indicate his contempt for the intruders, he pointed to the buffalo robes on his right, instead of the left-side place of honor for guests.

"Talk," he instructed in sign, scowling.

Frank's hands moved. "First, we want our weapons and horses watched. Returned when we leave."

"You want too much, white man. Talk."

"We didn't come here to fight," Frank said, in Comanche. "The pony soldiers' chief from the big fort by the mountains is camped on the Fat Grass. He comes in peace. Only fifty men with him. He waits there. He asks you to meet him and bring fifty warriors."

"All white men are liars," Black Star retorted, his fluid motions insulting. He was sticking to signs, Frank realized, refusing to talk Comanche, even though the white man spoke his language.

"The soldiers' chief is ready to smoke and talk," Frank went on, by sign this time. "With you. Black Star. Greatest Qua-ha-da chief. Greatest stealer of Tehanna horses, mules, cattle. Greatest Qua-ha-da fighter. Greatest chief on all the plains," Frank finished, his hand sweeping, taking in all directions.

Black Star sat like sullen stone. "What does he want?"

"Captives. He will pay for them."

"What captives?"

"Standing Bull, the young Pena-te-ka warrior, stole a young white woman, a yellow-haired woman. He left Old Owl's camp to sell her to you as a wife or slave. Before that, not long ago, the Qua-ha-das stole the yellow-haired woman's little sister in Texas. So the pony soldiers' chief will pay ransom money for both captives. Old Owl was taking that word to you when he died. We rode with him."

Black Star's sweeping hand hurled amusement, arrogance. "Are there captives in my lodge? Do you see a yellow-haired woman? A child?"

"A great chief like Black Star might keep his captives in another lodge," Frank said, in slow, distinct air pictures. "The soldiers' chief will pay green money when you give him the captives — heap green money," he explained, curving his hands. "It will buy heap blankets, heap guns. Heap white man's goods. Better than the trinkets the New Mexican traders buy cheap and sell high to Qua-ha-das."

Resentment fired the black stare. "Qua-ha-das own many horses, many cattle. They are not poor like the Pena-te-kas, who wait on the reservation for the white man to feed them bones and horns, or rotten hog meat. Qua-ha-das are not going down hill like the Pena-te-kas because they are fighters. Not women afraid to die."

What Black Star said was true, Frank signed. Qua-ha-das were mighty people. For that reason, as a matter of honor, the soldiers' chief had brought much money. All of it would be Black Star's when he freed the captives on the Fat Grass.

272

There was no response. Frank felt himself tighten . . . Maybe, he said, shrugging, resuming, Black Star was rich enough. He had no need for white man's money. Money wasn't important to a great chief possessing all the rifles he needed. Rifles that shot many times without reloading, that could kill a man almost out of sight.

Frank silenced his hands, his manner indifferent.

Black Star's head raised a trifle. He was scowling again, and there was, for the first time, a ripple of interest in the swart, constant vigilance. "Never before has a white man been brave enough to come to my village looking for captives. It is strange. A fool would not take the risk for another white man if the fool expected to live long. You claim a yellow-haired woman is here. Maybe you want her for a wife."

Frank's head shake denied it. He became indifferent again. He had no use for a wife, he indicated, pushing away. Least of all, he hungered for a Tehanna woman. Most of them, he understood, were light-skinned and therefore ugly. Poor workers. Once he'd had a wife, a good Ute woman in the mountains, now dead. No, he was just bringing Old Owl's ransom talk. Old Owl was his brother. Weren't they burying Old

Owl in the custom of his people when the Qua-ha-das captured them? Hadn't he told the Qua-ha-das to bring them to Black Star?

Star considered without the barest trace of reaction. It was as if he poked coldly at each meaning. Pressure mounted until Frank wondered if the Comanche intended to speak at all.

"Old Owl," Star said, finally, "was crazy to believe a white man. You are crazy to come here, Bloody Knife." He'd shown no recognition until now. He continued bitterly, "I have not forgotten. Five winters ago you killed a young Qua-ha-da war chief. Red Robe. My brother. My own blood brother!"

Absolute bitter hate, the savage, banked-up hate of a Comanche, surged in Black Star.

Something jogged Frank, late but there: Scar Jaw's relishing remark as they started for the village. Scar Jaw knew! Frank filled his lungs. He watched Black Star, fearful that his expression might hint of the churning in his belly, of the hammering rumbling high in his chest.

"Your brother killed two of my men," Frank said. "He tried to kill me. He was very brave. One of us had to die."

Black Star stood now and made the sign

for "done-finished," and Frank, followed by Jim Dan, filed outside to find the hunters gone.

"Remember," Frank said firmly, "we want our horses and rifles back." Chances were they'd never see their property again. But if there was one thing an Indian respected, even in a white man, it was control of fear. Likewise, what an Indian despised most in a man, any man, Frank knew, was the revelation of fear. You had to talk hard, whether you felt hard inside or not.

"You will stay over there until I decide when to kill you," Black Star ordered, his hands swift, severe, as he indicated a place in the timber. "My people will be watching. Don't run. If you try to escape, you will die that much quicker."

Frank faced him, equally unbending. "If we don't show up on the Fat Grass two sleeps from now, the pony soldiers' chief will take the money back to the fort. Then you can't buy rifles. I know you need rifles," he kept on. "When the Qua-ha-das captured us they didn't have many. Just a few old ones a white man wouldn't use."

Black Star's mouth thinned. He had nothing more to say.

They were out of earshot when Frank spoke under his breath. "They're alive, Jim

Dan! Star wouldn't come right out and say, but I'd bet on it. One thing's certain — he's money hungry. Needs money for rifles, and he knows he can't get it 'til he trades his prisoners."

The Delaware wasn't so certain. "Black Star rich Ingen. Plenty horses. Steal plenty Tehanna cows, mules."

"This ransom money's easier than stealing. Heap less risky than fightin' rangers."

Jim Dan looked resigned. "Black Star him gonna kill you. Gonna kill me," he said, a forefinger tapping his heart.

They settled down to an intolerable waiting. Frank scanned the countless lodges, dull gray against the black-holed trees. A hot wind rolled and afternoon heat fanned in, crowding, massed in the woods, trapped there, intensifying. Ten rods away, through the center of the village, trickled the little creek, fringed by willows. Frank could see squaws and children filling skin water bags and gathering wood. Apart from their lazy movements, their chattering, the camp was listless, in the grip of a sultry oppression.

He turned his eyes on Star's lodge again and, presently, saw the two squaws return. Why hadn't Henrietta been inside? Did Star have her in another lodge, hidden? But there wasn't enough advance warning for Star to hide her. Besides, why should Star conceal her from a white man he'd soon kill? In a way, Frank was almost afraid to find out about her, fearing the worst, and the confidence he'd felt after leaving Star wasn't big any more.

Qua-ha-das had their own special manner of indicating scorn for an enemy, and the most withering was reserved for the despised white man — to ignore him as though he fought no more bravely than a woman. Hence, so far as the Qua-ha-das seemed concerned, the two men might not have existed. Yet when Frank walked to the creek for a drink, he saw that he was being watched. Across the stream a single buck stood watching, staring silently until Frank turned back.

That was an hour ago. The chattering along the creek and in the woods had quit. The village seemed to be sleeping, waiting for afternoon heat to pass.

Frank first noticed a skipping ball of light in the branches of the tree opposite him. It flickered briefly and vanished, snapped off. He was curious, but pretended no interest.

It wavered back, fluttering, dancing, jerking to the same place. He lost it again, only to feel quick heat on his cheek and glare in his left eye corner, gone just as he became conscious of it. Still giving no sign, he spoke to Jim Dan, who sat facing the creek.

"You saw it. Where'd it come from, across the creek?"

"No. 'Long crick. In them willow."

"Uh-huh. Let's see if he keeps it up."

A minute passed and nothing happened. The shadow of a grin cracked Jim Dan's mouth. "You say him? Mebbe Ingen girl like strong white man. Say come on."

"Like hell. You mean come pick up wood, don't you?"

Once more it appeared, a continuous, vibratory light on Frank's cheek, hesitant and likewise insistent. No distinct flashes — yet urgent, quivering. As suddenly as it came, the light failed. Frank waited; it did not return.

Jim Dan had quit grinning. Frank said, "I'm going down there."

"Wait."

He waited, maybe five minutes. The signal, if it was a signal, wasn't repeated, and then he got up and made unhurriedly for the creek. Across it, an Indian was rising, the same Indian who'd watched him the first time, now moving, now stock still and staring curiously. Frank, going on, faced straight ahead, though all the while he was working his eyes to the sides, on the green willows, on the places where sunlight penetrated the timbered openings.

He saw nothing, left or right, and by the time he entered the willows and kneed down to drink on the sandy bank, he'd dismissed the mirror flashes. An Indian kid would be up to such a stunt, flashing his teasing hand-mirror to annoy a hated white man. Frank raised up and scrubbed his sleeve across his dripping mouth. His watcher was cross-legged, in shade, his interest hard to determine at this moment.

"Don't look around, white man. Don't look!"

He knew better than to look around; he kept facing the Indian, for a second doubting his own ears.

"Listen to me, mister. Do something while I talk."

The voice, low, like a hiss, sounded no more than a rod to his left among the willows. It was a young voice, hesitant and scared sounding. A white girl's voice that was somehow a trifle Indian in tone — the words faintly awkward and stiff at the outset — a child's voice, which filled him with surprise, for he'd hoped for a woman's voice if someone called him. Displaying no hurry, he peeled off his shirt and got on one knee and began scrubbing himself.

"Listen, mister. There's a white woman here. You got to help her run away!"

"A white woman?" he said, rubbing his nose to hide his lips, and on guard, both here and across the creek where the Indian watched. "What white woman?"

No answer came and the ruffling suspicion wouldn't leave him. Comanches were sly. Sometimes it didn't take white captives long, when young, to become Comanches in thinking and loyalty. He got up casually, half turning, toweling himself with his shirt.

"What white woman?" he said again.

"You don't know her. What you care long as she's white?" The pinched voice was growing stronger, more impatient, insistent. In it he sensed some of his own distrust. "You just help her get away. She's with Black Star's band."

"I can't see you," Frank hung back. "How can I trust you? Maybe you're Comanche?"

He heard the rustling of a crawling body. Feeling ripped through him as, from the edge of his eyes, he spied a blurred face low in the willows, a small, flattened figure, and pale hair like wheat straw. The impelling thought deepened for him to stride over to her; he throttled it.

"Can you see me now?"

"I see. Don't come any closer."

"Do you believe me?" the small voice asked. "I'm white. Look at my hair."

There was no longer any doubt and he said, "I believe you. Keep an eye on that Indian behind me."

"He's still squatted down."

"Good. Talk fast."

"I will. They'll come lookin' if I don't hurry." In that moment, in the young voice, he grasped the loneliness of a very small girl. "I told you enough. You just help her if you can. Pena-te-kas brought her in few days ago."

With a smashing excitement, he said, "I know Henrietta. I know you — Emily."

He heard a gasp. "You know us? Our names?"

"All about you. Now listen to me, Emily. I'm here to help you both, but I don't know what I can do yet. What lodge is she in?"

"Close to Black Star's main lodge. In the slave lodge, where I stay."

"Didn't Star buy her?"

"Yes. Bought me, too. But the white man still wants her bad. Him and Star been arguin' over her. She's better off with Star than him."

Frank was pulling on his damp shirt. "You mean the one-eyed white man?"

"That's him — the Red One. He's mean." Her voice, though still cautious, sharpened suddenly. "That Indian . . . he's comin' this way! You better go!"

He was thinking of her when, slow-paced, in no outward hurry, he turned away. The Comanche had halted at the stream's edge, as suspicious as a camp dog. He watched, keeping step as Frank walked along the bank, following until Frank left the creek and entered the timber. Some moments later, Frank was relieved to see him turn back.

Horsemen milling outside Black Star's lodge held Frank's attention as he walked on, horsemen where none had been when he went to the creek. He saw Star step outside, then another Indian of burly build. When Star pointed in Jim Dan's direction, the warrior mounted a big piebald and approached with a heel-clapping rush, drawing the other Indians after him. Star followed at a Comanche horseman's awkward walk.

Jim Dan stood; he grunted a warning as Frank came up.

Frank, watching the riders, felt a sudden pressure when he saw the thick-necked man on the piebald wasn't Indian. He was light-skinned, reddened by the sun, a white man trying to be Comanche, and falling short; in filthy breechclout and leggings, his braided red hair greased and shining and wrapped in rich beaver fur; in fringed moccasins ornamented with beads and silver jinglers out of Mexico. Like Black Star, he boasted a first-coup eagle feather.

But what held Frank's gaze longest, and the thing he kept going back to, was the flap of buckskin over one eye socket. This was the white man of the buffalo wallow fight, the Red One.

The white man halted short, gripping a slender hatchet of Mexican design. His one pale eye ranged over Frank, hostile, impersonal; then, by degrees, the white man stiffened to a closer attention. His eye enlarged, the stare beating out, boring, and suddenly Frank saw recognition flare and take root.

"You talk with the forked tongue," the white man growled in Comanche. "You're not after captives. You're a spy for the soldiers. Come here to find our camp."

A loathing, a taste like bile, ran bitter in Frank's throat.

"Talk white man!" he threw back. "Hell, you're white! You can't hide it! Talk up!"

Feeling fouled the reddish features.

There was a brimming wildness in the single eye, a furious, unreasonable cast.

Frank was surprised, and not surprised, when the man snarled in English, insisting, "I'm Comanch'. Great warrior — greater than Black Star."

Frank, seeing Star loom up behind, taunted him. "Tell that to Star in Comanche. He'll cut your heart out!"

"I ain't scared o' no man." The white man slapped his chest. It was an exaggerated gesture, even boastful for an Indian. A surly violence moved this muscular man, whose broken nose and flattened lips told of a bar-room brawler in the past. Here was a white man tolerated by the Qua-ha-das only because he was a ruthless fighter, an enemy of his own people. "Ask any Comanch'," he crowed, punching out the words. "They seen me fight many a'time. They know what I can do. Young men ride with me — foller me when I cry fer war parties. Listen! I ain't white no more — I'm Comanch'! My heart's Comanch'! I kill whites — I kill yellowlegs! I ride anywhere. Nobody stops me. I take captives. Mexico! Texas!" He beat his chest again. "I ain't scared o' no man! No man!"

Frank couldn't take his eyes off the coarse features. Through the discouraging years he'd often wondered just how he'd react when he met the man face to face. Would the ache to kill be as overwhelming as in the beginning? Would he falter when the time came?

Well, he knew now! He hadn't weakened in purpose, he'd just worn down. He yearned to smash and tear and rip.

Frank called, "You lie! You're yellow! You make Qua-ha-das hide you!" He spat in the dirt at the foot of the white man's horse, every word and movement as baiting and insulting as he could make them. "You hide — but I know you. Remember that cabin between Sand Creek and Denver! The Indian girl! The baby! Remember, Yeager! Hellyesyoudo!"

There was no warning.

Yeager reared the piebald and sent him leaping, forefeet slashing, and Frank wrenched to get out of the way. Moving, he saw the blur of black and white patches as the horse pivoted with him. He felt pain crash and shatter to all parts of his body. It was only a glancing blow, but the noise of it was shocking in the quiet. It lifted him up and knocked him spinning in a black world turned upside down. He dropped heavily, sprawled, on hands and knees, dazed, unable to place horse and rider. His mouth streamed blood. A hot iron was burning his right arm and shoulder, burning steadily.

A shout — his name — Jim Dan's shout, it had to be, helped bring him alert. He heard rather than made them out, then. Yeager'd rushed past. He was pivoting his horse, driving at Frank again. Yeager was lifting his hatchet high.

Frank dragged air into hurting lungs and rose as partial clarity returned to his ringing head. Star was smart. He was using one white man to kill another white man, maybe a rival. It explained why Star had waited.

When Yeager pounded in, Frank took two leaping strides as if to run. At the last second, he stopped and sprang back. Yeager swept past, too far out. Frank heard a swishing as the downing hatchet chopped air.

Hooting yells broke out. He saw that a crowd was growing around them.

He got set and planted the ground more solidly under his boots. He felt an inward flinching as he saw Yeager, with slashing fury, cut the piebald about and start galloping back.

Old instincts whispered. The same maneuver wouldn't work twice. Frank spread his feet and bent his knees, his half-lifted hands knotted. There was nothing in his belly, flat-pushed against his backbone.

Yeager whooped.

Frank stood on the balls of his feet. Dodging this way and that, he spread his hands to clutch, to grab. Yeager didn't change his course. He closed in straight, but under tighter rein. He'd run Frank down, his actions said. He'd swerve either way. He'd not be fooled again.

Less than two rods separated them when Frank leaped to his right as before. He saw Yeager hesitate, estimating, saw his readiness for the backward jump. Frank crouched as if to do so. He lunged, and then checked himself.

Daylight showed as Yeager struck emptiness, going wide. But this time he was hauling in much faster, recovering and shortening his turn.

The next moment was brief and violent, close in. Frank couldn't maneuver; he was being crowded too fast, more than a thousand pounds of horseflesh driving at him. Yet it was suddenly unthinkable to him that Yeager should ride him down this way, with ease; that Yeager should win again.

From a low, dodging crouch Frank shot up for the hatchet-swinging arm. He missed . . . and felt the quick lash of pain across his chest as he struck the piebald. He groped blindly, and caught. He had hold of an arm now and he yanked and heard the man cry out. He got a whiff of grease, of musk and sweat, as they fell scrambling, rolling, flailing dust.

Yeager struggled to tear free. He still had the hatchet and Frank drove the point of his shoulder into the hard belly while he fought for the weapon. He took an elbow in the cheek, a fist above the kidneys, a doubled knee that grazed his groin and rammed his lower ribs as he twisted away. He grunted at the pain; the broken face grimaced. The knee came up again, striking the same place. The single eye, pale as glass, watched Frank go down. There was a wildness in the ruined features, a broken noise in the corded throat.

Frank rolled and lurched up, gasping for wind. He feinted a grab for the hatchet and crashed his knee into the bigger man's crotch, then smashed his fist into the agonized face as it fell back. He hacked repeatedly at the weapon arm — numbing, sledging blows, and saw the hatchet break loose.

Before he could scoop it up, Yeager was upon him like a rooting boar, low, fast, mouthing the broken sounds. Frank felt hands on his face — gouging, tearing, missing, but ripping the skin underneath his eyes. He fought free with a yell of pain, so suddenly that he slipped off balance and fell on his haunches.

The wide body groped for him, ready to stomp and maim.

Frank kicked out with both boots. The double blow made a sodden splat; it caught the lunging Yeager full in the face. Blood flew. Yeager screamed. Blinded, he pressed both hands to his eyes, to his battered nose and flowing mouth.

Frank had no mercy. None for this bullying, murdering man. Wrenched up, he threw his body behind a slamming blow to Yeager's belly. It was a fast, vicious punch. Yeager's hands dropped. Frank shifted to the bloody mask of Yeager's face and punished it again and again, a monumental anger soaring in him, a power like God in his fists.

And suddenly it was finished. Yeager took one wobbling step and collapsed. He rolled and lay flat on his back without moving.

It took Frank a dull moment, swaying over him, to understand that Yeager wasn't getting up. And then, seizing the hatchet handle, he was spinning to kill Yeager.

Rough hands grabbed him from behind. He was thrown backward, off his feet, his arms jerked and pinned and the hatchet twisted away. Going down, he glimpsed Yeager's head lifting a little. The stir inflamed Frank. He battled the tangle of brown hands and arms. Once, in his fury, he tore loose, momentarily, but an avalanche of strong bodies bore him down and under to stay. When they had made him helpless, they hauled him up on his feet, still fighting, out of wind, and stood him before Black Star. Frank thought, They'll kill me now.

Star looked from Yeager in disbelief and stabbed Frank with a level glance. "You are strong," he said.

Frank gasped in Comanche, "Let me kill him! He'd kill me!"

"His heart is Qua-ha-da," Star said. "He is our brother."

"Brother?" Frank mocked. His lungs burned; he sucked in wind. "He'll bring you trouble."

"He fights the whites. That is all we ask."

"He's no good —"

Star made a peremptory sign for Frank to be taken away.

"I'll fight you!" Frank cried.

Star's high-boned face was startled.

"Until one of us dies!" Frank called, raising his voice. "You — the greatest Qua-ha-da, I'll fight you for the captives."

Star was tight-lipped, but his eyes were growing bright.

Frank felt the sweat come. "If you kill me, they stay here. If I kill you, I take the captives to the Fat Grass."

"Bloody Knife," the Comanche said, "you are going to die anyway."

Frank spoke louder, scattering a belittling scorn for the crowd's benefit. "Is Black Star afraid to fight? Has he forgotten I killed his own blood brother? Is Black Star a woman?" he demanded and combed his hands downward from his head, the mocking sign for woman.

He saw the words take effect. Star wasn't a coward. He intended to kill Frank in a manner and time of his own choosing. But it was now a question of honor for him to accept Frank's challenge. He couldn't refuse before his tribesmen. His sweeping motion was final.

"We fight!"

"That settles it," Frank said, scorning him. "Now?"

Star sneered. "When the sun rises. So the whole village can watch Bloody Knife die."

"You will die, not me. Is it knives or guns?"

Star's answer was to slap his belt knife.

291

★ ★ ★

The day was dying in banners of orange flames, the sun just about bottomed in its westward flight across the great sky.

Frank watched it moodily. He was more battered than he'd first believed. Every inch of him ached with a singleness of pain. That one smashing collision with the piebald had damaged him most. It took effort to raise his right hand halfway to his head; there the paralyzing agony trapped him, locked him. His whole right side felt swollen. To-morrow, he knew, he'd just be half a man — half when he needed every ounce of strength and likely a cunning few men had.

He sat stiffly, his head canted back as he rested his throbbing body against a cotton-wood trunk, watching the glum acceptance of Jim Dan. Neither had spoken; there wasn't need for words, nothing that words could do. They weren't tied, and neither was there need of that precaution, what with Qua-ha-da guards squatted in a loose circle, posted like so many copper images. Their amused stares said Frank would soon be dead. Likewise, Jim Dan. Maybe, since he was an Indian enemy, sew him up in a green hide and leave it in the hot sun to shrink and crush its victim. There were many ways.

Frank wasn't certain that he could handle

Star; that, if he did, the Qua-ha-das would let him take the sisters. But it was one more step toward a dim survival and he would go through with it. He was, he supposed dully, like a man crossing broken ice, stepping from one floating chunk to another, now nearing the far shore, now being carried back.

He groaned and sat up as an Indian woman set a kettle of light-colored boiled meat between him and Jim Dan, who waited for Frank to sample it first. Frank drew back at the rankish smell; then his mouth juices routed his queasiness. Ignoring his nose, he dipped in a hand and remembered he'd had no food since early morning and recalled how the stomach of a buffalo cow, which this was, and smelling a mile, could fill a man good. Between them they cleaned the kettle.

Faint light was hovering over the dusky land when he noticed them, three squaws walking abreast around Star's main lodge. His attention wandered, then returned as they continued in his direction.

At that instant he knew. The one in the middle, the one with the blanket over her head. The way she walked in graceful stride, tall, making the squaws appear shorter than they were. Yes, they were coming across to him, and he wondered. It meant, for sure,

293

that Star, in showing her, was confident of tomorrow morning. Mighty certain, Frank thought.

An upsurge of feeling crackled within him as they stopped several steps away, but he pretended not to recognize her.

As if on signal, the squaws crouched down, their smoky eyes like polished beads.

Henrietta took two forward steps and stood facing him.

He was afraid to look at her, afraid of what he might find in her face — certain despairing expressions he'd learned to expect after seeing the few women old Isaac had managed to bargain for or ransom free; gaunt, homesick wrecks of broken, lank-bodied women, mostly Tehannas, their hair ragged, their skins leather-brown and sometimes fire scars on their arms, who but for their light-colored eyes and hair would have passed for full-blooded Comanches, who long ago had quit crying but wept unashamedly when Martha Roberts held out her arms to them.

Slowly, very slowly, he looked up at her.

Henrietta Wagner was barefoot, her long legs slim and sun-browned beneath a loose-hanging buckskin dress far too large for her, and so short her knees showed. Despite wind and sun, sand and heat, the ivory coloring of her skin persisted and the blue eyes taking him in weren't what he expected at all, not subdued eyes. His glance held to her face and what he saw next struck him motionless. Her left cheek, up high, was swollen and discolored a reddish purple.

"Talk," she said haltingly, as if unsure. "They can't understand us."

Still giving no indication that he recognized her, he got up with a painful slowness and said, "You've had a bad time. I hate that."

"I'm alive," she replied simply.

He was looking at the bruised cheek again, feeling a quick, flinty anger. "You — you're all right?" he said, hesitating over it, and regretted the instant he asked.

He could see the patience of something deep and buried in her wide-set eyes, and suddenly what he knew was unbearable. He found his hands knotted, his chest pumping fast and hard.

"Yes," she answered, but he knew she lied. "I'm all right."

"You're brave to say that." He felt humbled and deeply shocked for her. "By God," he swore, "whatever happened I'll even it up for you when I fight Black Star —"

"But I didn't say," she broke in and faltered.

"I'll kill him!"

She gave him the oddest, the straightest, the most barren look he'd ever seen. "Star bought me," she said. "But I'm no more than a slave. He has several young wives — jealous wives."

"It wasn't Star."

She put off her answer. She made a gesture with her shoulder; her mouth was trembling and a mixture of fright and revulsion crept alive in her eyes. She clenched and unclenched her hands until the knuckles grew pale.

"Standing Bull, I guess." He avoided her eyes and stared down. When she didn't answer, he brought his gaze back.

"No," she said, and went on in her direct way, in a voice so low-pitched he strained to catch her words. "It was the white man who lives with the Qua-ha-das. He broke into the lodge where they were keeping me. Before Black Star bought me."

It was Frank who looked away, astonished that she could be so calm. "God damn his heart!" he swore, self-accusing. "I tried to kill him! They pulled me off!"

"It's over," she said in the identical, maddening tone of simple patience, and again he marveled at her.

"Henrietta," he said, touched for her. "That's Yeager. The man who wiped out my family. I won't get another chance at him."

"Don't blame yourself. It won't help."

"I want to get you and Emily out of here." And he added gently, firmly. "Tomorrow we'll see. If I kill Star, you go free. You and Emily. We'll see."

Gratitude enlivened her eyes, as luminous as he'd seen them that first day in Major Vier's office. She said, "You're hurt — yet you're going to fight him." She shook her head and he saw her wish to touch him. Her hand came up. She stopped herself, as if reminded of the watchers. She sized him up and down, looking doubtful and concerned for him. "Isn't there some other way? You're not able. If you were, I wouldn't want you to. You're not beholden to me!" When he said nothing, she spoke quickly. "I have money at home. Can't you talk ransom?"

"Star wants my hair. I killed his brother a long time ago."

"But I can pay him more money than he's ever had or will have!"

"Major Vier's waiting on the Fat Grass with a thousand dollars," Frank said. "I told Star. But his honor's at stake. That's how it is. Means more than money."

"Reuel?" Hope ran across her face.

"Reuel? He came after me?"

Frank nodded and told her about Carlos Vasquez, the pursuit and capture of the Pena-te-ka band, and Old Owl's death.

"Carlos," she said softly. "Thank God he's alive."

"Vier took the field soon as he could," Frank explained. "That night. He's pushed hard. I'll give him that much credit."

That pleased her, and he realized maybe he'd been unkind.

"Guess I'm late with the news," he said. "Seein' as how it is. You being his woman and all —"

The squaws rose. One of them grunted an order and yanked Henrietta's arm. She had time to give him an unfinished look before she was hurried off.

As he followed them with his eyes, he pondered Star's reasons for allowing her to come to him, even to be seen by him. Was it the Qua-ha-da's reckoning way, his hating Indian way, of dangling something desperately wanted before a white man's eyes — before that white man died?

CHAPTER 14

He could smell them before he made them out beyond the trees in the early morning grayness, people in motion. As the light came stronger, he saw what looked like the entire village converging upon a clearing west of Black Star's circle of lodges. Voices had a light distinctness, the sound of a holiday. The gathering was still going on when sunrise slashed the eastern sky and his guards ordered him to his feet.

He stripped to his waist with some difficulty, the damnable bruised stiffness clamping him again. He tossed his shirt to Jim Dan, and, to the guards' amusement, took several minutes loosening up, flexing arms and legs, rubbing sore muscles.

Then they'd wait no longer; they commanded him to go. He started walking, Jim Dan at his shoulder.

Past the lodges, spread out on a stretch of gentle slope, he saw a wide circle of waiting Comanches, dark and eager under the burnishing sunlight. When the crowd was slow making a path for him, he strode among them and by the force of elbows and shoulders opened his own way.

A withered old woman, three fingers hacked from one hand showing her family losses on the warpath, spat and screeched insults at him. He passed her by, stepped inside the circle and paced to the center.

At that point he stopped still, assuming a slouched posture. There was a span of time broken only by the mutterings of the crowd. Nothing happened. He sat on the ground, cross-legged, feeling the whip of excitement, of uncertainty.

At length, he saw Black Star approaching, moving slowly through the Qua-ha-das. Even after Star paused opposite Frank, in the crowd, he seemed an eternity removing his blanket, fooling with his leggings, talking with his friends. He was heaping up the pressure by making the detested white man wait.

Frank countered by staring as stony-faced as any insolent Qua-ha-da preparing for a fight. He had no particular feeling; he was afraid and he wasn't afraid. He wanted to get it over.

There was a little run of silence as Black Star made ready and stepped to the crowd's edge, as he entered the circle. His naked torso muscles were smooth and rippling, those of a man made like a statue. Behind the advancing Star stood Yeager. Except for his swollen, puffy features, he seemed as arrogant as ever. He posted himself in the first row of spectators and folded his arms.

Star stepped in close. Each hand gripped a long-bladed knife. He pitched with his right, pitched high, and Frank, legs braced wide, saw light catch the spinning blade.

He stepped back a pace and caught the handle deftly, and felt dismay. It was a butcher knife, one of the cheap Comanchero trade items, prone to snap on bone.

"Bloody Knife," Star cried bitterly, with a remembering relish, "you are going to die!"

And Frank cried back, "What of your word? After I kill you, will your warriors try to stop me from taking the captives?"

"You talk brave, Bloody Knife! You are the one going to die! If you kill me, you die!" Frank sensed a craftiness in the despising tone. "Better for the captives if you die. When a Comanche passes, his property goes to relatives and friends, it is our custom. But I have no fear that will happen to me."

Darkly, Frank understood. A chief's word of honor and influence died with him. He had no authority after death. If Frank killed Black Star, the Qua-ha-das would finish him; the captives, as the dead chief's property, might go to anyone. As long as Star lived, the sisters stayed in his lodge, under his protection, and Henrietta couldn't be touched again by Yeager.

If Frank died, none of this changed.

Frank faced Star. He motioned Star in, his manner insulting.

Star's answer was a sudden cutting swipe with his knife — *fight.*

Frank was shouting from high in his throat, moving on instinct. He saw Star take a crouched stance and circle in closer, gripping his knife with the point down.

Frank bent his knees, spread his boots for balance and held his body and head well back, extending his knife out and upward like a sword.

For a while they maneuvered around each other, both wary, Frank sizing up the lithe body shining like greased copper. Star was an old hand at this game; he revealed himself in his practiced, spring-legged circling.

All at once, the circle tightened. Star sprang in, slashing, but Frank dodged away, narrowly, in time. Spinning, the Qua-ha-da came in again, and again Frank avoided him. As yet, Frank hadn't made a cut at Star.

A scornful hooting broke out — fight! — white man!

Star grew bolder, as if suspecting Frank stalled or his heart trembled. Qua-ha-das called encouragement as Star attacked, rushing, feinting, rushing. Frank stood still; in the following moment, he made a low, sweeping thrust at Star's naked belly. He saw Star draw in. The stroke barely missed.

After that, Star displayed more caution. The cat-eyed circling commenced again. A spark of elation welled up in Frank that he'd lasted this long. He could, he'd learned by now, match Star's feinting swiftness. But Star's strength, once they locked grips, as they would, finally, was another matter.

Wild to finish it, Star pressed faster. He narrowed the circle. By sheer speed, he clamped on Frank's knife wrist — at the same moment striking downward.

Driving in and up, Frank caught the striking wrist. Blood pounding, straining, he stayed the blow. But he couldn't force the arm upward; he could not break the Qua-ha-da's unbelievable strength. Neither could he free his own weapon hand.

In another moment, Frank was alarmed to feel the thick wrist, greasy with sweat, sliding from his grasp. He tried to break his right arm free and could not. He gave a giant heave. It was futile. Star's strength was astonishing. Twisting violently, Frank heaved again . . . and felt the Qua-ha-da's grip give, tear, the fingers raking. But Star's other hand was wrenching free, swinging the knife, and instantly Frank felt a ripping along his left forearm.

He dodged clear, seized by a hot and murderous will to kill, vaguely aware they had fought to the crowd's edge. He wheeled to drive in, wheeled recklessly, and stumbled over a foot. As he went down, sprawling, he spied Yeager's face.

Star came in like a pouncing cat, knife ready. He struck out, a looping slash for Frank's chest. But Frank rolled, kept rolling, and spun to his feet. Star held up, breathing short, quick gulps. He made a half turn, muttering, and the encroaching crowd gave ground.

They set off circling again, the tempo slowed down. Frank's arm dripped steadily, but he had use of it. He played position mechanically, in and out, feinting, back-stepping, thrusting and dodging, slipping away . . . He had no idea of time and gradually objects took on a film of red haze. Star's eyes were like pits of black glass ever in front of him. He was just distantly mindful of the constant chorus of hoots. It dragged across him that he was tiring; he guessed he'd lost more blood than he realized. There wasn't much time left him. Whatever he did, there was no real way out, for him or for them.

He came to a flat-footed stop, too weary to circle. He hadn't that much strength to waste. He saw determination in the dark stare as Star darted in like a big tireless cat on swift feet. Frank shifted to meet him. For once, Star was too anxious. For a breath he was off balance, his chest unprotected.

Frank, to his surprise, let the chance pass. Too late, he saw the Qua-ha-da cover up and leap aside, a frowning bewilderment and then triumph in the smoky eyes. The crying of the crowd was a rising wind now in Frank's ears.

"Woman!" Star taunted. "Woman!"

At his slurring call, the circled watchers took it up. In a single voice, the Qua-ha-das took up the name and shouted it, over and over.

Frank stood. He motioned Star in with an empty-bodied wave.

Star paused, looking amused. His hesitation, however, was brief. He danced from side to side, closing the gap between them. When he swept in, it was with all the violence and intent to finish and kill now, now.

An instinct had hold of Frank. An instinct without thought telling him wait, wait, crouched, until the final pinch of time in which he could still act.

Star's knife hand swept up and Frank dived, dropping his own knife and going for Star's arm. His outflung hands clawed hard flesh; they dug and caught and hung on. He smashed into Star and struck the ground with Star's knife arm between his hands. He rolled up and crashed it, struggling, across his uplifting knee as he would snap a stick.

Star cried sharply. The knife fell away.

Frank scooped it up. Still lunging, he drove his knees into Star's belly. Star grunted and his face twisted, went blanched, and Frank battered his knees into Star again, brutally. Star's eyes were open, but he couldn't rise.

It was such an unexpected turn, Star down, his finely muscled body writhing, when moments ago he'd been primed to slash and kill, that Frank, bringing the knife up, was dimly surprised to find himself checking it.

It wasn't until he heaved to his feet that he understood Star was waiting to die.

In sudden motion, quite suddenly, Frank snapped the long blade across his knee. He came upright then — spraddle-footed, knees buckled, head slung down on his chest as he fought wind into his tortured lungs. "Look . . . Bloody Knife breaks the knife."

Star showed complete astonishment through a glaze of pain. "You won," he groaned. "Kill me."

"No more war between us." Frank was hacking to breathe. His legs and arms were shaking.

"Kill me . . . as I'd kill you." Star's flinty black eyes neither gave nor asked. He was ready to die; he would not whimper. "I will not beg. Kill me!"

"My heart is good." Frank had to pause for wind. "Here — here." He touched his chest.

Star groaned and stirred a little.

"Now I ask you for something." Frank took a deep drag of air. "Take — the sisters to the Fat Grass."

A deeper scowl worked into Star's suffering gaze. He propped himself up on one elbow.

"Together," Frank said. "We'll go together." Watching the hawkish features for some sign, one way or the other, he couldn't decide what might happen next.

He watched, he waited, as Star, heavily, with pain, got to his knees and rested his weight upon his good arm, his face distorted. Star was impassive again when he straightened to his feet.

"You did not kill me," he said, a bewildered wonder unsolved in his voice. "You are a fool. All white men are fools."

Frank listened, not moving a muscle, not knowing what to expect, unless it was all bad.

"But you are not a coward," Star declared. "You are a brave fool, and Qua-ha-das honor the brave." His gaze cut straight at Frank. "The knife is broken. Let it stay broken between us."

CHAPTER 15

It was still early morning when the Qua-ha-da party gathered and filed through the watching village, some forty-odd armed warriors, mostly older men. Not a single one painted, not a single pony tail tied up for war — which Frank took note as positive signs of Black Star's intentions. The sisters rode under strict vigilance in the cavalcade's center; they would until the exchange was made.

Frank, like Jim Dan, rode his own mount and carried his own weapons, all returned without explanation. He looked behind as he left the village, feeling harsh in his throat, reproving himself for leaving a dirty chore unfinished; he'd not get another chance hereafter. Yeager was passing out of his life for good. Why, he thought, did Yeager's kind have to live? Yeager had made himself scarce after Frank's fight with Star, and Frank was tempted to ask Star to fetch him forth. After hard reflection, he'd decided against such a request. Star, he calculated, wouldn't interfere in a personal feud; neither did Star have the authority.

309

Yeager was a headman among the Qua-ha-das, adopted by them as a brother, and therefore protected by them, accepted because he fought the whites. He had influence as long as his war parties were successful.

No, Yeager had to be put aside. At this moment, Frank considered grimly, revenge wasn't the important thing. Common sense ruled, instead, above all while Star's mood held, to hurry the sisters to the Fat Grass, in safe hands. Frank's ache to kill Yeager would have to wait, probably for all time, for there'd be no coming back.

Physical letdown set in as he rode along, dulling his sense of elation. He was a little woozy from loss of blood and the battering of two days. He felt very tired and the sun was soon hot. Vier, he thought. By God, he'd better be there, waiting. He'd better be ready. Not roaming around, playing it big. Once we go in, he'd better play it safe and quiet. No fuss.

Frank glanced at the sisters, and it occurred to him that he hadn't yet spoken to them. With Star mounting his captives last, there'd been no opportunity. They were still Star's property. You respected that possession, you were expected to.

Nevertheless, someone had told them the

news. Or they'd just guessed. They knew where they were going. It glowed in their faces with a singleness of grateful thanks; it increased their blonde resemblance to each other, he thought, as if the same soft light touched each sister at once. They held whispered conferences during the first brief tie-up at a stream crossing; they clung to each other or held hands. Always, they stayed close. Before Frank could ride back to them, the party was in motion. He turned his head and rode on, thinking of Major Vier.

The miles dropped behind and when the Qua-ha-das halted near the place where Old Owl had died, Frank, seeing his chance, reined across as the sisters watered their ponies.

"We'll make the Fat Grass by early afternoon," he said glancing at the sun. "Black Star's taking us back a shorter way."

Henrietta faced him, so warmly direct that he wasn't prepared. Despite the awful, ill-fitting dress and the drawn weariness that made her eyes seem unusually large, there was something not to be forgotten about her — bare-legged, shoeless, on the small, tough Indian mustang. Her yellow hair, which she had someway managed to keep clean, was blowing in the hot wind, and the glassy sunlight caught the deep blue glints of her eyes. Her mouth was tired, yet broad and full. He couldn't miss the swollen cheekbone, either. Just the sight of it kicked off his violence again, spoiling his hasty, unforgettable picture of her.

"We want to thank you," she said, with feeling. "We wanted to long before now, but you never rode back."

"Star's moving us fast."

"So we're thanking you now," she said. "It seems like a poor way to say it."

"You're going home. That's the thing."

"It's hard to believe after all that's happened," she said, and her wonder was rich and musing. "Yesterday, I was ready to quit." Her voice was musical in a way, he supposed, a woman would feel for her man far off, unleashing a surge of wanting she hadn't dared hope for during the hard-driven days on the trail and in the camp, and even now expressed haltingly. She seemed to estimate something for a long moment; presently a note of doubt dulled her tone. "You say Reuel's waiting?"

"He's there," Frank said positively, and wondered why she'd even question it. "With one company. Waiting for you to come in so he can give Star the ransom money."

312

A flicker of feeling passed over her that he couldn't figure. She was on the verge of speaking, he thought, when the Qua-ha-das stirred and moved back to the trail.

Black Star, riding a yellow mustang, angled away from the creek and into a perverse, heat-struck farness that offered nothing, rising and dropping brokenly under layers of sheeny fire-light that burned the eyeballs, punished the body and squeezed the heart out of stout horseflesh.

By early afternoon, jutting up through the quivering glaze, a butte formed in the distance. Frank recognized it. As they moved closer, the remains of a comb-like, red sandstone ridge became visible against the furnace sky, hulking and low, gathering sullen dead heat. Beyond that eroded mass lay the basin of the Fat Grass, and its one sweetwater spring and deep arroyos slashing half its once level floor of grass.

Star was looking off. He halted. At his grunted command a young Indian went smoking into the remoteness ahead.

"Is the pony soldier chief camped by the spring?" Star asked Frank while they waited for the young Qua-ha-da to return. Although Star hadn't sent out scouts during the day, there was about him, at the present, a freshening vigilance. He would not enter

313

the basin without looking.

"West of the spring," Frank said. "In the open. Out where you can see him."

"Fifty pony soldiers?"

Frank nodded. "Just a few more than you have warriors."

Star's smile was thin. "We are much stronger. One Qua-ha-da's heart is braver than all his enemies."

Before long, the scout returned at a run. Not many pony soldiers, he said. The Qua-ha-das counted about as many. He'd ridden close on the Fat Grass as Black Star had instructed him. Close enough for the soldiers to shoot if they wished to hurt him, he explained proudly. Instead of shooting, they waved at him.

Star looked assured. He rode back and formed his warriors in a single file. Next, in front of the line, he placed Frank and ten of his headmen, then the sisters and Jim Dan. When this was done to his liking, he took his party toward the ridge that masked the basin.

Emily Wagner's small face beamed as Frank glanced back. She was hollow-eyed, worked thin as a splinter; but she was going to be a pretty girl. She had her sister's large eyes, her sister's liveliness. Her hair, bleached almost white by sun, curled softly at the temples where the veins traced blue. She turned her attention to the gap in the ridge where they would pass through. Her gaze and Henrietta's mirrored an equal seeking, a hoping and longing about to be realized. As Frank watched, Emily's expression sobered; suddenly, she was crying without sound.

He jerked away, thinking. One thing spoils this. Emily was spared because she's too young. Henrietta wasn't because she's a woman. And it had to be a white man, at that, a man who don't deserve to live. Yet he's still alive — left to bring the same wrong to another family. Another young woman.

His mind fed on that and he felt a deep discontent. Why did he have to let the thing ride him when they were this close? If he'd killed Yeager, probably the outcome with Star wouldn't have happened and the sisters would be in the camp; at the best, ransomed years later like the broken women old Isaac had freed. Besides, wasn't Vier waiting in the basin? Hadn't Star kept his word? Hadn't both men? Nothing was going to happen.

He put the memory of it from him and concentrated on the barren trail, the heaved-up wilderness everywhere. Star, trotting, entered the gap and if Frank had any doubts they vanished when, looking for Vier's one company of cavalry, he found it at once. He studied the dark, elongated clump. Vier's men were spread out in a double line, dismounted.

Frank ran his glance around and returned to the company, his frown forming. Vier had shifted camp since Frank and Old Owl had left. He was nearer the far side of the basin, on a flat expanse of grass. Where he should be, Frank gave second thought. In the open, in full view where Star can see his strength and intentions. That's what counts today. He moved over there closer to water and better grass. Well, he belly-ached enough about it.

Riding down the crumbling slant, Frank saw a setting of complete calm. The basin seemed locked in an afternoon drowse. Heat devils danced and nodded, throwing distant objects in flickering, wavering images, unreal to the eye. Major Vier's waiting cavalrymen were indolent, blue-black lumps, motionless on the yellow grass. In here the wind, somewhat blunted and shut out, was like a stale breath, sluggish, heavy, and the packed heat hammered a man in lifeless waves.

They dipped in and out of a deep arroyo

316

that ploughed clear to the north rim and broke through. Southward, about midway of the basin's floor, the arroyo fanned out into stringers of gouged washes. To the east, where Vier's camp was posted, the tawny grassland was fairly level.

Star, walking his yellow mustang, turned and motioned and Frank loped up to ride next to him. When short of a hundred yards separated Qua-ha-das and troopers, a small detail of cavalry came out. Frank recognized the stiff, parade-ground carriage of Major Vier, followed by two sets of fours.

Frank scanned them again, feeling disappointment. Ed Niles wasn't among them.

When within speaking distance of the trotting troopers, Star halted and his fluent hands framed a sign — his right palm striking his closed left fist, two, three times, the sign for "smoke." He slipped to the ground.

Major Vier, likewise halting, raised his voice. "Mr. Chesney, I won't stand for any pussy-footing around. Waited long enough. Tell him I'll take the captives now. Money's in my saddlebags. He can have it all. That's what he's interested in."

"Star says smoke on the ground first," Frank replied distinctly, with warning. "Makes the peace solid. It's Comanche

317

way, Major. Only way this will work today. Come on." He dismounted before Vier could protest.

Vier's hesitation was just momentary, but it was there, and, Frank worried, a poor start for a touchy ransom council. As the Major stepped down, his straight-through attention was shifting from Star to Frank, to the sisters and the silent headmen, and back to Star. He straightened, erect and inflexible as always, flung reins to a horseholder and unsnapped the set of saddlebags on the back of the cantle. Stiff-legged, he went forward to meet Black Star.

He could have stepped from his tin bath tub at Fort Hazard just minutes ago. For Frank was seeing the old Vier — brusque, cold, impatient, commanding, the faint yet unmistakable fastidious air clinging to him as he faced the Qua-ha-da chieftain.

Star, with ceremony, offered his hand.

Vier had the look of a conqueror as he clasped it briefly, gingerly, and stepped back, hands struck straight to his sides.

And Frank thought, His Majesty's Cavalry, no less. His Majesty's Horse. Accepting homage from a gut-eatin' Comanche. That's how it is to him, the bastard, and Star sees it.

Afterward, they all squatted on the grass

and a headman brought a lighted red sand-stone pipe to Star, who pointed the stem toward Grandmother Earth, offered smoke to the sky and the four great directions and passed the pipe to Major Vier.

Vier's face bore sweat, and Frank swore silently. Don't dab it. Not in front of Star.

Rather hurriedly, Major Vier made short work of the same ceremonial gestures and returned the pipe to Star, who sat in silence, his usually non-committal dark glance steadily on the pony soldier chief.

"What's he waiting on?" Vier demanded presently, his impatience a goad upon Frank. "There's a thousand dollars in these saddlebags — government money."

Frank spoke to Star, hoping to speed up the exchange, "The pony soldier chief is ready to hand you the ransom money for the prisoners — a thousand heap dollars in American money," and drew the size of a greenback in his left palm.

At the moment, Star was showing more interest in Major Vier than the money. He said with some puzzlement, "I cannot re-member when a white chief came to Qua-ha-da country and brought no more pony soldiers than these."

"The yellow-haired woman is going to be his wife," Frank said. "Many soldiers would

319

make it hard to talk peace."

Star returned a curious look. "Is it because you have no horses to give for a wife, Bloody Knife? Is that why you don't take the yellow-haired Tehanna woman for yourself? I do not understand you white men. You speak one way and the meaning is another. But today it is good that we travel the same peace road like brothers, instead of trying to take each other's hair. I can sit here in the sun and not have to look behind me."

Having spoken, Star rose and signaled, "Come on."

The sisters hesitated and then, uncertainly, rode toward the parley group. Not a Qua-ha-da followed. The only horseman in motion behind them was Jim Dan.

Major Vier motioned the sisters to the rear. Not until they rode past did he hand the greenbacks to Star. A moment after Star took them, Vier turned on his heel. He had gone but a step when Star, yet holding the pipe, called to him.

Vier wheeled on Frank, his compressed lips betraying nervousness. "Now what? He want some horses to boot?"

"He's trying to give you the peace pipe. Take it."

Vier was sweating again, reluctance hard upon him.

"Take it," Frank prodded, though holding his tone level. "By God, you take it, Major. Yes, you damn well better take it."

The Major's black jaws were like damp mud, moist in the light. Nevertheless, he faced Star and when the Comanche held out the pipe, again in unhurried ceremony, Vier accepted. The white man and the Indian stared into each other's eyes. There was this moment and then Vier pivoted and marched stiffly to his horse.

Star's expression was far away as he turned, his glance resting on Frank. "Bloody Knife," he said in sonorous, flowing Comanche, "let the knife stay broken."

Frank nodded, feeling an incompleteness, and watched Star go to his horse.

It's over, Frank thought. Over. Over mighty quick. But hard to believe a man's own eyes. Almost too fast, too easy. For he'd had his own doubts up to the very last, until Vier took the pipe; fearful that Vier, with his damned rudeness, his damned importance, his damned Majesty's Manner, might someway anger Star and the parley would blow sky high.

A looseness came, a sense of gratitude for which he had no exact words. He was watching the sisters and Jim Dan, and Vier and Vier's detail, riding for the dismounted company — trotting now, trotting faster. It was actually over; it was finished and he was thankful.

Something brittle on the hot wind, some crash of sound, bit into his eardrums. A sound that had no place here. Something was crackling inside him as he flung around. He looked, he dropped his jaw and stood rooted.

Cavalry was climbing out of the deep arroyo behind Star's band. Cavalry so close Frank could see Captain Parkhurst and Lieutenant Ed Niles leading the advance, deploying the first double file. Carbine shots rattled. Powdersmoke bloomed in dirty gray puffs.

For a stunned moment, he couldn't move. Then clarity crashed through him. He understood everything — Vier's cooperation, Vier moving camp, Vier's hurry to quit the parley ground, cut the talk short. Vier had brought up the main command to ambush the ransom party, while Star kept his word.

Frank was yelling in warning at Star. His voice fell lost in the din, unneeded. He glimpsed Star's accusing, astonished face as the Qua-ha-das, vaulting, scrambling to ponies, began scattering like quail. In one stride, Frank was at his horse and in the saddle, hanging on, in a slamming run for Vier's camp. He was free for the moment.

It was then he heard it, a new and menacing sound that turned the blood cold, paralyzed the mind. It pierced even the growing gunfire, the clatter of running horses. He swerved to look.

Shrieking Comanches were streaming like phantoms out of the ghostland of eroded washes to the south and southwest, rushing for the snarl of troopers leaving the arroyo. They came in bunches like howling wolves, led by a burly man astride a big piebald war horse.

Yeager! It burst over Frank that Yeager also meant to betray Star. To break the peace.

Frank looked at the arroyo. Parkhurst, quick to sense danger, was swinging in alarm. His tangled command was almost caught.

Frank, running on, saw the opening in front of him suddenly close, racing shapes cutting him off from Vier's company. So it came to him as he turned that Star's warriors were no longer scattering. They had some kind of order now. They were attacking.

An Indian loomed in front of Frank, war club swinging. Frank rolled in the saddle and slammed his horse's shoulder into the lighter pony, and saw the pony, knocked off balance, spill its rider.

Indians were crying and wheeling through the dust and smoke, charging Vier's company as well, charging, firing and wheeling on to circle and come in again. Frank shot point blank at a glittering face; it dropped away, slowly, then abruptly, lost from sight.

The pressure against Vier's position seemed to grow. Frank sensed this as he saw Parkhurst's command still struggling to free itself of the arroyo, and more Indians piling east to join Star's warriors. Over on his right, Frank spied troopers trying to drive a wedge through to Major Vier. He saw this fight developing, and bogging, and he pressed that way, low in the saddle.

He never got there, for again the terrible pressure shifted as more Indians slipped between. He had the sensation of being caught in a whirlwind, unable to break clear. All at once, his turning horse brought him face to face with a Comanche. Frank had that instant to see surprise dilate the man's eyes. The Indian jerked, flinging up his rifle. Frank fired and his bullet tore through the naked chest, and in the quickness of a drawn breath he watched the man topple and die before he struck the dusty ground.

Somewhere, somewhere deep in that smoky confusion ahead, a brass voice was bellowing commands. The voice never weakened; it guided Frank, and drew him on, as steady and dominant as a beating drum, the one unchanging thing around him.

Frank worked on and presently came to the fragments of a company, still mounted, holding fast just this side of the arroyo, forming around a hatless, russet-faced officer on horseback whose shock of white hair trailed loose on the wind.

It was Captain Parkhurst, everywhere at once, standing fast here so the remainder of his command could fight clear to rally on higher ground. Behind Parkhurst, bobbing shapes of horses and troopers kept climbing through a fog of brown dust.

Frank, taking his place in the irregular line, heard Parkhurst's iron shout, "Where's Lieutenant Niles?" There came no answer and Parkhurst bawled again, "Where in hell'd he take Company M?"

Frank saw a trooper rush up to Parkhurst and point in the direction of Vier's camp. Parkhurst shook his head with a savage rejection.

Qua-ha-da lead whipped around them. With a sudden sharp cry, the man on

Frank's right pitched sideways. The Indians were firing and racing in, pressing in with a boldness that came from sure knowledge of victory. They'd caught the hated yellowlegs still snarled in broken ground, and there they determined to smash them. They were sliding around to Frank's left, going on for slashes at Vier's out-numbered skirmish line and circling to strike Parkhurst again.

Dust rolled heavier and suddenly the Qua-ha-das pressed in closer, wheeling past. Frank fired at the wavering, ducking, dipping targets. Gunsmoke made an acrid taste on his tongue. As one knot of dark figures swept past, there was another to take its place in a dead-on run. They kept swarming in smothering rushes, their bullets and arrows striking marks. Now and then a trooper fell and horses ran riderless, and presently the line began caving in under increasing pressure.

Wall-eyed with fright, a cavalry mount bolted straight for the crush of Indian ponies, its ashen-faced rider yanking futilely on the reins. There was the thud of colliding horseflesh, a horse's high scream and then horse and trooper disappeared, engulfed.

An Indian, painted yellow to his waist, darting in swiftly, engaged the trooper nearest Frank, hand-to-hand. Another

Indian veered to join.

Frank's bullet knocked the second Comanche loose from his horse, and he ducked around, too late to help. A shot exploded and the grappling trooper was falling shoulder first, his brown, blurred visage a boy's slim face, tortured with shock and agony. Frank caught the Indian wheeling and blew a hole in his chest. He saw the shape fade and disappear beneath hoofs. But the last thing he saw was the twisting image of another young face, anguished beneath its bold streaking of black and ocher, younger even than that of the boy-faced trooper a split-second past.

On each side of Frank the line was ragged, unfilled. An unhorsed Comanche sprinted forward, taking bobbing aim. Frank saw him jerk and spin like a crazy dancer. But the reeking field kept growing Comanche horsemen, crying fighters riding like demons . . . Frank's carbine was empty; no time to reload. He used his revolver point-blank. Heat banked against him. Dust fumed thicker and became a low-hanging pall and the smell of powdersmoke bit his throat.

"Forward!"

He sensed the change before he saw it take form, a stiffening of the weakling line.

Next he saw it strengthen, some of the gaps filled. Troopers started yelling full voice.

Parkhurst had retrieved his men from the arroyo, rallied and deployed them. Now he had them attacking.

Frank moved with them, forward for the first time. As the line struck the sliding current of the Comanche attack, it hesitated. It showed, feeling, fighting its way, but it did not stop. This was to Captain Parkhurst's style and liking — the open ground and an enemy he could feel at arm's length. So he hammered his line straight-on.

For a while the Indians stuck in front, firing and rushing by, weaving in and out, slipping to the off side of their ponies, yet giving ground. Then there weren't so many as before. Dead ponies dotted the Fat Grass. In another minute, Comanche horsemen were shrinking farther into the background, still sullenly wheeling and firing, but drawing back, nevertheless.

At once, Parkhurst battered his way left, aiming to hook up with Major Vier, and thereby touched off another hot fight.

Through the roiled dust and bright stabbings, Frank could see an isolated company of dismounted troopers. Caught in Parkhurst's enclosing maneuver, the warriors there started pulling out and scattering. Not far beyond, where Vier was, more Comanches were breaking south.

In the last wheeling bunch, Frank thought he saw Star's yellow mustang. There was no sign of Yeager's piebald.

Gradually the firing dropped to a surly scattering. The Comanches were going off and the grimy gunsmoke was lifting. Parkhurst gave chase, but did not follow through the eroded gates of the south ridge. There, wisely, he held up and swung back.

To Frank came the belated realization that it was over, over beyond doubt this time. He took a swinging look around and was instantly appalled. Despite Parkhurst's manful bludgeoning, there was as much defeat as victory here for Major Vier's command, though the Comanches had lost heavily as well. Loose cavalry mounts mingled with Indian ponies. Here and there lay a warrior or trooper on the trampled ground. It was hard to tell where one company's stand had started or ended. Horseholders were collecting mounts; details were bringing in the wounded.

Two M Company men carried Ed Niles across and lowered him gently. Frank came down from the saddle.

"The Lieutenant tried to bust through to

Major Vier," Sergeant Tinsley explained. "We got close."

Ed Niles' eyes were open. He was showing pain in a dull white face; his breathing was uneven.

Frank bent over him. "Where you hit, Ed?"

"Up high — I think."

More troopers passed, leading horses and packing in more wounded. A surgeon hurried up. He unbuttoned Ed's jacket and shirt. Frank dropped his glance, bit his lip. He looked up to see the doctor's slight shake of his head.

Sergeant Tinsley's low, growling curse was the only sound in the hush locking the little group. Frank was too stunned to speak. He watched the surgeon make Ed as comfortable as he could, watched each unavailing motion.

"I hung on to your watch," Frank said in a husky tone. He was pinned here by a terrible conviction that he could not, would not, accept, meanwhile not wanting to leave and yet worrying about the sisters and Jim Dan.

"Keep it," Niles groaned, but managed a faint smile. "Knew you'd make it back. Some sight, Frank, old hoss. Watched you through my glasses . . . riding in with the captives. Wasn't a bit impossible for you, was it?"

"I was lucky. Ed — you're talking way too much. Be still."

Ed shook his head. "Want to talk. You know, we just about reached Major Vier. Anyway, we took some pressure off him. He was partly over-run, looked like. We had to dismount . . . fight on foot." Pain checked him; then his voice picked up. "Scared me for a while. But we didn't turn tail; not even when they piled in on us. Didn't know what I'd do — never in a big scrap before. Just skirmishes. Makes a man feel good inside. Glad I didn't hump up."

"You sure didn't." Frank was intent on the painted face, gray under its whisker stubble.

Ed Niles had an odd, quiet look. He was getting weaker. But he said, "Went on through the black cave — clear through and came out."

"Ed," Frank said and glanced warningly at Sergeant Tinsley. "We got to make you some shade."

The sergeant crouched closer. "Sure, Lieutenant. Let ol' Sarge Tinsley put up a blanket."

"Rather talk." A growing slackness ruled Ed Niles' raw-boned body. His angular face was leaden. Yet a certain gladness gathering in his eyes seemed to give him strength. "Frank, dispatch detail found us before we left the Pena-te-kas." He took an open-mouthed breath, another. "Louise didn't go home. Had the baby . . . a boy. Named after me." He managed a bare, proud smile. Then the inertness caught him up.

Frank shifted so as to shade Ed with his body.

"She sent word. She's waiting . . . Louise . . . th' boy. Hear me?"

"I can hear you, Ed. They're both back at the post, waiting for you. Like you knew they would."

Only Ed's eyes could speak for him now.

"Just like you really figured," Frank said, trying to hold him on. "Like we said. Listen, Ed, we're going to take you home. Understand?"

Frank waited for Ed's voice. Then he knew there wasn't going to be any answer. He watched as slowly, wearily, Ed Niles turned his head aside.

After a time, Sergeant Tinsley coughed and stood up.

"Ed," Frank tried. "Ed —"

It was as if he watched a lone candle of flame, infinitely fragile, jerking, struggling in a gusty wind, as if he had watched it flicker one more time and go out and now he waited for it to catch again. Suddenly pulling forward, he called, "Ed!"

"No use," Tinsley said. "The Lieutenant just can't hear you any more."

Frank didn't know how long he was fixed there before he raised up — empty, all hollowed out inside like an old log. But he was aware of one thing: he'd remember the look of weary happiness on Ed's face — as Ed spoke of his family — he'd remember and carry that with him as long as he lived. Once more he bent his head and the angular features got blurred in his vision. He had a savage, uncontrollable bitterness, then, and it sent him walking across the scarred, hard-fought ground. He bumped into a trooper and trudged on, his head down, moving blindly.

Somebody called nearby. Frank paid no heed. The call came again, bellowed like an order, and Frank heard his name. It jarred him back to his surroundings. He turned and saw Captain Parkhurst, alone and dismounted, the wreckage of the afternoon like scoured tracks across his ruddy face.

"Didn't work, did it?" Frank said with a brutal damning.

"What do you mean?" Parkhurst said quietly.

"Why, Vier's ambush — when he ordered you to ambush Black Star's ransom party."

Parkhurst bristled a little. But bite was lacking in his voice. "You tell me something. Where'd all those other Comanches come from? Black Star knew. He must have known. If he didn't plan it that way, who did?"

"Captain, Star didn't know. I'll swear to that. A white man led those young Comanches. Stirred 'em up."

"White man?"

"Yes, a white man — renegade. You saw him on that big piebald. You couldn't miss him, out in front. Star got doublecrossed twice today. He's Comanche, all right, but I hope he got away. And I think he did. Got away with the ransom money Vier aimed to get back when you took Star prisoner — because Star kept his word."

Frank, finished and turning to go, held up at the curiously compelling tone of Parkhurst, who was saying in a lowered voice, "Come with me a minute. I want to show you something."

They had to walk just a short distance.

First, there was the Comanche's half-naked shape, the red smear on his chest, and his rifle — and then Major Vier a few steps farther, flat on his back.

Cold shock ran over Frank as he stared.

He hardly recognized Major Vier's shattered face. Vier's hand still gripped the revolver pointing at his head. Frank, glancing again where the Indian lay, saw that the rifle pointed away from Vier.

"See what I mean?" Parkhurst said, distressed. "I wish — but the Indian couldn't have done it. Probably fell or crawled here after Vier died. I can't see Vier shooting the Indian, then killing himself." Parkhurst chewed his lower lip, thinking out the story. "Vier had Company A with him for the parley; it was cut off. He saw that M Company was stopped, if he saw it at all. But he certainly knew he was cut off and he was in a position to see how the battle was going. Everything looked lost from here. So . . ." Parkhurst spread his hands.

Frank was still staring hard. In his mind's eye, he could almost picture Major Vier's final moments . . . Vier watching the ruin of his whole career passing in tattered review before him, watching the bitter, tag-end pieces passing him by on the yellow Fat Grass — driven, broken by the crying demons on horseback.

"Cut off — you said," Frank grunted, looking around. "Yes, cut off like Monahan was. But nobody tried to reach Monahan,

335

even when Vier knew —"

Parkhurst was swearing softly, interrupting. "I keep thinking how this will look to the men. Commanding officer — well, any officer for that matter."

Frank opened his mouth and closed it again, thinking of Ed Niles. A sudden thought grew, kept growing. Why not?

There were some things men had to believe in. He knew that now. Why let one man dirty such beliefs for others?

Why not leave that much for the good men who came after?

Time would swallow everything — the old hatreds, the bitter wrongs on both sides, the high hopes that had been raised and lost.

Yes, why not?

And quickly he was stepping to the Indian's body, and nudging with his boot and pointing the Indian's rifle, just right, upon Major Vier. Another moment, still quickly, going over, he drew Vier's stiff arm outward and placed the barrel of the revolver Vier held in a line on the Indian's bloody chest.

Frank looked around as he finished. No one seemed to have noticed. There were too many dead and wounded. What he'd done wasn't perfect, but it would pass battlefield inspection.

Parkhurst's gaze was alive with a stunned

comprehension. "All right," he said swiftly. "Yes — it's all right." He stabbed Frank with a questioning look and said curiously, "What about Monahan? What was it Major Vier knew?"

Frank hesitated, said, "They're both gone — we'll leave it there," and was surprised that the words had come from him.

He moved in a tired trot, circling his glance, hurried by a sense of lateness. Details were combing the littered field from A Company's stand to the arroyo. He looked for a woman's tall figure among the straggling men and loose horses and found no sign of her. He saw where A's flank had folded, where dead horses lay thickest. His steps slowed and he was filled with a swelling sense of loss. He passed a trooper whose still face was upturned to the sun; he stopped and spotted a detail busy toward the rear. He went that way.

He saw nothing different from the other burdened knots of men until a trooper, moving aside, revealed a small figure in buckskin. It was Emily. She was standing by a man on the ground — a man in hand-me-down clothes with a dark, wide-boned face and long black hair. Jim Dan had propped his back against the rump of a dead horse. Frank hurried over.

"What's the matter, Jim?"

Jim Dan's black eyes evaded Frank's. An angry blotch of crimson had spread over the thigh of the Delaware's straightened-out leg.

"We'd better take you in," Frank said and looked around. "Henrietta? Where is she?" The black eyes slid away again. He turned to find Emily's dismal face.

She told him, "The white man — he took her off again," and with the telling she was rubbing her eyes, suddenly in a choking weeping.

"They came in behind us," a trooper said. "Grabbed some horses, too. Fight was about over. Wasn't a big bunch."

"Pena-te-kas," Jim Dan groaned. He gave a puzzled shake of his head, indicating the Pena-te-kas had fled in the direction where the sun rises.

Frank's jaw fell. "East?" Since it was of no importance at the moment, he dismissed it. "Some of Standing Bull's runaways?"

Jim Dan nodded miserably. "Heap Qua-ha-das rubbed out today. White man no more Qua-ha-da chief. Medicine go bad. No good. Him Pena-te-ka now." His defeated expression turned more mournful, apologetic, self-damning. "Jim Dan no bueno fighter. No bueno."

"Never mind." Frank was gentle as he got his arms under Jim Dan's shoulders. He said to the others, "Give me a hand."

They carried Jim Dan across where the overburdened surgeon, in shirt sleeves, was giving first attention to the worst wounded. As soon as he could, Frank searched out the busy Parkhurst, told his story and asked for ten men.

"We can spare a platoon," Parkhurst said.

"Ten's plenty. We can move faster; less fuss. M Company men if I can have them. Ed Niles' old company. Sergeant Tinsley. An extra horse for each man, Captain. We'll switch off."

Parkhurst dropped his shoulders. "I don't envy you, Chesney. Looks pretty hopeless to me."

"I don't know," Frank said. "We're not far behind."

"Well, you have my permission."

Meanwhile, Parkhurst said, he would care for his wounded and bury his dead and start for Fort Hazard tomorrow. Frank's detail would have to catch up.

Frank was cinching up when a figure slipped to his side and spoke. It was Emily — alone — she had approached like a Comanche, quiet as woodsmoke, without a whisper of sound.

She took in his two horses and the troopers making ready. "You'll bring Henrietta back, won't you?" she said, hope big in her eyes.

"Fixing to try." He finished cinching and looked down at her. "Keep an eye on Jim Dan for me."

The blue eyes got bigger. Her small mouth was grave. She gave him a slow, firm nod.

A rod away, he heard Sergeant Tinsley bark the detail to saddles. Frank started to mount, then paused.

Emily was looking up into his face. And of a sudden, with a certain shyness but in which also lay a child's absolute faith, she reached up her thin arms to him and he bent and kissed her cheeks.

She whirled, running, gone as swiftly and silently as she'd materialized, like a Comanche.

CHAPTER 16

The afternoon was pure hell, the tortured land ablaze. Frank moved the detail as fast as he dared for the safety of the horses, already wearied at the start. The eleven rode craftily, like raiding Indians, each man leading an extra horse, traveling in a silence interrupted only by the stumbling of tired hoofs and the swearing of red-eyed troopers whose minds lay on the sweet-water spring left behind on the Fat Grass.

Sometimes in the deceptive distance, mirages flickered between earth and sky, distorting everything, shimmering and wandering from one quicksilver lake to another, lakes that were always beyond them.

Eleven chasing a whirlwind across nothingness, racing the killing sun and hating its punishment and yet aware of its need; for the race would be ended by sundown. Nightfall would cover the tracks; morning too late to catch up. Time and distance were all that mattered now. Past sundown Frank closed his mind.

By now he had formed a picture of the band they followed. He figured fifteen bucks, eighteen at the outside. One bunch of tracks stood out, tracks of shod cavalry mounts taken in the surprise dash on A Company's rear.

Less than an hour of this, of heading into desolation, and Frank called a halt, flagged down by a mounting sense of contradiction. Horse smell and the stale sweat of troopers became an almost tangible stain on the stifling air as he considered the tracks with a great deal of thoughtfulness. He raised his glance, on where the tracks ran. A brokeness met his eyes, an infinity of cruel distance stretching on and on. He blinked and stared hard and long, hand shading his smarting eyes. This time, he said silently, we're after a white man.

"What's wrong?" Tinsley asked. He was a middle-aged man possessed of large, thorny hands and gray eyes that looked white against his rawhide skin.

"We're headed wrong," Frank told him flatly.

Tinsley didn't understand. "There's the tracks. Plain."

"Sure. Smack into bone-dry country. No pony water inside two days' hard travelin'."

Tinsley weighed that, puzzled over it while he worked his tobacco-lumped jaw.

Frank said, "Old Owl circled in from the

north — time he brought Vier to the Fat Grass. Went around this dry stretch."

The sergeant nodded, as if tracing it out in his mind.

"I figure these tracks turn north if we follow 'em long enough," Frank said.

"North?" Tinsley wasn't differing so much as he was seeking to reason it out. "Why not south?"

"Burnt out, same. They got to work back to the breaks," Frank said. "This east business is just a feint to wear us out. Leave us still trackin' when it gets dark. If we are, we're finished. Never catch 'em."

"Water," said Tinsley. "Hell, they got to have water."

"Recollect that spring north of the Fat Grass? In that crooked canyon?"

Sergeant Tinsley sat up straight; his blood-shot eyes blinked. "Cap'n Parkhurst camped us there, comin' in night before last."

Frank nodded, reminded that Major Vier had had Parkhurst close behind all the time. He dashed the thought swiftly, said, "They'll circle in there, I figure. Camp to-night." He worried a look at the sliding sun. "These extra horses, we can start swapping off, Comanche style. Get there first, if we ride hard . . . God pity her if I'm wrong."

Sundown wasn't an hour off when Frank, in advance, reached the watering place. No unshod ponies, he saw, had passed here since Parkhurst's command, following the trail of Major Vier's one company, had stopped on its way to the Fat Grass. He waved in the troopers, long ago beaten into silence, through the narrow cut and into the canyon, forking left and right, split by the tiny trickle that dropped from a high lift of rock and ran like a weaving thread of silver between war-paint walls laced with squatty cedars and boulders.

The horses, crazed for water and now smelling it, tore the reins from the troopers' grasp and piled forward. Frank let his mounts go and afterward got down to drink. For a long time there was just the rapid, sucking murmur of bottom-dry horses and the brittle chinking of curb chains. Pushing up, hurried, he noted his stranger's face in the greasy reflection of the water — gaunt as a wolf's, sunken eyes in black cavern sockets. A red-eyed, stubbled, dangerous man about come to the end of his jerk-line.

He called to Tinsley, "Let's get these horses out of sight. Canyon makes a bend down there," he pointed.

Horse-holders swept the mounts away.

With a cedar branch, Frank dusted out

their tracks in the sandy passage of the cut. Coming back, he laid troubled eyes on the fresh prints they'd made milling along both sides of the stream. On second thought, he decided maybe the dingy light and the crazed rush for water would hide what he could not.

Tinsley and Frank discussed the ambush; they picked a stand in the cedars opposite the cut, a couple of rods up the sloping canyon wall. Thicker cover lay up stream; this they passed over in favor of a better line of fire and the early moments of surprise, when dulled riders and horses satisfied thirst. Then Tinsley called the detail together.

"You will not," he said, "fire 'til I give the order. Watch out for the young woman. She's what we want. Single her out first thing. There's a dozen or so outlaw bucks in this bunch. Get in the first lick — keep whittlin'. If you see some buck tearin' off with the young lady, shoot the horses." Sergeant Tinsley spiked his glance all around and continued:

"First mother's son that makes a damn-fool racket, I will brain on the spot. Now git your hind-ins up there."

Tinsley spread the detail and Frank started up the slope. Without any warning, his knees buckled and he had to put out a hand to brace himself, oddly astonished at his weakness. His head throbbed. He had a fever in his slashed arm; he could feel it. He was like a used-up horse as he climbed on and posted himself behind a cedar near Tinsley.

He waited, and waiting wasn't his liking now. Time was a precious thing, dwindling and wasting away by degrees, its loss marked by the skidding sun. As nothing happened, he began doubting himself and his judgment for coming here, for taking this gamble. He concentrated on the gap and through it until his eyes blurred from the strain. He waited and watched some more, seeing nothing and hearing no more than the still-hot wind or the scrape of a restless trooper's boot. His mind fumbled at dreaded alternatives. Had Yeager doubled back? Did Yeager know of another water hole? Frank mulled at them, he picked at them, he pulled them apart and thought of what he might do in Yeager's place — and was left unsure. Each time he returned to Old Owl's knowledge of the country, the knowledge of a Plains Comanche, an old Comanche. He had to accept that — trust it; it was all a man could hang to.

He almost dozed, steeped in his own misery . . .

He came alert with a sudden upfling of his nodding head, startled by the clack of a hoof on loose rock. Light was fading beyond the gap, the late strokes of the sun dulling to a thickening haze.

Frank pressed forward, in a moment picking up the shoeless trot of a weary pony. Pony and Indian loomed outside the gap; they kept jogging on and presently the walls of the cut flanked them. Inside the canyon the Indian drew still. His pony fought its head for water and the Indian, still looking left and right, let the pony drink. A brief interval and he whirled and rushed back over his tracks.

It seemed a long time.

Several minutes ago the Indian had vanished. Had something spooked him? Pretty soon, the canyon would turn to a formless river of black shadows. Then, Frank thought, how did you tell white woman from Comanche?

"Christ!" gruffed Tinsley. "Reckon they'll ever come? Light's gettin' poor."

"They'll come," Frank said. "Let 'em all ride in to water." There was yet another spell of waiting, and the canyon fell duskier.

When they came, it was all at once, in a drumming shuffle rising out of the dimness, traveling through the early twilight that laid a faint sheen on coppery bodies. They came in a somewhat scattered, irregular bunch, extra horses adding to the clatter, with the noisy confidence of tired riders returning to a familiar haunt. Frank caught slurring, soft-toned calls in the Pena-te-ka tongue.

He strained for sight of her — and located her by the yellow blur of her hair, near the center, her cavalry mount roped to Yeager's big piebald. She rode with drooping head; her hands were tied.

Sergeant Tinsley let them ride in all the way — let them mill and fan out a bit along the trickle and the horses settle to drinking, delaying until Frank got alarmed. At that moment, Yeager and Henrietta passed behind two bucks.

"Fire!"

Carbines crashed, mingling with Tinsley's brass shout and the higher, stricken crying of the Pena-te-kas. Riderless horses switched around, instantly milling, some bolting. Carbine fire quickened to a steady rattle, blasting off the canyon walls.

Frank lost Henrietta in the churning confusion. But the spotted flashes of Yeager's horse sighted her for him again. In the sooty light, he picked up the big piebald going at a jerking run down canyon, Yeager yanking on the rope of Henrietta's slower animal.

Frank fired twice at the piebald. It ran on full-flight. Ran on and suddenly broke into a plunging fall. As the horse started down, Frank drove to his feet and piled down the slope and hit the canyon floor running.

He saw Yeager bouncing up, rifle swinging. He saw Yeager's frantic sidewise glance. Light threw a greasy shine on his battered features; his mouth was a tight slash. And then he swung on down the canyon and ran dodging.

Frank got too eager. He snap fired — missed. He pulled up short and threw the Spencer to his shoulder. He fired again, deliberately.

Yeager stumbled, floundering with the sound of the shot.

Frank was upon him in the limit of a hacking breath. As Yeager attempted to spin up and point his rifle, Frank shot him again. The slug took Yeager in the chest, knocked him flat. He lost his rifle. He made a savage grab for it. Frank worked the Spencer's lever again and felt the carbine jar in his hands. Yeager fell back; he stayed down. Frank stood over him and kept cocking and firing.

When the carbine snapped empty, he stepped over and peered down at Yeager, at the dirty smear of the eye patch. During the fight he'd had no emotions. Now he waited for the stored-up hate and the vicious pleasure to strike up. But they never came. He looked for a long count, without the smallest twinge of regret, and felt nothing much. Nothing more than if he'd just killed a dangerous animal. He had no particular elation. His ears were ringing. He was very tired. Over-used.

He thought in a strange, dull way, Well, it's done with. For them. Her.

Finally, he turned his back on Yeager's body and started, heavy-footed, up the canyon.

He saw the fight was about over, almost a rub-out. He could hear several horses slamming off. A last flurry of scattered shots rang out. After that, the canyon was quiet and the voices of the troopers took over, flat and unnatural sounding now, troopers doubling back and forth.

He heard a man call, "Couple bucks got away."

"Let 'em go," Tinsley ordered.

Tinsley was leading Henrietta away from the trickle and the lumped Pena-te-ka dead. He had one thick arm cloaked comfortingly around her shoulders while she sobbed out her wild, convulsive relief.

Frank tramped across and when she lifted

her head and noticed him, she put out her hand to touch him, and he held her without speaking, feeling the trembling of her body.

"Emily's all right," he told her. The rest, he decided, will have to wait. The part about Vier.

Tinsley left them to collect the detail. Frank guided her to a flat rock and as she dropped to it, he said, "You're not hurt?"

She shook her head, no hesitation now, but decisively. This time, he knew, she wasn't lying. Yet she looked on the edge of collapse, her weariness a dark stain across her drawn face. As if to reassure herself, she took his hand again and he sat beside her.

"They circled around to throw you off," she said, matter of factly. "How'd you know to come here?"

"About the only place they could water. We took a chance." So great a chance, he doubted he'd take it again under the same circumstances. He hesitated, thinking to himself, prompted to tell her about Vier's death and not knowing how to start.

Sergeant Tinsley came up. "Got two lads boogered up a little," he said regretfully. "Chesney, I'm for makin' a fire up the canyon a ways. Risky, maybe. But by God, we got to have coffee."

"Only thing to do," Frank agreed. "No

Comanche's coming back here tonight."

Full night moved in directly and he watched from nearby as she lay on the horse blanket. He could tell she wasn't sleeping, for now and then she stirred, turned or lifted an arm. He had the feeling that sometimes her eyes sought him. Watching her restless turnings, he concluded he could delay the telling no longer. And yet he waited a little while more, dreading what he had to do, feeling the lonely wind come rising along the canyon, feeling it come cool and calling of far-off stretches, freighted with an inexpressible sadness tonight. He thought of Ed Niles and the troopers so still on the yellowness of the Fat Grass, and for some reason he thought of Black Star and the broken knife.

He got up and stood a moment. When he stepped across, she took his hand and drew him down alongside her, murmuring, "I can't sleep. I keep thinking."

He studied her gently, with sympathy, in the indefinite light of Sergeant Tinsley's mesquite root fire. Strung out around them all but two men standing sentry duty slept like battlefield dead. Picketed horses stamped; the stream was a slender luminous streak splitting the canyon floor.

"Don't like to bring bad news," he began,

wishing to comfort her, to break it in a less direct way; but as he spoke he realized there was no other than the direct telling. "Reuel Vier is dead," he told her.

She dropped her head a trifle and lifted it, still holding fast to his hand. He waited for her outcry; he waited and felt surprise when she made no sound. It was peculiar to him, as if she sat there without feeling.

"He died like a soldier," Frank went on, and found the lie rolling off his tongue like something rehearsed. "Happened in close. Quick, I guess. Way it looked, Vier and the Indian shot about the same time."

She seemed to regard him with a curious attention.

"You'll always remember him," Frank said. "Will it . . . come between you and another man, say, when you think what might have been?"

"Frank!" Her voice laid into him sharp; her long fingers tightened. "You needn't try to cover up for Reuel!"

"Cover up?"

"Yes!"

He was totally unprepared. He sat back, sensing the driving will of her.

She said, "First of all, I know he planned to ambush the ransom party. We all saw what happened."

353

"Just about anything goes in an Indian campaign," he said and left it there, unresolved.

She leaned to him, and he could see the flashing of her eyes. "I saw the Indians break the soldiers' line," she said. "That's when Reuel shot himself — I saw it! Oh, his men didn't see. He was alone, behind them. He . . . he died like a coward, Frank. When his men needed him the most."

"You knew all the time."

She went on, softly, "You tried to make him a hero because you thought I loved him. You wanted to leave me that memory, didn't you? Well, I never loved him. I feel sorrow and pity for him now, but I never loved him."

She came to him, she waited with her face upturned, and a vast impatience grew upon him. He placed his mouth to her lips and felt the sudden intensity of her wish for him. She pulled her head away, she laid her face by his cheek.

She said, "I love you. Will you take me home right away? My place in south Texas? Take Emily and me?"

"Soon as we can. And maybe the little Mexican boy. His father's dead."

"Yes. Yes."

"I'll make you forget," he said. "I made a

354

big mistake that night. Next day when I went to tell you I'd help, it was too late. When they took you, I knew I had to go on as long as —"

She was there against him, and the force of her lips wouldn't let him finish.

The employees of Thorndike Press hope you have enjoyed this Large Print book. All our Thorndike and Wheeler Large Print titles are designed for easy reading, and all our books are made to last. Other Thorndike Press Large Print books are available at your library, through selected bookstores, or directly from us.

For information about titles, please call:

(800) 223-1244

or visit our Web site at:

www.gale.com/thorndike
www.gale.com/wheeler

To share your comments, please write:

Publisher
Thorndike Press
295 Kennedy Memorial Drive
Waterville, ME   04901